Victor Watson

OPERATION BLACKOUT

CATNIP BOOKS
Published by Catnip Publishing Ltd
320 City Road
London
EC1V 2NZ

This edition first published 2015
1 3 5 7 9 10 8 6 4 2

Text copyright © Victor Watson, 2015
Cover design by Will Steele

The moral rights of the author and illustrator have been asserted.

A CIP catalogue record for this book is available from the British Library.

ISBN 978-1-91061-100-5

Printed in Poland
www.lfbookservices.co.uk

www.catnippublishing.co.uk

Prologue

A man with a glass eye is relaxing with his boss in an office somewhere in central London. Somewhere secret.

Outside in the streets the cold spring sunshine is bright. But in this office there are no windows. It is underground, in a cellar, perhaps. However, the leather chairs are comfortable, there is a pot of coffee on the mahogany desk, and a coal fire is burning in the grate. Charles Preston likes his luxuries.

The one-eyed man hands over a large black folder. 'It's all there,' he says.

His chief takes the folder and studies it for a moment. 'That girl,' he says. 'Tell me about her.'

The one-eyed man takes off his eye patch and rubs his face where the elastic has pressed into the skin. 'Ah!' he says slowly. 'The girl!'

He leans towards the desk and pours black coffee into his cup.

'She was at the heart of it,' he says. 'Hannah – Hannah Conway. Ten years old.'

'A determined girl, I think.'

'Very! Her mother died when she was little. Her father is in the Navy.'

'Her *risk*?'

Silence for a moment. Then the one-eyed man says slowly, 'High. *Very* high.'

- I -

Hannah Conway: High Risk

Now don't you worry about your gran, love.

When old Mrs Ritchie said that, she knew her gran was dead. Sometimes it's what people don't say that carries the meaning.

She'd been pulled head first out of the rubble by a couple of firemen. She was naked and covered in plaster dust. And she couldn't stop coughing, and spitting her mouth clean. Blood ran down her leg from a cut on her left hip.

You have to be a good girl and stay with me for a few days.

Mrs Ritchie took off her coat and wrapped it round her. With her arm around the girl's shoulders, she led her among the fire engines and ambulances, and through the confused and frightened people. The girl was dry-eyed and shivering, and her hair was in rat's tails from the rain, which poured pitilessly down.

The clouds were lit red and orange by the fires burning under them. And the *noise*! An endless menacing roar of exploding bombs, planes thundering overhead, buildings collapsing, people shouting meaningless things.

There'll be no air raid tonight, they'd said. *Because of the bad weather.*

They were wrong. She'd seen it all before, night after night since September. But she and her gran had always been lucky. Their house had always survived. Now she had nothing and no one, and for the first time she was scared.

As she was taken away, she looked back. Her grandmother's house was an uneven heap of fallen rubble, with only the back wall still standing. The upstairs lavatory was still attached to the brickwork, but it sagged forward as she watched, wrenched itself free of its fittings, and crashed heavily down into where the kitchen used to be.

It fell suddenly quiet. The bombers had gone, and the monotonous roar of their engines was fading as they thundered away across central London.

She was naked inside Mrs Ritchie's coat. She didn't care about that, but her feet hurt because she had no shoes, and the streets were cold and littered with broken glass and brick.

Now what? she thought.

*

Her name was Hannah – Hannah Conway. She was ten.

It was December, 1940. She should have been evacuated like other kids, but her gran was ill and she'd stayed behind to look after her. That night, she'd helped her to have a bath

6

and had got her back into bed when the sirens sounded. She'd planned to get in quickly and have a bath herself, before the water got cold. That was why she had nothing on. When she heard the first of the bombs screaming down, and the thump of explosions, she grabbed her case and got under the kitchen table. That's what Gran had said she should do.

She kept the case ready-packed. It was very small, hardly bigger than a sandwich box. In it were her ration books and a half-crown. She was holding it when those men dragged her from the rubble.

Mrs Ritchie took her to her house, cleaned away the blood, gave her something to eat, and put her to bed. She lived near Woolwich Arsenal. 'It's the Arsenal those bombers are after,' she said. 'And the docks.'

Looking back, Hannah realised that Mrs Ritchie must have been very brave to go out during an air raid to check on them. 'I *knew* that lot fell on your street,' she said later. She was kind too, in her way. But she wouldn't let Hannah go to Gran's funeral. She said it would upset her. Did she think she wasn't upset anyway?

She had no clothes. So Mrs Ritchie went to the local street market and bought some second-hand things – a raincoat with a belt, a pink nightie, a grey gym-slip, a white blouse, a grey woolly jumper, and a pair of dark blue knickers. There was only one of each, and so on Monday afternoons Hannah wore the nightie while everything else was washed, dried and ironed ready for next morning.

She didn't mind having only one of everything. But she wished Mrs Ritchie had got her some socks.

Mrs Ritchie's house was a lot smaller than her gran's. And her gran's house had been smaller than the one she used to live in with her mum. That was in Southampton. Would her next home be even smaller? she wondered.

She was with Mrs Ritchie for about three weeks, over Christmas. It was a miserable time. There were no lights in the streets because of the blackout, and Mrs Ritchie had no decorations in the house either. There was no Christmas tree. It was a half-dead Christmas that year. The baby Jesus seemed a long way from London.

Mrs Ritchie tried her best though: in Hannah's stocking on Christmas morning there was an orange, a bar of nutty chocolate and a red woolly hat. And they had Hannah's favourite kind of sausages for Christmas dinner. Best of all, though, was a book – *A Little Princess* it was called, and it had belonged to Mrs Ritchie when she was little. Hannah knew from the pictures that it was the sort of book she would like.

Hannah wanted to be hugged and cuddled. But Mrs Ritchie didn't go in for hugging. What Hannah really wanted was to have her gran back, and their house, but she knew that was impossible. Nothing would ever be the same again.

Gran had told her once that when she was a toddler she

used to get her words muddled. *Hannah wants a huggle*, she used to say. And they had huggled a lot. Even in those last few weeks – when the old lady was almost too weak to get out of bed – Hannah used to lie beside her on top of the blankets and they would hold each other tight.

Well, there weren't going to be any more huggles. It was a sad lesson to learn. You just have to bottle the sadness up and try to keep it inside you.

She used to think of her father when she was low-spirited. He was a captain in the Royal Navy, always strong and bright and brave, somewhere on the Atlantic Ocean, escorting convoys. But it was more than a year since she'd seen him. Now, when she thought about him at all, she imagined him in the middle of a huge grey ocean storm.

A few days after Christmas there was a terrible air raid, heavier than any of the others. It went on all night, wave after wave of bombers. As usual, they went to a nearby air-raid shelter, Hannah with her suitcase. The shelter was in a cellar under a bus station – an enormous place, with hundreds of people. There was an old man with an accordion. He played lots of songs and everyone joined in. She knew the words of the songs but she just sat and stared, like an idiot. After a while, despite the poor light, she hunched her shoulders and read her book, with the loud song-singing billowing around her.

'You'll ruin your eyes, doing that,' Mrs Ritchie said. There was a woman nearby, sitting on a collapsible chair. They exchanged looks, and the woman raised her eyes to heaven.

'Kids!' she said. 'But what can you do?'

When the all clear sounded, everyone left the shelter – but the moment they stepped outside they knew that night's raid had been different from the others. In the early dawn darkness, a weird red glow lit up the whole sky. It seemed as if all of London was on fire. Dimly in the dusky, billowing smoke the dome of St Paul's stood clear and untouched – but it was hard to believe anything else had survived.

People stood in the street, staring in disbelief. It seemed to Hannah that she had inside her brain a tiny secret camera, which took a picture of that scene, at that moment. It was there ever after, that picture, in her head for always.

She heard someone say, 'I'd like to tie that bastard Hitler to one of his bombs and drop him from two miles up.'

When they got home they found Mrs Ritchie's house had been flattened. *So now she's just like me*, Hannah thought, *bombed out, and homeless*.

Mrs Ritchie didn't make a fuss. People didn't, at that time. She just said, 'I'm sorry, ducks, but I'm going to have to hand you over to the authorities.' She was going to live with her sister in Shrewsbury, and she couldn't take Hannah there.

So there she was, with nothing but the clothes she'd got on. In her small suitcase she had *A Little Princess*, a half-crown folded inside a clean hankie, her identity card, and her ration books. No one ever went anywhere without their ration books.

Now she'd been bombed out twice. *Things always happen in threes*, people said. But how could she be bombed out a third time when she had no home?

-2-

An Interview with the Schuldirektor

Konrad stood stiffly in front of the Master's desk. His feet were together, his arms by his sides.

'Konrad Friedmann,' the Master said. 'I have some bad news for you. Prepare yourself!'

Konrad swallowed, and said nothing. He knew boys at the academy were expected to display iron self-control.

'Yesterday, your father killed himself.'

Konrad's heart leaped into double-time and the blood rushed from his face. But not a muscle in his body moved.

'That is *not* the bad news,' the Master continued. 'The bad news is that yesterday six senior members of the National Government attempted to assassinate the Führer. Six *trusted* members! Your father was one of them. He was a traitor to the Fatherland!'

Again Konrad waited, inwardly tensed, hardly managing to breathe.

'The other five were taken outside and shot. Herr Hitler allowed your father the option of killing himself. Do you know why the Führer was so generous?'

Of course Konrad knew why! But his mind was in a white daze of confusion. He could not make himself speak.

'You are related to Herr Hitler – and that is why your father was allowed the privilege of committing suicide. For the same reason, your mother and sister are only under house arrest, though they are suspected of being co-conspirators.'

'But my sister is only seven,' Konrad said. His voice sounded strange in this new world that had suddenly been created.

'The authorities believe they knew what was planned – yet they said nothing. Their loyalty to the Third Reich is in doubt.'

A bright memory of his life at home came vividly into Konrad's mind. How his mother and father had despised Adolf Hitler – and what he had done to Germany and Austria. How ashamed they were to be related to him! How they loathed this war he had started across the whole of Europe.

'That was the bad news,' said the Master. 'Now the good! *You* are to be given a chance to redeem your family from its disgrace, and save the lives of your mother and sister.'

Konrad frowned briefly, in puzzlement.

'The Führer has a task for you. It is a great honour. If you refuse it – or if you fail – your mother and sister will be shot.'

From the street below, the wheels of a tram squealed against the rails as it turned into the Schwedenplatz.

'You are to go to your dormitory and pack your things. One small suitcase only. You will return to this room in half an hour to learn the nature of your task.'

'Sir?'

The Master looked startled. Pupils were not expected to ask questions. 'What is it?' he barked.

'How did my father . . . ?' He could not bring himself to say the words.

'He swallowed a poison capsule.'

Konrad inwardly breathed a sigh of relief. At least he could spare himself the torment of imagining his father firing a bullet into his head.

*

When he returned to the Schuldirektor's office, there was someone else – a man in military uniform. Konrad knew at once that this was a senior officer of the Gestapo. Also, there were two armed soldiers at the door.

Having to prepare for such a sudden departure had kept Konrad occupied. But he was unable to stop thinking about his mother and father. They had believed that Germany was caught in a vast and brutal insanity. The Academy had been a refuge for him, and he did not want to leave. It was stern but not cruel, and life there was orderly.

'Konrad Friedmann!' the Gestapo officer said. 'You have a chance to retrieve the honour of your family! Will you accept the challenge?'

'Yes.'

He was corrected. 'Yes, *sir*.'

'Yes, sir.'

'Good! Then pay close attention! In the east of England there is a building, on an airbase. In it, the British are researching a new and highly developed codebreaking facility. That building must be destroyed.'

This seemed to Konrad like something from a storybook. What had British codebreaking facilities to do with him?

'Herr Friedmann, you are to be parachuted into the area to blow up this building.'

Herr Friedmann? Konrad managed to retain his stiff body posture, but he was unable to conceal the amazement and disbelief, which showed in his face. 'Sir, I am only twelve.'

The Master intervened. He was annoyed. 'This is a great opportunity for you, Friedmann, to show your loyalty to the Third Reich,' he said. 'It is given to you only because of your family connection to Herr Hitler – a personal favour, a *family* favour, from the Führer. Do you understand?'

Konrad bowed his head. 'But I know nothing about explosives,' he said.

'Good!' the officer exclaimed. 'Good! That shows the right attitude! A willingness to learn! You will accompany me now. I will take you to a training school run by the Abwehr. You will have three weeks in which to learn about explosives, and how to make parachute jumps.'

The Master spoke again. 'Do you accept, Friedmann?'

What choice had he got? Irrationally, he recalled a family photograph in which, aged about two, he sat on cousin Adolf's knee. 'Yes,' he said. 'But why me?'

'You are a clever boy,' the officer said thoughtfully. 'I hope you are not too clever. Your master has explained that one reason is that you are a member of the Führer's family. But the other reason is that you speak perfect English and with a perfect accent.'

How did he know that?

'That is correct? You were educated in England – before the War.'

'Yes, sir. I had an English grandmother and we lived with her.'

'And you went to an English school until you were ten.' It was not a question. The Gestapo officer knew this already. 'If you succeed, your mother and your little sister will be allowed to live in peace.'

'But how will you know?' Konrad said. 'How will you know if I have succeeded?'

The officer smiled at the boy's naivety. 'We have our agents in Great Britain,' he said. 'We know everything that happens there.'

'What will happen to me afterwards?' Would there be some kind of pick-up, a rescue operation?

'You must lie low until the end of the War. It will not

be long. When we defeat Britain, you will be reunited with your mother and sister.'

'But I won't be able to stay with my English grandmother. She died in 1939 – and the War might last for years!'

'It will not. By next year Great Britain will be part of the Third Reich!'

Half of Konrad's mind was British – and it rebelled against this absurd notion. But, in the maelstrom of his feelings, the thought of getting out of Germany was like a light brushing of cool air on a fevered face.

'No one will suspect you. You will succeed because you are a child, and because your English is perfect.'

'But, sir! This is crazy! I am just a schoolboy!'

There was a silence. The officer's face softened a little and, when he spoke, his voice was gentler. 'Yes,' he said sadly. 'It *is* crazy. The whole world has gone mad! And we are all caught up in it. To send a schoolboy on a sabotage mission is just one small madness in the universal lunacy.'

The Master disapproved of this kind of talk. 'Friedmann,' he said, 'I am glad you have decided to show your loyalty to our great homeland, and to wipe out the shame of your father's treachery.'

Konrad ignored him. The Master was irrelevant now, already part of a world that had gone for ever. 'If I am captured?' he said.

The Gestapo officer's shoulders stiffened and his face

hardened as he recovered his military self. 'Have no fear,' he said. 'The British will not shoot a schoolboy. They are sentimental about children.'

-3-

The Man with the Glass Eye

Hannah didn't remember much about the next few days. Mrs Ritchie took her to a local policeman's house but she didn't stay there long. The policeman was out at work all night during the air raids, and in bed all day, exhausted. He was too tired to deal with some homeless child. And his wife didn't want her there, that was obvious. So she left.

She crossed to the north side of the river on the Woolwich ferry. That was easy because it was free, and she used to do it on her way to school. She spent a few nights in air-raid shelters, and she usually got a bite to eat there. But she was hungry most of the time, and cold because she'd lost her mac and her woolly jumper. She couldn't remember what happened to them. So all she had on top of her vest and gym-slip was an old black jacket that had belonged to Mrs Ritchie.

Still, it was friendly in the shelters. She would choose a nice-looking family and sit close to one of them. If she was lucky, they sometimes shared their sandwiches with her. *Perhaps I can live like this until my dad comes back*, she thought.

She imagined the joy each would feel when he found her.

He would pick her up, hug her tight, and swing her round. The way he used to.

On the ninth or tenth night she got lost. She knew she was somewhere near the Royal Docks. But when the air-raid sirens sounded she couldn't find a shelter. It was raining, and she was very cold and she'd had nothing to eat all day. She came across a bombed-out warehouse and went in, hoping to find some part of it with a roof still intact. It was pitch dark and she had to feel her way carefully across the debris on the floor.

She could already hear the Jerry bombers coming. Any bombs dropped here, she thought, would be wasted. There were no intact buildings left.

She had the fright of her life in there. You do – if you think you're completely alone and then you find you're not. She was concentrating on finding somewhere sheltered from the rain where she could hide until the raid was over. But she heard the scrunch of a footfall on broken glass. There was someone there – standing quietly in the dark. 'What do *you* want?' he said.

She was scared stiff. What she *didn't* want was some strange bloke in a bombed-out building! Her eyes were used to the darkness after all those nights of blackout, and she could see he had an enormous torch. People usually carried torches because of the blackout, but *small* ones. His torch was as big as a car headlight.

She should have made a dash for it. But she knew she couldn't run across all that rubble in the dark without stumbling. So she stood her ground and said nothing.

'Who are you?' he said. He was in front of her, close up, tall and powerful, with that massive torch swinging in his hand. 'What's your name?'

It was a harmless question, she thought. But she realised afterwards that she shouldn't have told him. 'Hannah Conway,' she said warily. 'What's yours?'

He laughed. A strange, menacing sort of sound it was too. *Cycle-tops*, he said – or something like that.

He took out a packet of cigarettes, and chose one. Most people smoked, if they had some money to spare. The cigarette hung between his lips while he felt for a box of matches. Out came the matches from his coat pocket – and out came a folded piece of paper, which fell to the ground.

As he raised the lighted match to the cigarette, it briefly illuminated his eyes – one alive and restless, the other glassy and still.

She stared at it, transfixed. *Oh, you poor thing!* she thought. She didn't say it – it would have been rude. It was a common enough thing after all, just an unlucky man who'd had an eye injury. Perhaps he'd been shot in the War. But as his one eye stared glassily into vacancy and the other glanced down at Hannah, her heart raced. She was sure this man could see deeper into her with his one good eye than most people could with two.

'Why are you staring?' he demanded.

His words reminded her of Mrs Ritchie. 'Why are you always *watching* people?' she'd said to her once. 'You make me nervous in my own house! Following every move I make with your eyes like that!'

The man blew out the match and the darkness enveloped both of them. She stooped to pick up the piece of paper he'd dropped, intending to give it back to him. But at that moment the Jerry bombers were upon them, right overhead, like a roll of thunder.

It was a familiar sound. Night after night she'd heard it, all through the winter. But that night she was more scared of the glass-eyed man than the whole German Luftwaffe.

He shouted above the noise of the bombers. 'Tonight I'm half expecting to meet my maker. I hope I don't take you with me. I'm sorry about that, Hannah Conway. That's your bad luck!'

What? What did he mean?

'So I'd clear off if I were you!' he said. 'Sharpish!'

Then he seemed to forget all about her. He switched on his torch and shone it straight up into the sky. She couldn't believe what she was seeing! They'd all had it endlessly drilled into them that no one should ever show a light after dark – yet this bloke was deliberately shining a powerful torch into a sky full of enemy bombers.

She backed away from him because she was beginning to understand what he was doing. Somewhere up there, enemy bomb-aimers would be looking down, searching for that light. And the beam of it was as powerful as a miniature searchlight. The place they were in was already badly blitzed – but he wanted to help them drop even *more* bombs.

At that moment two air-raid wardens burst into the building from the street. They must have seen his light, Hannah thought. One of them shouted, and then they made a rush to catch hold of him. But the glass-eyed man was faster than they were, and he broke free and got away.

One of the wardens gave chase, but the other stayed to look after Hannah. 'You look a right mess!' he said. He knelt down in front of her, holding her shoulders, studying her in the light of his torch (a *small* one). She knew she looked a terrible sight, with her hair all wet and her bare legs sticking out from under Mrs Ritchie's old jacket.

She told him what had happened. Then, of course, he wanted to know why she was out all alone in an air raid. It was a long story and she could see he had other things on his mind. They had to shout because of the roar of the bombers overhead.

He stopped listening. 'Come on, love,' he said. 'Hold my hand, and I'll take you to a shelter.'

He did, and it was a good one. It was a cellar under a bombed-out factory. She got a mug of soup there, and a bread roll. A boy snatched the roll out of her hand and ran off, but the soup was delicious. That was why she didn't go in chase of the boy – she couldn't risk spilling a single drop of that soup.

They had a piano there. She couldn't believe it! Not just an ordinary old upright, but a grand piano! And everyone was having a sing-song!

But she didn't join in the singing. She was too tired, and she couldn't stop shivering. Just before she fell asleep, she remembered the bit of paper and pulled it out of her pocket. Typed on it was a list of about thirty names, just surnames. Some of them had hyphens in the middle, and three of them had been crossed out. And beside each name was a number. Hannah thought they were telephone numbers. When she folded it up, she saw two words written on the outside – *Great Deeping*.

Great Deeping, she thought. *What does **that** mean?*

She shoved it back into her pocket. She always kept lists.

-4-

Back to School

Everyone was turned out of the shelter in the morning. Hannah had no choice but to wander the streets. But later she remembered that the new school term should have started by now. If she went to school, she thought, someone there would tell her what to do.

Hannah was not a Londoner. She'd been born near Southampton. She'd moved to London when her mother died. She was six when that happened. After that, she lived with her grandmother. Before her dad went back to sea he'd found a small private school close to the Custom House. She liked it there. There was one teacher she especially liked, Miss Amery, and once the thought of her got into her head she couldn't stop imagining her. *She'll be pleased to see me*, Hannah thought. *Perhaps she'll take me home to live with her.*

It took her all morning to find the school. She was shivering and headachy, and she kept feeling dizzy. The trouble was that the bombing had changed the streets. It was hard to find familiar landmarks. Several times, when she found a street she recognised, she wasn't allowed in it because of unexploded bombs. When she did finally get there, the school was deserted. There wasn't a soul to be seen. And there was a notice on the door.

The pupils and staff of St Marcellina's School have been evacuated to a place of safety in the country.

The whole school! And she'd been left behind! She couldn't believe it.

One of the best words in the language is *we*. If you can use that word a lot, you're very lucky. *We sat round the table . . .* or *We all met up and went to the shops . . .* or *We waited eagerly to see what the new teacher would be like . . .* Because if you can use the word *we* it means there are people you belong to. You're connected.

It came into Hannah's mind then that she belonged to nobody. Her gran was dead, Mrs Ritchie had gone away, and now even her school had been evacuated. She was totally abandoned. Disconnected.

There was a bench in the playground where they used to play hopscotch. The rain had smeared and muddied the chalk lines. She sat there and began to cry. It was the first time since her gran had been killed. Normally, she didn't go in for crying because her dad always warned her against self-pity. 'It does no good,' he said. 'You just have to face what's happened, and decide what to do about it.'

People said she was hard, because she never cried. They said she had no feelings.

But that day she did cry. There was no one to see, so perhaps it didn't count.

When the War started, she'd asked her dad what was going to happen to her. He said, 'You're going to *survive*, that's what's going to happen. Remember that – *your job is to survive*. And I intend to survive too, so that we'll both be here when it ends.'

That had been a bad time. Her mother had died ages ago; she was used to that. But that autumn, in 1939, there was a new trouble: three weeks before War broke out her best friend moved away. Then her dad had left too, and gone back to sea.

She would have to survive without a mum, without a dad, and without her friend. And it occurred to Hannah then that her father might already have been torpedoed somewhere in the Atlantic. Many had been.

She sat up straight and wiped her eyes. The rain had stopped, but there was a bitter east wind and it was too cold to stay there in the empty playground.

She was so hungry that her stomach hurt.

In the streets, there were crowds of people everywhere; a second evacuation. Before Christmas, lots of evacuated children had changed their minds and come home; others had just come back for the holidays. But the bombing was as bad as ever, worse on some nights, and so now they were going back to the country, crowds of them. There was a school – another school – all walking in a crocodile. They wore purple uniforms, and carried suitcases and gas masks. Some teachers and parents were walking with them.

Hannah tagged along behind them. No one took any notice of her. Once she fell over, and one of their teachers helped her up and gave her a hard-boiled sweet.

She followed them all the way to Liverpool Street station. There was confusion there, with crowds of anxious people milling around and getting in each other's way. *I'll need money for a ticket*, she thought. So she opened her suitcase to find her half-crown. But someone knocked her from behind and all her possessions fell out and were scattered around. She had to get down on hands and knees to save her things, and all around her there were the legs and feet of hundreds of hurrying, frightened people.

She retrieved everything, except the half-crown.

She tried to get to her feet but she never managed it. Everything went woozy and she passed out. She didn't know how long she lay on the ground, only a minute or two probably. When she came round, someone helped her to stand up and supported her to a seat. 'I have to get back to my lot,' he said. 'You'll be OK now.'

She didn't feel OK. It was a big station, and very noisy. All the different sounds merged into one big throbbing roar. It made her head hurt. Everything she looked at seemed to be ten times clearer than normal, and everyone was moving in slow motion.

She stared around, at faces mostly. How strange they all seemed! The porters and ticket collectors looked menacing and she wondered what they were secretly thinking. Could you really trust all those anxious mothers fussing about their children? There was a boy – about Hannah's age – carrying his younger sister. He looked concerned, as if he was comforting her. But how could you tell what he was *really* thinking? He probably bullied her in private, for all anyone knew.

They could all be acting a part, lying with their faces. How could you trust anyone? How can you ever know?

As she pulled Mrs Ritchie's old jacket closer round her, she remembered that she'd spent some of the half-crown at a tea wagon. And she'd put the change in the pocket.

When she felt for it, she pulled out two shillings and tuppence. And with the coins there was that folded paper, with those names and numbers typed on it.

In the end the money didn't matter. With so many children crowding on to the trains, and so many confused and worried grown-ups all over the place, and railway staff who had probably been up all night because of the air raids, no one seemed to care about tickets.

So which train should she get? There were lots, and Hannah forced herself to study the destination boards. She couldn't concentrate and her eyes wouldn't focus. But she did notice that the train at platform six would stop at a place called *Great Deeping*.

The two words jumped out at her. It must be the name of a place, she thought, and then she remembered it had been scribbled on the back of that scrap of paper with the list. Was that just a coincidence? Or did it *mean* something?

She was too exhausted and confused to work it out. But that was the train she got on – the train to Great Deeping.

She climbed into one of the carriages and found a seat. The heating wasn't working and it was cold, but the corner seat was at least comfortable.

She was almost asleep when the guard on the platform blew his whistle. There was a slamming of doors, like small bombs exploding, and the crowded train began to move. Towards Great Deeping, she supposed. *But it doesn't matter where I go,* she thought, *because I don't belong anywhere.*

-5-

Training School

Konrad Friedmann sat back in his seat as the car took them through the outskirts of Vienna and into the country. The Gestapo officer sat beside him. Two uniformed soldiers were in the front, one driving, both cut off by a glass partition.

In Konrad's heart, excitement warred with wretchedness and confusion. 'May I ask a question?' he said.

He was corrected. 'May I ask a question, *sir*.'

'May I ask a question, sir?' Konrad said.

'Of course.'

'Is it safe to carry explosives when making a parachute jump?'

The Gestapo officer's face softened. He had sons too. 'You will not have to take your own gelignite,' he explained. 'You will be instructed where to find it.'

Konrad thought about this and decided that it was an unsatisfactory answer. 'But, sir,' he said, 'if there is someone in England who can provide me with explosives, why can't *he* blow up the building? Why take all this trouble to send *me* there?'

'Are you regretting your decision?' the officer said.

'No, but I want to understand.' He realised he'd forgotten the *sir* but this time he was not corrected.

The Gestapo officer took a deep breath. He was reluctant to confess the truth to this perceptive boy. 'We have not enough skilled operators in Britain,' he admitted. 'We have not been able to find anyone in that area who knows how to use explosives. There are plenty of Nazi sympathisers in Britain but they are mostly enthusiastic amateurs. There is a good deal of *muddle*. Some of them are probably highly intelligent, but they have no professional training.'

Konrad digested this information.

'But *you* will have the training. And you have three other important qualities: you speak perfect English, you are clever, and you are a not a grown-up.'

Konrad was still not satisfied. 'Within a few hours of my father's . . .' he hesitated '. . . crime, someone had thought of me and worked out this plan!' It was beyond belief.

'Not *someone*. It was *me*!'

'But . . .'

Konrad was not allowed to continue. Perhaps the officer was already regretting that he'd shared his doubts about the British Nazi-sympathisers. He grew irritable and no more questions were permitted. But Konrad worked it out. They had suspected his father's loyalty to the Führer *in advance*, and had this plan ready. Or, more likely, they intended to use the son as a hostage to guarantee the good conduct of the father. But his father had forestalled them.

Konrad liked to understand what happened to him.

The car pulled up before some wrought-iron gates. Security was checked, and the gates were opened. Armed guards saluted as the car passed in. There was a long drive across open parkland, with grass and scattered trees, and distant buildings. Konrad saw a group of about ten men, all gazing upwards. As the car drove slowly past, a paratrooper landed close by the watchers, and everyone cheered and applauded.

'Welcome,' said the officer, 'to the Waldbrand Training School. I shall not see you again. I wish you luck!'

*

There were sixteen other students at the school, all grown-ups. Three women and thirteen men. The fact that Konrad was a schoolboy was ignored. He was always addressed as either Friedmann, or *Herr* Friedmann. The atmosphere was friendly and everyone showed a kindly interest in the progress being made by other students. As far as he could tell, this kindliness was sincere.

But kindliness was not the same as trust. Konrad observed from the start that there was one unwritten rule: *ask no questions*. No student ever asked other students about their past, or the missions they were being trained for. And no mention was made of the fact that their missions would involve a good deal of killing. But that, Konrad told himself, was what happens when your country is at war.

There were three extended lessons every day. Konrad was to study explosives in the morning, parachuting in the afternoon (this was the one he looked forward to with the greatest excitement), and in the evenings he was to work on his cover story.

There were two main meals every day (with much better food than he'd had at school) and he had a bedroom of his own. This amazed and impressed him.

He asked the commandant if he might attend his father's funeral, but it was not allowed. 'It would distract you from your work,' he was told.

Konrad thought of his mother and sister, and wondered if they would be allowed to attend.

'Sir,' he asked. 'Has my mission got a codename?'

'Indeed it has! It is *Operation Blackout*.'

Konrad found this helped. His life had been thrown into confusion, but he found the codename enabled him to focus his thoughts upon a clear and single purpose.

Seventeen missions were being planned and prepared for at the Training School. Operation Blackout was only one of them.

*

The other students were staying at the school for many months. They had to learn about every kind of explosive, and even how to use chemicals to make them. But Konrad's teaching was concentrated on only one explosive – gelignite. That was all he needed to know.

Gelignite, he learned, was a safe explosive because its chemicals were inert until detonated. He was taught how to place the sticks for maximum damage, and how to wire them up to a detonator. None of this was difficult. At the end of his first morning he was allowed to plan and lay out a single stick of gelignite sufficient to blow up a small rosebush. As he pushed the plunger down into its box, he felt it engage with the magneto inside – and a fraction of a second later the gelignite made a discreet little pop and the distant rosebush flew in fragments into the air.

On his last morning there was a test he had to pass: he blew up an entire building. The grounds had many outbuildings – stables and sheds mostly. Everyone came to watch, standing around quietly and wishing him luck. He did the job very carefully, checking all the time for maximum destruction. When he pushed down the plunger, the stable building erupted upwards with a roar and clouds of dust before crashing back down into a spread of rubble.

Birds rose cawing and screeching into the air. Everyone applauded and patted him on the back. Konrad had reminded himself from time to time that people get killed when buildings are blown up. But at that moment he couldn't stop himself from enjoying a feeling of personal triumph. Anyone would!

*

He was going to have to make a parachute jump. Not a big one, only from around 1,200 feet. But *in the dark*. The afternoons were devoted to preparing for that.

The first afternoon was devoted to jumping from a wall ten feet high. Then fifteen feet. Finally twenty-five feet. He had to learn how to roll and relax as he landed. He was good at it, but at the end of the first afternoon his joints felt battered and sore. After three lessons of this he had to go into the grounds and jump from the same wall – after dark. This was more difficult because he tensed his lower body in readiness for the hard landing which he could not properly see approaching.

But he improved. One afternoon in his second week he was driven to a nearby airfield and fitted with a parachute. He climbed aboard a Junkers. 'Anything a grown man can do can be done by a boy of twelve,' his tutor said. These words stiffened Konrad's resolve.

The moments before jumping were very bad. But floating down with the silk parachute rustling softly above him was a delight, almost an ecstasy. But quickly over. In no time he was landing – in exactly the same manner that he had used when jumping from a high wall.

'Perfect!' his tutor said later. 'It only remains for you to do it at night.'

'There is nothing here but open ground,' Konrad said. 'But in England there will be trees, and telegraph wires, and rooftops.'

'Where you are going to be dropped,' the tutor said, 'there are none of those things.'

-6-

Oliver Pickens

'Mum! I'm gooin t the station.'

'What – *now*? Thas pourin wi rain and pitch dark! Wodya want to goo there for?'

'I like seein the train come in. There's a lood of vacuees comin in at six.'

'You must be daft, boy! Well, dew you make sure you're back in time for supper! Or you oon't git none! *And* yew'll git a clip round the ear from yer dad, probly.'

Ollie shuffled on his mac, pulled a woollen balaclava over his head to keep the rain off, and went outside for his bike. Fixed to the back of it there was a two-wheeled wooden cart. He'd made it the previous summer out of a crate and two pram wheels. He was good at that sort of thing. It was used for carting coal, billets of wood for the fire, taters, carrots, anything. Whenever he used it he remembered he'd made it himself.

Ollie knew why he liked watching the vacuees. He half envied them, that's why.

Great Deeping station was two miles away and – with the

wind and the rain – it took him half an hour to get there. When he arrived he found small groups of people waiting, and someone had hired the local taxi-bus. He stood in the darkness away from everyone else, holding his bike.

When the train steamed in, Ollie sighed with pleasure. He watched the crowds of London children getting out of their carriages, peering into the darkness, slamming the doors behind them. The only light came dimly from inside the compartments, and in less than two minutes the doors were shut and the train was pulling away. Ollie watched its red rear light fading softly into the wet, gusty night.

Most of the kids knew where they were going. They'd been back to London to visit their families. One or two of them were being met, most hurried off into the town in twos and threes. But there were a few new ones, and they were rounded up by a couple of women in uniform, who shepherded them into the bus. Names were called out, but there was no fuss. One child was crying, a boy of about six or seven.

In less than ten minutes it seemed like all the evacuees had gone. And everyone else, too.

But Ollie knew different. There was one they'd missed. A girl, standing in the darkness under the steps, as if she didn't want to be seen.

Ollie stood still, concentrating. Nothing could be heard but the high roaring of the wind and the lashing of the rain. He pushed his sodden balaclava back from his forehead –

and watched to see what she would do.

But she didn't do anything, just stood there, as if she had no wish to go anywhere. So after a few minutes Ollie went over.

'Yew all right?'

No answer. She just stared at him, a sorry little thing, he thought. 'Hev ya got anywhere to goo?'

*

She had nowhere to go. She didn't even know why she'd come to this place. Besides, she only half understood what he was saying.

'Come yew on then! Yew better come wi me.'

But she didn't move. Decisions were beyond her. This was the lowest point she'd sunk to.

'I'm Ollie.'

Ollie? What sort of name was *that?*

'Suit yerself then,' Ollie said. She watched him mount his bike and pedal off. In no time at all he was lost in the darkness.

She wanted to be left to her misery. Her face was wet, her hair was in dripping rat's tails, and her clothes were soaked and shabby – all of them, not just Mrs Ritchie's old jacket. Even her shoes were sodden. If she'd had socks, they would have been soaked too. Her feet had been frozen for days. She was hardly aware of the state she was in, hardly aware of the long night ahead. She was only dimly aware of anything at all.

There was a light approaching the station forecourt. A pale cycle light. This time, the boy cycled right up to her, and – still standing astride his bike – he pointed to the wooden cart and said, 'Get yew in there!'

Still she didn't move. 'No one een't goin to *hurt* yew!' he said. She was making him feel stubborn. If she didn't make a move herself, he wouldn't keep trying. 'If yew take all night about it, we shan't be hum for supper.'

Since her gran died, she'd had no control over her life. None at all. She'd just *drifted*. She'd drifted into being looked after by Mrs Ritchie, drifted away from the policeman and his wife. She'd drifted through the blacked-out streets, and in and out of air-raid shelters. She'd drifted to her empty school. And finally on to a train to this place just because she'd happened to find its name scribbled on a scrap of paper.

But now she had to *choose*. It wasn't much of a choice, between this weird boy and staying by herself all night. But it was a choice of sorts.

No more drifting.

She stepped forward and climbed shakily into the sodden handcart. There was just room to sit with her bare knees pressed under her chin. She could feel the wet on the wooden floor of the cart soaking through her knickers to her buttock-bones. She couldn't stop shivering.

She held on to her case, and Ollie set off, labouring a little because of the extra weight.

*

She would never forget that ride. It was as if she'd died and was being taken on a journey to the underworld.

They overtook a couple of groups of evacuees, huddled and stooping in the wind and rain. No one said anything as they passed.

Apart from them, there were no people. The only living things were the wind in the black sky, and the slanting rain. And the hissing of the tyres on the wet road. The boy just cycled on, his shoulders rising and falling in front of her as he pushed down on the pedals. He was like a figure in a dream, taking people on hopeless journeys.

At one point the cycling stopped. A boy – another boy – appeared out of the darkness. He and Ollie spoke briefly. Something about a cat.

'You can't miss it – it's only got three legs. We haven't seen it for days.'

A girl appeared out of the wet darkness, huddled and stooped against the rain. 'Tibby! Tibby! Where *are* you?'

'She's an evacuee,' the boy said.

'I just picked her up at the station!' Ollie said.

'Not the girl in your cart! The *cat*. The *cat's* an evacuee.'

The girl came closer. 'She had her leg blown off by a bomb,' she said.

'Well, if you see it . . .'

Their words were insane. An evacuee cat? Were they looking for its leg? wondered Hannah.

'I gotta git this kid hum,' Ollie said.

The boy and the girl stepped back into the shadows, and Ollie set off again, pushing hard down on the pedals.

Nothing made sense to Hannah. The people seemed insane, and what they said was mad. Had she come to a special town for mad people? Were they all lunatics?

It was a long and windy street where the houses were huddled close in the darkness. There was a level crossing, then a river bridge. After that there were no more houses, just a smell of wet grass and wet fields. The wind became more regular, a long continuous roar on one note. And the rain falling from the huge dark sky swept across her face like wet curtains at an open window.

She'd never imagined a place as empty as that. It was like being out at sea in the middle of the night in a small open boat. She thought briefly of her father, but she pushed the image of him out of her mind. Thinking about him no longer helped.

They turned right along a narrow lane. In the feeble light of the boy's cycle lamp she saw a signpost – *Deeping Old Bank*. The lane wound on, with a high grassy bank on one side.

The boy called back to her. 'Nairly hum!'

Home? How could this be home, in this vast and streaming emptiness? Who would want a home here? She felt like a ghost.

There was a bridge, made of slatted wooden planks, so the

wheels of the bike and the cart clattered like a machine gun, *rat-tat-tat*.

He had to help her out of the cart, she was so stiff and weak. There was a house, a solitary building with no neighbours. Its walls were grey and   . The next minute she was inside, clutching her case, shivering.

They were in a small, dark passage. Then there was a room, with strangers, in the yellow light of an oil lamp on the table. There were two people: a girl of around four or five, seated at the table holding a spoon upright in her fist, and a woman at a long black range.

'Wodyew come in that way for? Woss wrong with the back door?'

Perhaps it was the sudden warmth – or the smell of food – that made her feel faint. Hannah thought she was going to pass out. She held on to the door post and managed to stay upright.

The woman turned and stared. 'Wotchew got there?'

'She was at the station. She een't got noowhere to goo. I couldn't leave er.'

The woman was Ollie's mum, and Hannah found out later that her name was Mrs Pickens. She moved a saucepan aside so that it wouldn't boil over. Then she came over to Hannah and looked her up and down. 'Well, she can't stay ere. We een't spoosed to have vacuees – that posh woman *said*! Cos we live too far *out*!'

44

She folded her arms. 'Dew yew git those wet cloze orf!' she said. '*All* on em! *Now!* Ollie, git upstairs and find my ole dressin gown, that thick one.'

Was she supposed to do it there? In front of them? But Ollie had gone, and she could hear him clomping about overhead. Mrs Pickens went back to her stove. So Hannah began to undress – and that made her shiver even more as she peeled off each soaked and sodden garment. The girl at the table was staring at her, but Hannah was beyond caring.

She heard an outside door open and shut.

'Thas *him*!' Mrs Pickens said. 'He allus knows jus when to show up.'

A man came into the room, small, wiry, unshaven. He walked around the table and was halfway across the room before he saw her. Hannah held her arms tight over her front but she couldn't hide all of her. Everything in the room seemed to freeze at that moment. He glared balefully at her – but she was too weak to feel embarrassed. Or even bothered.

Mrs Pickens hadn't been bothered either, she thought afterwards.

He didn't say a word. There was a wooden clothes horse by the stove, with a bed sheet draped over it. He picked it up and stood it in front of her like a screen, and then ignored her.

Then Ollie came back, with the dressing gown. He passed it to her and said, 'Wotcher, Pa!'

Mr Pickens grunted. He went over to his wife and Hannah saw him jerk his head back towards her, signalling a question.

'Ollie found her,' his wife said. 'Down at the station.'

She turned back to the table. 'Oonly she can't stay ere! We een't got nuthin for er.'

Yet Hannah saw that she was laying out five plates for supper. She was enveloped in the dressing gown by then, and so when Ollie said 'Come *on*!' she went over to the table and sat there with them. She kept being gripped by fits of helpless shivering.

But what a supper! Rabbit pie, it was – though she didn't find that out until later. And mashed potatoes, with gravy and sprouts. When she'd finished, there were seconds. And then roly-poly pud with custard.

She had one bad moment when she thought she was going to die. There was a hard, tiny ball in her mouth, some kind of pellet. It scrunched her teeth and she spat it out on to her plate. Then there was another – and she thought her insides had started to break up and were falling out of her mouth.

The third one pinged on the plate when she spat it out. Everyone laughed, and Ollie said it was the shot that killed the rabbit. Actually, *not* everyone laughed: Mr Pickens was stony-faced all the time.

*

'Ollie,' Mrs Pickens said. 'Dew yew put this child to bed. *Now!*'

Hannah stared. But when Ollie had lit a candle and jerked his head at her to come, she followed him. He opened what looked like a cupboard door, but behind it there was a narrow staircase. Up they went in the candle shadows, and along a dark passage to a door at the far end.

The little room seemed completely empty.

There were no rugs, just bare floorboards. There was no furniture, just a solitary wooden chair. There were no curtains at the window, only the blackness of the night. There were no bookshelves, no pictures on the walls. There was a tiny black metal fireplace, but no coal, no wood, no cinders even.

But there was a bed, narrow and inviting. Its pillow was clean and its sheets folded neatly back. And over the blankets there was a faded yellow eiderdown.

'Hev ya got a nightie?'

She shook her head, feeling ashamed.

'Pyjamas?' Again, no.

'Wait yew here a minute.' He left the room and came back a moment later with a boy's shirt, grey, with long tails. 'Dew you put this on,' he said. 'I'm tew big for it now. That useter be rough an hairy, but that een't any more cos thas bin worn and washed soft. So yew'll be all right.'

At the door he turned. 'Doon't forget to bloo out that candle afore you goo to sleep. Night, night!'

Outside the wind walloped and thumped against the walls

of the house, and rain lashed against the windowpanes. She stood the candle-saucer on the empty windowsill and shivered as she took off the dressing gown. But the shirt was clean and warm, and she blew out the candle and climbed into bed.

Ollie had put a hot-water bottle where her feet would be. It was lovely! Pure bliss!

She'd heard bad stories about what happened to evacuee children. She'd heard people say they were beaten, and treated as slaves. But she was too exhausted to feel scared, and too confused to work things out. She just turned on to her side and drew her knees up with the hot-water bottle tucked into her stomach. Sleep washed over her immediately.

-7-

Feelgood's Tea-Room

In a side street in Kensington, London, there was at that time a small tea-shop. It was called Feelgood's Tea-Room. Regular customers called it simply Feelgood's. The street had so far escaped any damage from the Blitz, and – in spite of rationing – the tea-room staff offered a wide range of cakes, home-cooked biscuits, and sandwiches.

The clientele was mostly women – women of all ages, well-dressed and confident. But there were also smart elderly gentlemen in long overcoats, and occasional officers in the RAF or the Army, home on leave. Navy officers too.

It was a thoroughly British tea-shop.

But one afternoon in early January, the customers sipping their Earl Grey tea and taking delicate bites from their Chelsea buns would have been surprised if they had been able to see into the flat upstairs, where the owner of the tea-shop lived. Miss Stephanie Feelgood – slim, trim, with her hair bobbed to expose her elegant neck – was sitting at her desk, lost in thought.

Feelgood wasn't her real name. People started to call her that when she bought the tea-room. But she liked it, and continued to use it.

In front of her was a large notebook, and she had been writing in it. She had been writing in German. It was not against the law to write in German (or speak it, or think it). Of course it wasn't, even though Britain was at War with Germany.

Nevertheless, the customers downstairs would have been surprised if they had known. *German?* they would have said. *Surely not!* Everyone hated Germany in 1941.

Miss Feelgood closed the book, tucked it into the back of a small drawer in her desk, locked the drawer using a key on a chain around her neck, and dropped the key discreetly inside her pale blue blouse. Her movements were swift and precise.

There was a quiet knock on her door and a visitor was admitted.

Mrs Lufton was an apologetic woman, with drab clothes and colourless hair. There was nothing about her to attract attention or interest. She was anonymous. And yet, surprisingly perhaps, she held a very senior position in the War Department Inspectorate.

They sat, facing each other. 'I've received orders,' Miss Feelgood said quietly. 'We've been instructed to find a supply of explosives.'

Mrs Lufton thought for a moment. 'We can do that,' she said softly.

'Tea, dear?'

'Yes, please. What kind of explosive?'

'Gelignite.'

'It's for a building, then. But do we have anyone with the necessary skill to blow up a building?'

'Of course we don't! You know perfectly well that most of our members are idiots! We have a chronic shortage of experts. Fortunately, *we* are not doing the blowing up. The Jerries are probably parachuting in a trained saboteur. They're being secretive about that. Our job is to get hold of the explosives – *and* one of us will have to supervise the delivery.'

Exciting, Mrs Lufton was thinking. *A proper mission! At last!*

'Who will you send?'

Miss Feelgood sprinkled some white powder into her tea and stirred it in. 'A flavoured sweetener,' she murmured. 'I picked it up in Berlin before the War. Would you like to try some in yours?'

Mrs Lufton was not a fool. No power on earth would ever persuade her to drink anything that Miss Feelgood had put powder in.

'Cyclops,' Miss Feelgood said thoughtfully. 'I'm sending Cyclops.'

'Why Cyclops?'

'He's been a very bad boy,' Miss Feelgood said slowly. 'He's got us into trouble.'

'Oh, *no*! What's he done?'

'The list. *Our list!* He has let it fall into the hands – would you believe it! – of a child. Some ragamuffin he came across in the East End.'

The visitor straightened her shoulders and her small grey face hardened. 'How?'

Miss Feelgood explained. 'He knows perfectly well that lists should always be memorised and destroyed,' she said. 'It has all our names on it – including *yours*!' she added venomously.

'I suppose it could happen to anyone.'

'Not to me,' Miss Feelgood said.

It was true. Miss Feelgood did not make mistakes. And she had no understanding of people who did. Mistakes were foreign to her nature. That was why she was their leader.

'Do we know the name of this child?' Mrs Lufton asked.

'Yes. But no thanks to *him*. He refused to tell me.'

Mrs Lufton was filled with amazement and envy that anyone would dare to refuse an order from Miss Feelgood. 'Why?'

'Some nonsense! He said he didn't want the name of an *innocent child* to get mixed up with ours.'

'Then how did you find out her name?'

'Quick thinking, of course!' she said. 'I ordered him to trace her whereabouts – and recover that bit of paper.'

It was obvious that Mrs Lufton did not understand. Miss Feelgood watched her contemptuously.

'Then I followed him. It wasn't difficult in the blackout. Even you could have done it.'

Still Mrs Lufton failed to understand. 'Where did he go?'

'He started at a police station, but that didn't work because he told them he'd lost *his daughter* during an air raid. They refused to help unless he could prove he was her father. Then he went to a Women's Voluntary Service centre, but they were shutting up for the night and told him to come back next morning.'

Mrs Lufton said she found it hard to believe that a missing girl could be traced that way.

Miss Feelgood ignored her. 'At the third attempt he was inside longer, talking. That looked hopeful, I thought. So when he'd left I went in myself and asked if my husband had been there, looking for our missing daughter. *Ah!* they said. *You must be Mrs Conway! I'm sure Anna will turn up. Try not to worry.*'

'So her name is Anna Conway?'

'Yes. Or Hannah Conway, perhaps.'

'Where does she live?'

'There's a problem about that. According to Cyclops, her home was destroyed before Christmas, and she moved in with a neighbour. Then that house too was blitzed and the child stayed for a couple of days at the home of a policeman. Then she disappeared. There is no trace of her.'

'Have you checked the official casualties?'

'Of course. Her name is not among them.'

'It is very unlikely that a child would know what the list was. Or would even have bothered to keep it.'

'It is equally possible,' Stephanie Feelgood retorted, 'that she might have guessed what it was and taken it to the police. If she does that, we'll all be hanged for treason.'

Mrs Lufton turned pale. 'That is very unlikely,' she said. 'Most adults are too stupid to have given the list a moment's thought – and children are even stupider.'

'It is my experience,' Miss Feelgood said icily, 'that stupid adults are far more stupid than sensible children. *I* was not a stupid child. I would have known what that list was.'

It would be a mistake to think that these two women liked each other. They didn't. They worked for a common cause, that's all. 'Then what is to be done?' Mrs Lufton asked.

'She must be found,' Miss Feelgood replied. 'Around New Year thousands of children were leaving Liverpool Street station. This girl was in that area – and it seems likely to me that she joined those evacuees and left London.'

The visitor waited. Miss Feelgood continued. 'You have access to official evacuation lists.'

'I've never seen any!'

'You are an inspector. *Insist* on seeing them! *All* of them! I'm sure they need to be inspected.' She emphasised the consonants as she spoke, so that each word came out like a tiny piece of broken concrete. '*M*eanness and *sp*ite are your *sp*eciality. This is a chance for you to be *parti*cularly *m*ean and *sp*iteful.'

'And *if* I find out where she is?'

'Cyclops got us into this mess. It will be his responsibility to get back the list.'

There was a perceptible pause. Mrs Lufton waited. '*And* deal with the child?' she asked.

'Yes,' Miss Feelgood said quietly, 'he's a murderous brute. And I've never entirely trusted him. So when he's dealt with the girl, I may have to deal with *him*.'

This conversation was still running through Mrs Lufton's head as she walked downstairs and through the tea-room where Miss Feelgood's patriotic customers were innocently enjoying their teas.

-8-

'There's Nothing Here!'

Hannah slept through most of the next day, until the evening. Ollie brought her some supper on a tray. 'I bin an ad a look at yew from time t time,' he said slowly. 'But yew bin fast asleep all day.'

It was a fried meal – bacon, eggs, and bubble and squeak. It was delicious. Ollie sat on the bed and watched while she ate it. Afterwards she said, 'Where's the lav?'

He grinned at that. 'Out in the backyard!' he said. That didn't surprise her; plenty of places in London had the same arrangement. 'But there's a jerry under the bed.' He bent down and pulled out the chamber pot. 'I'll empty it later – but yew'll ha to dew it y'self when yew're better.'

Then he left her to it. Hannah remembered her gran, who used to be amused by the word *jerry*. She found it funny that the word for a chamber pot also meant a German. *I'd like to piss on all of them!* she used to say. She could be rude, her gran.

But Hannah felt dizzy out of bed. So, when she'd done, she got straight back in and went to sleep again.

On the second morning it was Mrs Pickens who came up,

not Ollie. 'Yew feelin any better?'

She *was* feeling better, a lot better. She felt a lifting of the spirits because the morning sun was shining into the room. She hadn't seen sunlight since before the War. (She knew that wasn't strictly true, but that's what it felt like.)

Mrs Pickens found her clothes from somewhere. 'Yew cn take your pick an come down as soon as yew're ready,' she said. 'An yew'll need a good wash. All oover! Best place for dewin that is in the kitchen. Thas the warmest place. And there oon't be anybody there cept me!' she added as she left the bedroom.

Mrs Pickens had taken away Hannah's old clothes – such as they were. Hannah laid out the new stuff on the bed. There was a pair of shoes, ankle socks, stockings, and rubber bands to hold them up (but not proper garters). Elasticated knickers, vest, skirt, blouse, a grey gym-slip and a woolly jumper. And a mac.

For three days she never left the house. And in time she began to help with cleaning and cooking. Mrs Pickens didn't talk much but she seemed to like Hannah. And as the days went by Hannah told her what had happened in London. Some of it, anyway.

She paid close attention to Mrs Pickens, and slowly she learned to understand those gloomy predictions she made. 'This bacon eent never gooin to be enough for five people!' she'd say. But there was always enough bacon. 'I dunno how we're gonna keep warm with oonly this amount of coal!' But the kitchen was always warm. 'I don't know where yew'll end up, but yew can't stay ere.' But Hannah *did* stay there, and no one seemed to mind.

Except Mr Pickens. He never spoke to her, not once. He didn't say much to any of them, just the occasional grunt. She'd catch him staring at her, *glaring* would be a better word. How he could glare! His look was sometimes so malevolent it almost made her flinch.

Hannah usually tried to influence people and make them like her. She was good at it, but she got nowhere with him. And yet his family didn't seem to be troubled by him.

He could make his meaning clear without saying a word. Once, at supper, he looked long and hard at the toad in the hole on Hannah's plate. Then he looked at the others' plates. She knew exactly what he was thinking. There were six Brussels sprouts on hers, and only four on Betty's. Mr Pickens reached across, speared one of Hannah's sprouts with his fork, and plonked it on the little girl's plate.

'Betty doon't like sprouts,' Mrs Pickens said calmly. Hannah felt humiliated and angry but she didn't say anything.

Luckily, he was out for most of the day. He went out before she got up, and he came home at around four o'clock. He fell asleep then, in an armchair by the range. After supper, he would go out to a shed that was behind the house. She didn't know what he did there, and she didn't care as long as he stayed away from her.

She learned the geography of the house. She worked out which things were kept in the cupboards, what each of the rooms was used for, and where the candles and oil lamps were stored. Her body was learning too – how many steps there were on the stairs, and how low you had to stoop when you went out to the back scullery.

One morning she went outside for the first time. It must have been a Saturday, because Ollie showed no sign of going to school.

Ollie said, 'Dew yew put on suffin warm and then I'll show yew round outside.'

Wrapped up with woollen scarf and gloves, Hannah followed him into the open air. Betty came too, like a quiet little animal. 'Ollie! Dew you pull up a few leeks for supper!' his mother called out.

The frost outside was like an electric shock. She'd never seen such a big pale blue sky, or such brilliance. It was a huge, transparent morning, white and dazzling, and every surface was frozen like rock.

She looked around in dismay. 'There's nothing here!' she said. She'd never seen such emptiness.

'Ah, thas all yew know!' Ollie said.

I've hurt his feelings, she thought.

Around the house there was a small garden, and the earth was as black as coal. There were dry frozen puddles on the path and they cracked like gunshot when they were trodden on.

There were a few rows of sad-looking green things, which Ollie said were the leeks. He didn't try to pull any up. 'They're fruz into the ground,' he said. 'There'll be noo leeks tnight unless the weather changes. We'll ha to hev sprouts agin. Hev ya ever picked sprouts when they're fruz on the stalk?'

Well, of course she hadn't! And he knew she hadn't. He was getting his own back. She didn't even know they grew on stalks! If she'd thought about it (which she hadn't) she would have supposed they grew in the ground, like tiny cabbages.

'What's that?' she asked him. There was a massive, long bank of black earth, about six feet high, with neatly sloped sides. Someone had been digging at one end, there was loose straw about, and some old sacks had been laid across the hole.

'Thas a tater clamp,' he said.

She hadn't a clue what he was talking about, but she didn't let on.

'Let's goo up on to the riverbank,' he said. He led her along the garden path and up the slope to the bank. There was a bridge, the one they'd crossed on the night she arrived.

She was expecting to see a river under the bridge. The bridge was real enough – a wooden slatted construction, wide enough to take a vehicle. But there was *no river*! There was no anything! She couldn't believe her eyes. A bridge that went over a non-river! Two grassy banks wound their way together between the fields, high above the landscape, with a wide space between them. But there was no water there, nothing but a tangle of dead grass, bleached and flattened by the rain.

Nothing in this weird place was ever what she expected! 'Where's the river?' she said.

'Oover there!'

Ollie pointed across the flat fields. About half a mile away there was another riverbank, only that one seemed to be as straight as a ruler. 'They moved it,' he added. 'About a hundred year agoo.'

She was going to have to learn this place like a foreign language. She only half understood what the people said anyway – and it was the same with the landscape. She could make no sense of it.

They stood on the bridge, the three of them, leaning on the rail in the brilliant sunshine. Hannah thought of her father. *Standing on the bridge* meant something different to him, and she could imagine him doing it.

Ollie pointed out the features of his homeland. He was still smarting because she'd said there was nothing there.

Beyond the new river a couple of miles away she could see a few rooftops and a church. 'Thas Great Deeping,' Ollie said.

'Is this Little Deeping, then?' she asked.

'No. This is the Old Bank.'

Downstream (only there *was* no stream) he pointed towards a big airbase. You couldn't see it, but it was there, he said. 'Thas Norfolk oover there.'

'Is this Norfolk? Where we are?'

'No. We're in the Isle of Ely. An thas Ely Cathedral.' He turned round and pointed in the opposite direction.

She'd heard of that. But there was a haziness on the horizon and she could see no sign of the cathedral.

'An they're our neighbours,' he said, pointing slightly nearer.

Neighbours? The nearest was a quarter of a mile away! In her gran's house the neighbours had been on the other side of a wall, and you could hear them talking.

There were five houses, three on one side of the Old River, and two on the other where the road was. She stared at them. Each one was tucked up close against the riverbank.

In a field about half a mile away there was a tiny figure leading a big horse. Betty tugged her sleeve and said quietly, 'Thas Pa.'

'He's spooster be ploughin today,' Ollie said. 'But the ground's rock hard, so he'll aveter find suffin else to git on with.'

But Hannah had had enough. That huge sky was exhilarating and very lovely. But the emptiness made her nervous. It almost *hurt*. She'd known when she got on the train at Liverpool Street that she was going a long way from London. But this was like being sent into exile – and then banished again, even further away.

Her woollen glove had stuck to the frost on the wooden railing. She pulled it free and asked to go back in, pretending it was because she was cold. Again she thought to herself, *there's nothing here*!

-9-

Barnaby Hamilton

The evening lessons became Konrad's favourite activity. His teacher was called Fraulein Eva. Her surname was never used, and she seemed to have no military rank. She wore civilian clothes. She was attractive, quick-witted and quiet.

She had her secrets, Konrad thought, and he liked that.

'If you are picked up by the British police, you must not be Konrad Friedmann,' she said. 'I am going to change you into a different person. This will be possible only because you have no trace of a German accent.'

'A real person?'

'Yes. His name was *Barnaby Hamilton*. If you are arrested by the authorities, he is the person you will be.'

Konrad waited. The smoke from Fraulein Eva's cigarette curled slowly towards the open window, and out into the darkness.

'You must leave Konrad Friedmann here in Austria. Nothing of him will travel with you to England. That is imperative.'

'How old was he?'

'About the same age as you. A few months before War broke

out, he ran away from his boarding school and was never seen again.'

'He might have died.'

'No death has been reported. Nothing is known about him after that. In any case, you will become Barnaby Hamilton.'

'The police will question the headmaster.'

'He is dead.'

'The deputy headmaster then.'

'He came to Germany in 1939 and joined the Nazi party.'

Their source, Konrad thought. *He was probably the school's German teacher.* He could see it all.

'The boy's family?'

'He had no family. There was an elderly aunt who paid for him to attend the school. She died in 1939. There was no money left and the boy's future was uncertain. That was another reason for running away.'

'The teachers?' he said.

'There were only five teachers. It was a small school.'

'But the police will contact them. A photograph will be sufficient – they will know I am not Barnaby Hamilton.'

'One was killed in the London Blitzkreig, two are our prisoners of war. The other two are in the British forces overseas.'

'They can be contacted.' *I am talking like a spy*, Konrad thought.

'Yes. But it would take some weeks to locate them and get

64

photographs sent out. And for them to be questioned. There will be enough time for you to complete your mission.'

'Boarding schools always have a housekeeper.'

'She too came to Germany.'

'With the deputy headmaster?'

'Correct.'

'And the groundsman?'

'There was no groundsman. The pupils themselves kept the sports field in good order.'

Not a very good school, Konrad thought. 'I will need an identity card.'

'We are preparing one.'

'Is there a photograph of Barnaby Hamilton?'

'Only one. It is a picture of a soccer team. Barnaby is one of them.'

'What subjects was he good at?'

'Maths, science, history.'

'And bad at?'

'None. But English and art bored him.'

'His character?'

'Moody.'

'That was because he was unhappy.'

'It doesn't matter whether he was unhappy or not.' Fraulein Eva spoke sharply.

But it does, rather, Konrad thought. 'Was he well behaved?'

'He had a certificate for good conduct.'

'Have you got it?'

'We are making it.'

'When did he start to attend this boarding school?'

'When he was seven.'

'Then I will need to know . . .'

That was when the lessons started in earnest. Young Barnaby had once had parents, but no brothers or sisters. Konrad needed to know about next-door neighbours, the distant aunt, his home, his bedroom, the garden, toys, books. The list was endless. Then there were the details of life at the school – his best friends, the school rules, the punishments, which boys slept in his dorm. And Konrad learned every detail, even the tiniest. What was not known had to be made up. Every evening he learned a little more. And every evening Fraulein Eva interrogated him, trying to catch him out.

His daily lessons became a game. She had taught him the rules and then they competed with one another. But she told him nothing about herself. That was part of the game too. Some boys might have fantasised about her private life, imagining details. Not Konrad. He *liked* the way she enclosed herself in secrecy.

She never once trapped him into making a mistake. 'You win,' she said. 'Every time.' But it didn't matter, because his victories were her triumphs too.

*

Konrad's days were so full of activity, and he slept such a deep and exhausted sleep at night, that he was able to set aside the dilemma that troubled him.

But it was always there. What would he do when he arrived in England? Half of him was British, and he didn't think he could bring himself to blow up a building that was part of the British War effort. Especially if there were people inside it.

His waking hours were filled with the need to prepare himself for Operation Blackout. But at the back of his mind he always knew that when it came to it, he might not be able to carry it through. He also knew that, if he didn't, his mother and sister would be taken away and shot.

He never for one moment doubted the Nazis would do this.

*

On his last evening he was summoned to Fraulein Eva's office so that he could be finally transformed into Barnaby Hamilton. Every detail was perfect. There was a slim leather wallet, polished by use. In it was Barnaby's identity card, rubbed and dog-eared. And his good-conduct certificate.

There was a photograph, worn and shabby, showing young Barnaby in a goalkeeper's woollen jersey and gloves, standing proudly with his arms folded and one foot resting on the ball. Around him the other players were lined up, with a lean, beaky man wearing specs. Konrad knew them all by name and history.

There were also a couple of old school reports, folded so sharply that they were beginning to fall apart into small squares.

There was an almost-new raincoat ('You stole it from a shop,' the Fraulein explained), boy's short trousers, and a dark green school blazer with a coat of arms on its breast pocket. It was worn and shabby, a brilliant work of art, with holes in the elbows and frayed cuffs.

But Konrad's heart jumped in dismay. Had they made a mistake? Or was he being tested? For the blazer fitted him perfectly.

'I ran away from school two years ago,' he pointed out. 'I have grown. *So has my blazer, apparently!*'

Fraulein Eva was furious, either with herself or with the unknown person who had made the clothes. Someone would be working all night to correct the mistake.

All that painstaking preparation, Konrad thought – it might all have been wasted because of one small oversight.

At breakfast the next morning, everyone shook Konrad's hand and wished him luck. Fraulein Eva said, 'From this moment Konrad Friedmann has ceased to exist. Barnaby Hamilton is going to England! You must leave behind everything that belonged to your former life.'

But Konrad had no intention of leaving everything behind. There was one precious item that he smuggled out. So he too made a mistake; one small error of judgement.

-10-

Officially on the List

On a bright morning when she was in her bedroom, Hannah heard a car, out of sight, winding its way slowly along the narrow road on the far side of the Old River. When it reached the wooden bridge it stopped, and the driver made her way on foot over the bridge towards the house.

'I'm Mrs Daisy Ollerton-Handy,' Hannah heard her say when Mrs Pickens opened the front door. 'I'm one of the County Organisers of Evacuees.'

Now I'm for it! Hannah thought. She crept downstairs and stood in the shadows in the kitchen.

Mrs Pickens folded her arms and stood with her head slightly on one side. 'How-ja-dew!' she said. Polite, but not welcoming.

'I believe you have an evacuee here?' The visitor spoke a language that everyone was familiar with. It was the language of people who organise things.

'Thas right! We dew.'

'Mrs – Mrs *Pickens*, is it? May I come in? There are some matters we must discuss.'

So Mrs Pickens let her in. 'Take a seat,' she said, and indicated one of the chairs at the kitchen table.

'Is the child here?'

'I'm here,' Hannah said, and stepped forward.

'She should be at school.' Mrs Ollerton-Handy was nervous, Hannah could tell.

'Noo one een't told us which school she's gotta goo tew.'

'I see. What is your name, child?'

'Hannah Conway.'

She deliberately didn't say *miss*, or *ma'am*, and she could see that Mrs Ollerton-Handy noticed. But the way she'd looked round the kitchen had annoyed Hannah.

'What happened to you?'

Hannah spoke quietly, almost in a whisper. 'We got bombed out. My grandmother was killed – and they pulled me out of the rubble.' She didn't waste words.

'You lived with her? Yes, I see. Where are your parents?'

'My mother died when I was six. And my dad, he's in the Royal Navy. I don't know where. Somewhere in the world.'

'His rank?'

'Captain.' Hannah always felt proud when she said that.

Mrs Ollerton-Handy leaned back thoughtfully in her chair. 'This girl is not on any of our lists,' she said to Mrs Pickens. 'Still, that doesn't matter provided you don't mind having her.'

Mrs Pickens raised her chin a little. 'We never did mind

havin vacuees,' she said, 'only yew lot said we weren't sposed to ave none.'

'Only because you live so far from . . . so far from anywhere else.'

'Well, she een't got noowhere else to goo.'

'No,' Mrs Ollerton-Handy said slowly. 'How did she end up here?'

'Ollie – Oliver, my boy – he found her at the station. Arter all the others ad gone.'

'A chance evacuee,' Daisy Ollerton-Handy said, smiling a little.

'It wasn't chance,' Hannah said. 'He found me and brought me here.'

'I meant that he just *happened* to be there when you –'

Hannah felt stubborn. 'No!' she said. 'He *decided* to ask me if I wanted to go home with him. That's not chance!'

She knew what was going through Daisy Ollerton-Handy's mind. *Well*, she was thinking, *not* your typical evacuee! But she wasn't an unkind person, Hannah thought. She rose to her feet, thanked Mrs Pickens, and said Hannah's name would be officially added to the list. 'But she'll have to go to school.'

'Ah, but which one?'

'How old are you, Hannah?'

'Ten. Nearly eleven.'

Mrs Ollerton-Handy made a decision. 'She must go tomorrow to the local school at Deeping,' she said. 'And later we'll find out if she's clever enough to go to the High School at Ely.'

'Noo one from down ere ever goos to the High School,' Mrs Pickens said. Then she said to Hannah, 'Thas some posh place. In Ely.'

'Have you got your ration books?'

'Yes.'

'Identity card?

Hannah ran upstairs to find her identity card.

'Gas mask?' said Mrs Ollerton-Handy, when she came back down.

She shook her head. 'I lost that . . .'

'I have a spare one in my car,' she said.

'She oont need noo gas mask,' Mrs Pickens said. 'Why would Jerry want to bother about gassin us lot, out here?'

'He probably wouldn't, but he might want to gas the airfield. And that isn't far away.'

Hannah disliked it when people talked about *Jerry*, meaning all Germans. Even her grandmother used to do it. She understood why everyone hated Germany but it made her feel uneasy. She'd spent six weeks in Germany before the War, and it was the best time of her life. But she'd learned not to talk about it. When she told some of the girls at school, Louisa Carstairs had spread gossip that Hannah was a Nazi spy.

After that she kept her German holiday at the back of her thoughts, along with her other secrets.

Mrs Pickens sniffed. Still, when Daisy Ollerton-Handy held her hand out, she took it and said goodbye.

When she'd gone Hannah said, 'It's going to mean a lot of trouble, having me here. I'm sorry.'

'Yew een't no trouble,' Mrs Pickens said. 'We like havin yew here.' But Hannah knew she was thinking to herself, *What have I let myself in for?*

-II-

Erased

Deep underground, in the basement of a government building in central London, a group of twelve women worked every day – volunteers trying to impose order on confusion.

In charge of them was Lady Rainns, who – like them – was doing her bit for the War effort. She was none too pleased – and neither were her fellow volunteers – when their work was interrupted by a visitor one dark and wet afternoon. They were even less pleased when they learned that she was from the War Department Inspectorate, and had come to inspect them.

No one likes to be inspected. It makes you feel you're not trusted to do your job.

However, there was nothing for it; they had to pretend they were pleased to see her. 'Where would you like to start?' Lady Rainns asked.

'Well,' Mrs Lufton said, 'your work is to keep a record of all the children who have left London. So perhaps I should inspect those records.'

'*All* of them?' said Lady Rainns.

'Of course not! Let's say –' Mrs Lufton paused as if selecting a railway station at random – 'Liverpool Street. Yes, I'd like to see details of the children who've been evacuated from Liverpool Street station since Christmas.'

So Mrs Lufton found herself a little later in a very dark corner seated at a table with several books filled with handwritten names. There was one for children who had gone to Ely, another for a place called Littleport. And one for somewhere called Great Deeping. And several others.

The books were full of crossings-out and rewritings, as the women in the basement did their best to record the constantly changing locations of the evacuees. They refused to *stay put*, those tiresome children! Some just came home. Some moved to different addresses. Some went to join aunts and uncles who lived in Wales or Cornwall. Some got lost altogether.

Some had come back to London for Christmas and been killed in the bombing.

Mrs Lufton could see that the task of Lady Rainns and her helpers was almost beyond them. She was relieved when she was able to escape at last. She joined them for a cup of tea, thanked them, said their work was admirable in difficult circumstances, and fled.

Out in the chilly darkening afternoon she hailed a taxi. As she leaned wearily back into her seat she ran over in her mind the events of the afternoon.

She'd never expected to find what she was looking for. But she'd found a name at the bottom of the Great Deeping list –

added lightly in pencil, in different handwriting, with a later date: *Hannah Conway – the Old Bank.*

Odd, thought Mrs Lufton. Old post offices and old rectories were sometimes converted into private homes. But she didn't think she'd ever heard of an *old bank.*

On the table there'd been a small wooden box with pen nibs, pencils and other dusty odds and ends. In it she'd found an eraser, and quickly and efficiently made use of it.

There was no longer any record of Hannah Conway. She'd been rubbed out.

-12-

Mucker Bailey

Walking home from school took an hour.

One bitterly cold day in Hannah's second week at the school in Great Deeping, the darkness was already closing in when they set off home. They were just crossing the railway line when Ollie said, 'There's Mucker! Comin to meet us.'

'Mucker?' Hannah said. 'Who's Mucker?'

'Mucker Bailey. He's my mate. He lives next door.'

That would be why she'd never met Mucker Bailey before – *next door* was a quarter of a mile along the riverbank!

'Why is he called Mucker?'

'Dunno. His dad's called Mucker too.'

'What's his proper name?'

'Cyril. But noo one never calls im nothin but Mucker. Cept teachers.'

Mucker Bailey was ambling along the empty fen road towards them. He seemed to be about Hannah's age, and he walked with a kind of slouch.

'Wotcher, Ollie.'

'Wotcher, Mucker.'

'Is this your vacuee?'

Hannah didn't like being talked about as if she wasn't there. So she said she was, and told him her name. 'Have you been ill?' she asked him. 'I've never seen you at school.'

'I doon't goo t school much,' he said. 'I reckon I'm a bit thick, y'know.' He was grinning. Did he really think he was stupid, wondered Hannah, or he was being sarcastic?

'Don't you get into trouble?'

'No. They send the tendance officer round from time t time, and I goo t school for a day or tew. Then I stop at hum agin. *They* doon't care! They make out they dew, but they doon't rairly.'

Hannah could tell that Ollie wanted her to think well of Mucker. 'He's ever so good at rat-catchin,' he said proudly. 'You should see him in action!'

'What I really like is *planes*!' Mucker said. He started telling Ollie about a German reconnaissance plane that had flown over that morning. 'But I like bombers best,' he said to Hannah.

'Every time a heavy bomber goos over he wets hisself,' Ollie said.

'Is he scared of them?'

'No! He *likes* em. Thas why he wets hisself.'

Hannah stared at Mucker. 'What's your mum say?'

'She doon't know! I doon't goo hum till thas dried.'

Mucker's house was the next one along the Old Bank and he persuaded them to go with him to see his ferrets. Hannah didn't need much persuading. She'd never seen a ferret, and Ollie was willing.

On the way there Ollie told her how one day last summer Mucker had got a tomato seed stuck inside a hollow tooth. 'That ole seed, that started to *grow*!' Ollie said.

Hannah didn't believe a word of it. But they both said it was the truth. 'I ad to goo t the doctor to have the seed taken out,' Mucker said. 'And the doctor said, if they'd left it where it was that would have growed right up through the back of my nose and into my brain.'

And Ollie said, 'And the roots would have growed downwards until they come out at the other end.'

Hannah only half believed this fantastic story. 'What happened?' she said.

'Doctor, he had a thing with a little hook on the end. He hoiked out the seed all right. But the tooth come away as well! *Bleed?* There was blood everywhere!'

He pulled his top lip upwards and sideways, and showed her a gap. It was not a pleasant sight.

But it wasn't Mucker's tomato seed that made her remember that day, nor his ferrets.

Although they *were* something, those ferrets! Mucker took them round to the back where there was a wash house, attached to the scullery. Just a lean-to, with an earth floor. It was dark in there but Mucker had a torch, and she could see there was a lot of clutter. There was a table, Mrs Bailey's mangle, and what looked like a rabbit hutch. In the hutch there were two ferrets.

Hannah thought they were lovely. Mucker took them both out and let her hold one, and it was as soft as silk. And so active, never still for a second! She reckoned the ferrets were cleaner than Mucker was, but she didn't say that.

'They allus wake up at about this time,' Mucker told her.

'What are they called?'

'Love-me and Leave-me,' he said.

On the wall a couple of dead rabbits were hanging with their heads down. They had already been gutted. 'Love-Me got them two smornin,' Mucker said. 'I gotta take one on em to Mrs Murfitt at the railway house tnight. She'll give me tew bob for that.'

'What about the other one?'

'Thas for us. My ma'll skin it and cook it up tomorrer, and what's left'll goo into a stew the day after.'

For the rest of her life Hannah remembered the dead rabbits – and the ferrets that had caught them. She had only to close her eyes and concentrate – and she could see and smell and remember what it was like in that dark little wash house. But what happened next truly gave her the horrors. Perhaps that's why she remembered the scene so clearly.

Mucker's mum came in from the house. She was a big woman you wouldn't want to quarrel with. 'Wotcher, Ollie,' she said. Ollie told her Hannah was his new evacuee.

'My name's Hannah Conway,' she said.

Mrs Bailey looked thoughtful for a moment. 'Hannah Conway?' she said. 'Thas a funny thing! There was a man round here this morning lookin for yew.'

Hannah's first thought was that her dad had come home. But that was impossible. Even if he had, he wouldn't know where she was.

'Queer bloke,' Mrs Bailey said. 'Big and tall. Built like a lighthouse. And he had only one eye.'

'Where was it?' Mucker said.

'On is face, you daft twerp! Where dyew think it was?'

'Was it in the *middle* of his face?'

Mrs Bailey folded her enormous arms and glared at him. 'He ad *two* eyes but one of them was made of glass. Is that clear enough for yer? They were where you'd expect a pair of eyes t be, yew bloody-grut moron! One on one side, and one on the other!'

Hannah felt as if she was turning white in the light of the candle, and Mrs Bailey stepped closer and asked her if she was all right.

'This man, did he really say my name?'

But even as she asked the question she remembered. He'd told her his name was Cycle-tops, or something like that. And she had told him hers. What a fool she'd been!

And now he'd come to find her. What did he want? What had she done?

*

They walked back along the top of the riverbank, Ollie and Hannah, and Mucker too. Ollie kept talking about ferrets and rabbit-catching, but all Hannah could think about was the fact that Cycle-tops had come all this way to find her. The memory of him in that dark, bombed-out building in the rain was bad enough – but the thought of him *there* was truly frightening. How had he found out where she was? That was sinister. And *why*? That was even more sinister.

The big empty landscape was fading into shadow. The flat fields and the distant scattered houses were slowly swallowed by the dark.

Back at Ollie's house, Mr Pickens was in the backyard, digging out spuds from the clamp. They went short of lots of things, those fen people, but never potatoes. There were spuds everywhere.

He straightened up slowly with one hand on his back, and glared as they went past.

Inside, Betty took Hannah's hand. She'd been crying. 'What's the matter?' Hannah asked her.

Mrs Pickens came in from outside with a bucket of muddy potatoes. 'That there tendance woman as bin, and she says Betty's gotta start school. I told her she's oonly six, but she says thas the law.'

Betty looked hopefully up at Hannah as if she could

do something about it.

'An I said thas too far for a littlun to walk. All that way! Then *she* say thas my problem, not hers. Bloody ole cow!'

Hannah started to wash the potatoes in a bucket of water, and Mrs Pickens took up the old knife she always used for peeling.

She was in a glum mood. 'Thas the way people treat us,' she said. 'They forgit all about us for ages, then they come down on us like a ton o bricks for breaking some rewl they've made. That reminds me – someone come asking for yew.'

Of course Hannah knew who she meant. 'A big man with a glass eye. Ever so polite he was! But who is he, and wha's he want yew for?'

Ollie's dad had come in. 'We doon't want her bringin a load of London riff-raff down ere,' he said. And that was remarkable, because in the three weeks she'd been there that was only the third time he'd mentioned her. Even then, he hadn't spoken *to* her.

Nobody took any notice of Mucker and he sat down beside the clothes horse and watched what was going on.

'Lord, gal!' Ollie's mum said to Hannah. 'Yew look as white as a sheet! Who *is* this man with oonly one eye?'

So Hannah told them everything about that night in London. She'd always been good at telling stories, and she had them paying attention. None of them had ever seen a bombed-out street. They'd never seen London at night, with bombs screaming down. They'd never even *been* to London! *Ever!*

So she made a good tale of it. And she told them how she'd stumbled on this man in the dark, and his glass eye, and the torch he'd shone up into the sky.

And she told them about the list he'd dropped.

'D'yew think thas what he wants? This list?'

What else could it be?

'Hev ya still got it?'

She ran upstairs and fetched it, folded inside her identity card. They could make nothing of it. It was just names and numbers. Ollie's dad peered at it, frowning.

Hannah hated the list. She wished she'd never seen it.

'I reckon we should take this to the police,' Mrs Pickens said. 'That means trouble!'

'I got a better idea,' Mr Pickens growled. He screwed the paper into a ball and was going to throw it on to the fire. But Hannah grabbed his wrist and stopped him.

'Yew daft ole fool!' his wife said. 'If yew burn it, whas she gooin t tell im when he comes askin for it?'

'She could just tell im she lost it,' Ollie said.

They were all staring at Hannah as she placed the crumpled bit of paper on the tabletop and smoothed it out. 'It wouldn't have mattered anyway,' she said. 'I learned the list by heart. I thought it might be important.'

She felt very lonely that day.

-13-

The Scene of the Crash

On their way home one afternoon Ollie and Hannah saw Mucker coming to meet them again. He was in great excitement. 'Didya hear it in the night?' he yelled before he'd even reached them.

'Hear what?' Ollie said. 'I never heard nuffin.'

'Did yew?' Mucker said to Hannah.

But she hadn't heard anything either. She didn't know what he was talking about.

'A plane come down in the night – further along the bank!'

'Are you sure?' Ollie said.

When they got home, Ollie got his bike out with the cart attached, and Hannah climbed in. They followed Mucker along the lane that went winding beside the riverbank, further out into the fen.

The road was still made of tarmac, just. But grass grew in the middle of it, and it became muddier and muddier the further they went. Finally the road died out completely and changed into a grassy track.

And what a sight they found there! There was a massive

low-loader belonging to the RAF. And Mucker had been right. There *was* a crashed plane – a German Junkers, Mucker said. The airmen had winched the wreckage on to the back of the truck with chains. It was tangled and ugly, and smeared with black mud. One wing was tangled and crushed, the other stuck up high above the cab of the truck.

There was a long and slightly twisted scar in the earth, where the wrecked aircraft had been hauled across the ploughed field.

Mucker and Ollie got as close as they dared, hoping to see a corpse or two inside. But the RAF men sent them packing.

'We'll goo back later and see if there's any bits left in the field,' Ollie said. 'We might find a finger or a leg or suffin.'

'Or a head,' Mucker suggested.

Tempers were short. It had taken the men all day to get the plane off the field. And because there wasn't enough room to turn the low-loader around they were going to have to reverse the truck all the way back to the main road. More than two miles, Ollie reckoned.

There was a good deal of swearing, and the men were red-faced and sweaty.

The three of them cycled back ahead of the reversing vehicle. When they got to the wooden bridge across the empty river, they stood there and watched the truck go by, whining and revving, and occasionally getting it wrong and having to draw forward and start again.

-14-

Mrs Lufton Takes Tea with Mrs Feelgood

About a week after her inspection of the evacuation lists, Mrs Lufton was again in the room above Feelgood's Tea-Room in London, taking tea.

'As far as the written records go,' Mrs Lufton said, 'Hannah Conway has been eradicated.'

If Mrs Lufton expected Miss Feelgood to say *well done* for finding Hannah Conway's name among the lists of evacuees, she was disappointed. But Mrs Lufton did not expect that. Miss Feelgood never said thank you. And she never gave praise.

'It's only her name that's been eradicated,' she murmured. 'It is strange the girl should have gone to Great Deeping.'

'Strange? Why is it strange?'

'Because,' Miss Feelgood said slowly, 'Great Deeping is mentioned in my orders. We have been instructed to arrange for the gelignite to be delivered there. To Great Deeping.'

'It's just a coincidence,' Mrs Lufton said.

'But it's still odd.'

'Coincidences are always odd.'

Miss Feelgood stirred her tea. 'It's convenient, actually,' she said. 'I can kill two birds with one stone.'

'In a manner of speaking,' Mrs Lufton said.

Miss Feelgood stared at her. 'I've sent Cyclops there,' she said. 'He phoned last night to report back to me. He has located the girl – this Hannah Conway. It's all working out rather well. But he hasn't got hold of the list.'

'I see. But . . . ?'

'I plan to go down to this place, Great Deeping. I have to check on the explosives in any case.'

'Would you like me to go with you?'

Mrs Lufton got a cold look in reply to that question. 'No, dear. This is a job for the person in command. I doubt if you would be up to it.'

'Why wouldn't I?' *I do wish my voice wouldn't squeak when I'm cross!*

'Because, if that girl has any idea of the meaning of the list, Cyclops will have to *deal with her.*'

'But then he will have a hold over us,' Mrs Lufton said slowly.

'Yes.'

'So . . . ?'

'So *I* shall deal with *him.*'

Their words remained in the air like delicate wisps of poison. Invisible and deadly.

I wish, Mrs Lufton thought as she watched her companion raise her teacup to her lips, *I wish I could deal with you.* But she knew she wasn't brave enough to try.

'I shall go down as an Inspector of Evacuees – and I'll use your name.'

'*What?*' Mrs Lufton's face had gone white and she half rose from her chair.

'There's no need to get into one of your panics. You heard what I said.'

'But any –' Mrs Lufton hesitated – 'anything you do while you're there will be blamed on me!' Her voice squeaked.

'All you have to do, dear,' Miss Feelgood said calmly, 'is to get yourself a good alibi.'

'An alibi?'

'Yes. Make sure you are *seen* in London. Or *anywhere*. It doesn't matter where, as long as it isn't Great Deeping. So that you can't possibly be accused of anything that might happen there. And just don't make a fuss! Leave it to me.'

-15-

Hilda Pritt is Mystified

'Hilda? Will you come for a drive with me? Just a few miles. Something I want to show you.'

'I say, Teddy! Are you flirting with me?'

'No I'm not. This is serious.'

These two had known each other since childhood. Now, Teddy Rayburn was a group-captain in the RAF, commanding the air base a few miles from Great Deeping. Hilda Pritt, who flew planes for the Air Transport Auxiliary, had arrived at the base that morning and was due next day to pilot a crippled Armstrong to be repaired in the north of England.

That was what the Air Transport Auxiliary did. They delivered planes – damaged planes, repaired planes, new planes sometimes. Hilda had flown in one of the new ones that morning.

Group-Captain Rayburn drove Hilda out to the perimeter of the base and stopped his car beside a big low-loader parked on the grass. On it were the remains of a mangled plane, battered, crumpled and smeared with black mud. It was an ugly sight.

'Gosh,' Hilda said softly. 'Someone's broken their plane! Poor blighters! What happened to it? Shot down?'

'No. Something went wrong with the altimeter probably. It was a dark night. And the pilot didn't know he was almost on the ground.'

They got out of the car, and as Hilda approached the wrecked aircraft she said in surprise, 'It's an old Junkers! A bomber! I thought they'd given up using that model.'

'It wasn't carrying bombs. It had been adapted for dropping parachutists.'

'Was it spotted? Was there an alert?'

'No. It slipped through somehow.'

'Crew?'

'All dead.'

There was a large brick building nearby. 'What's that building for?' Hilda asked him. 'I've often wondered.'

'Nothing really,' he said vaguely. 'It was just an admin block.'

'Admin?' Hilda said. She didn't believe him.

He hesitated. 'I'm not allowed to talk about it. But I can tell you that it was a *very important part of the War effort.*'

Hilda felt a sudden rush of affection for Teddy Rayburn. She remembered when he used to come and stay with her younger brother. They'd been about seven, and she was ten. She used to put them to bed and read them Beatrix Potter stories. How could that small boy with the tight blond curls have turned into this tall handsome man commanding one of the biggest airbases in war-time Britain?

She teased him a little. 'Come off it, Teddy!' she said sweetly. 'If it was so important, why was it shut down?'

'Because,' he said quietly, 'the Germans found out about it.'

She stopped teasing. 'How?'

'We don't know. Someone somewhere was feeding information to German High Command.'

They both looked around them, as if that someone might be close by, observing, eavesdropping.

'How absolutely *beastly*!' Hilda muttered. 'To think that we might be surrounded by hordes of spies!'

'Not hordes, I think. But I daresay there's *one* somewhere, keeping an eye on the airfield.'

Hilda looked around, in every direction. She couldn't help herself. But she could see no one skulking in the undergrowth, watching through binoculars.

'Come on,' Group-Captain Rayburn said. 'Get in the car. I want to show you where that plane came down.'

He drove them out of the airfield and across the fen towards Great Deeping. Then he took a narrow side road running like a ribbon alongside a winding riverbank. They passed a couple of isolated houses built up close against it – and the road went on and on and on.

Grey houses, grey landscape, grey sky, Hilda thought. *Jolly depressing!*

Teddy stopped his car at the edge of a ploughed field where the narrow lane finally petered out. A few yards away they could see ugly scars crossing the plough ridges in the black earth.

'It was upside down,' Teddy said. 'Broken its back. Over there.'

Hilda, a pilot to her fingertips, worked out what had happened. 'He came down in the field over there,' she said quietly, pointing. 'And he might have been all right – but he nose-dived into that ditch, and the plane somersaulted and broke in two.'

'That's about it,' Teddy said.

'But why . . . ?'

'There's something else.'

'I say! Can we get back in your car? It's bally freezing out here!'

'Yes, OK.'

When they were inside the car, he said, 'We believe the plane was carrying a passenger.'

'How do you know that?'

'There were signs on board that someone had made a jump.'

Hilda took this in. 'They were parachuting in a spy?'

'Perhaps. But there are signs that this passenger was a schoolboy.'

'A *schoolboy*?'

The captain opened the glove compartment of his car and

took out something wrapped in brown paper. 'Open it.'

It was a small white prayer book, with handsome ivory covers and a gold cross stamped on the front. It was the sort of prayer book that was given on special occasions. It was in English.

'Read what's been written on the flyleaf.'

8th October 1938. To my beloved son, Konrad, on your tenth birthday, from your proud father, Helmut Friedmann. That too was in English.

'It couldn't have belonged to any member of the crew.'

'No – not unless he was twelve years old.'

'Precisely. But there's more. I contacted the War Department. And it turns out that they know this Helmut Friedmann.'

Hilda stared.

'In January there was an attempt to assassinate the Führer. A group of senior staff in the military. One of them was Helmut Friedman. They were all shot, of course. Immediately. Except that Friedman was allowed to swallow a poison capsule.'

Hilda pulled a face. 'Why wasn't he shot with the others?'

'Because he was related to Herr Hitler.'

Hilda was quiet for a moment. 'And you think that man's son was flown here by a German plane?'

'Sounds crazy, I know.'

'What did the WD say?'

'Not very interested. Said I was to keep my eyes peeled for a boy wandering around.'

'Heartless blighters!'

'Apparently our intelligence chaps had not picked up any info about Jerry plans to drop a schoolboy.'

'Do they usually?' Hilda was amazed.

'Apparently they do,' Teddy said. 'But I can't stop thinking about it. This boy might be wandering helplessly about . . .'

'Or he might have injured himself in the jump.'

'Or worse.'

Hilda couldn't help herself. She scanned the darkening fields, half expecting to see a crumpled shape, lying motionless on the cold earth.

-16-

Rabbit Thief

Another of Ollie's mates was a girl called Abigail. She lived beside the railway crossing because her mum's job was to open and close the gates. Most afternoons she walked home with them after school, as far as her house.

Abigail's best friend was called Molly Barnes, but she was away from school, feeling ill.

That afternoon the weather was bitter. It was drizzling and cold, and darkness was already falling. They walked stubbornly homewards, with their heads down against the cold and their hands clenched inside their pockets. Mucker Bailey was with them that day. It was one of his rare appearances at school.

'Keep your eyes peeled for a cat,' Abigail said.

'What for?' Ollie grumbled. 'There's cats everywhere.'

'You'll know this one if you see her. She's only got three legs.'

'Is she yours?' Hannah asked her.

'No, she belongs to Adam.' Adam Swales was an evacuee who lived with Molly.

'Is she lost?'

'Run away,' Abigail said cheerfully. 'She's an evacuee, like you. A bomb blew her leg off and she was evacuated.'

The night Hannah had arrived someone had talked to Ollie about a missing cat. It came back to her, like a forgotten dream, full of rain and wind and darkness. Vaguely she remembered it – an evacuee cat. And a missing leg.

'Someone saw her on the railway, near my house,' Abigail said.

'If you're Molly's friend, the cat might have followed you home,' Hannah said.

Abigail shook her head. '*I* think she's on her way back to London,' she said with conviction. 'She's a clever cat, and she knows she came here by train.'

'Yew think she wants t catch a train?' Ollie said. He was sarcastic and bad-tempered that day because he had his little sister Betty to keep an eye on.

'*No!* Don't be daft! She'll probably walk back to London, following the track. That's what animals *do*.'

Well, Hannah thought, cats might be able to manage long journeys on foot, but little Betty was finding the walk too much for her. 'My legs are tired,' she wailed. Ollie and Hannah coaxed her, and teased her, and held her hands and swung her. But Abigail lifted her up and over her head, and sat her astride her neck. 'I'll ride you past the next three lamp posts,' she said, 'and then you have to walk as far as the crossing gates.'

Betty loved it.

'I'll give ya a ride arter that,' Mucker said.

But Betty pulled a face. 'I don't like his fingers,' she whispered into Abigail's ear. But they all heard.

'Mucker,' Abigail said. 'What's wrong with your fingers? Show me!'

Mucker held out his hands and Betty hid her face in Abigail's hair because she didn't want to see. His hands were red with cold because he didn't have any gloves, but they weren't any grubbier than most boys' hands. It was his fingernails that Betty didn't like.

'Mucker Bailey, why do you bite your nails like that?' Abigail demanded. She sounded like a schoolteacher.

'Dunno.'

'Well, you want to stop it! If you chew them all away, you'll have horrible soft pads at the end of every finger when you grow up.' She made the word *pads* sound like something in a horror film.

They all pulled a face. *Yeugghh!*

'All right, if yew say so,' Mucker said calmly. 'I'll stop.'

When they got to the level crossing, Abigail went in for her bike. She was going with them to Mucker's house that afternoon for one of his rabbits, and she planned to cycle back afterwards.

They crossed the railway and then the bridge over the river – the *real* river, not the empty one.

Once they were on the other side, it was as if they had

crossed a boundary into a different country. The darkening clouds were lower, the wind keener, the silence more complete. Even the wet seemed to be wetter.

Hannah picked up Betty and gave her a ride on her shoulders. When she was tired, Abigail sat Betty astride the saddle of her bike, and wheeled her along.

It was a long slog and by the time they crossed the wooden bridge over the empty riverbed it was fully dark. Going into Mrs Pickens' warm kitchen was lovely. Betty knelt down in front of the fire as close as she could get, and they all crowded round as they took off their wet things.

But there was a surprise. Mucker's mum was there (*Mrs Mucker* Ollie called her – but not to her face) and she had some strange news. Someone had stolen one of the dead rabbits that had been hanging on her wash house wall. 'In broad daylight!' she said. 'Would you believe it? When I went in t dew the mangling that wuz there. Later, I went to answer a call o nature, and when I went back agin, that *weren't*! Now, what d yew make o *that?*'

Hannah went hot and cold all over, thinking it was something to do with the one-eyed man. But why would he want to steal a dead rabbit? It didn't make sense.

'Are my ferrets all right?' Mucker asked.

'Noo one een't ever gooin t mess around wi your bloody ferrets!' his mother said.

'Praps it was Loopy Lavvy,' Ollie said.

Loopy Lavvy? Who was she? Hannah wondered.

Abigail had a different theory. 'It might have been Tibby,' she suggested. She grew more convinced the more she said. 'She's been seen near the railway, so perhaps she's made it this far. She must be really hungry!'

'That was on a meat-hook,' Mucker said. 'How could a cat jump to the top of a wall and unhook a full-grown rabbit?'

'Let alone a three-legged cat,' Ollie said.

But Abigail was stubborn. 'It might,' she said.

'This missin cat yew're on about, that carries money about, I spose,' Mucker's mum said. 'Cos whoever took that there rabbit, paid for it!'

They all stared in surprise. *Paid* for it? It seemed unlikely – but Mrs Bailey held out a pound note with a torn hole in it. 'That was stuck on the meat-hook,' she said. 'Instead o the rabbit! Do yew still think that was your *cat*?'

Mucker's face brightened. 'A pound for one rabbit! Crikey! Thas a fair ole profit!'

'I've come all this way for nothing,' Abigail said. 'My mum will be none too pleased.'

Hannah felt sorry for Abigail and when she left she walked with her to the bridge. They stood there for a few minutes, in the dark. 'Do you get scared?' Hannah said to her. 'Going all that way on your own, in the blackout?'

'It's always pitch dark out here at night,' Abigail said. 'Blackout or not.'

'Still . . .'

'I play a game. I pretend I'm in the middle of enemy territory. Surrounded on all sides by danger! I have my trusty steed, and we just have to press on. Then when I'm on Deeping Bridge – the proper bridge – I can see the cowboy fort on the other side, where I'll be safe. Once I've crossed the railway I shall be back in civilisation again.'

She stopped pretending. 'Mum's doing a fry-up tonight.'

'Do you want me to come with you?'

'But then you'd have to come back here on your own,' Abigail said.

Hannah had an idea. 'When you're on the bridge, flash your torch at me – then I'll know you're safe.'

Abigail liked the thought of that. 'We're not supposed to shine torches,' she said.

But neither of them believed there were spies hiding in the fields, waiting for Abigail to flash her torch.

'Three flashes,' she said.

'Not too quickly,' Hannah said. 'In case I miss them.'

'OK. Three *long* flashes.'

Hannah stood on the bridge for about fifteen minutes, and all that time the bitter wet drizzle poured over the windswept fields. She never once took her eyes off the place where she thought the Deeping Bridge was. She felt very lonely out there in the dark. For all she knew, the one-eyed man might be close by, watching her every move. But she'd promised.

They came eventually, those torch flashes. Only a tiny light, mind, hardly any more than a spark, and a long way off. But there they were, three long flashes. Abigail was safely in sight of home.

As Hannah turned back towards the house, the front door opened and Ollie's mum was there. 'Come yew on in!' she called from the doorway. 'Yew'll git perished o cold out there!'

Hannah hurried down the bank and crossed the vegetable garden. But before they went inside, Mrs Pickens pointed towards Great Deeping. 'Before the War,' she said sadly, 'we could stand on the bank and see the lights o the town. They useter look really pretty, twinklin away! Especially on a warm summer night.'

She put her arm around Hannah's shouders. 'Ah well,' she said. 'Let's git back inside!'

-17-

Konrad's Landing

It was luck that Konrad found the rabbit, and conscience that made him pay for it.

The drop had been exact. When he saw that he'd come down about a hundred yards from the target, Konrad was impressed. The German in him felt proud.

But it had been a bad night. He'd had no idea of the altitude of the plane, and because of the dark he'd not been able to see the ground rising rapidly up to meet him. His mind was not braced, his body was not relaxed in the way he'd been taught. He landed badly, and his left knee – most of his left side, in fact – ached painfully.

He remained where he had landed all the rest of the night, wrapped in his parachute, under a small leafless tree. There was a cold wind from the east and, despite his flying overalls and the school clothes and raincoat, he shivered uncomfortably all night. And his left leg hurt. Time passed slowly.

His equipment included a small torch, a small hand-shovel, a box of candles, dry rations for two days, a sharp pocket knife, a groundsheet, matches, a blanket, and money.

He'd asked for a gun but they wouldn't let him have one. 'If you're captured and found to carry a gun, they'll know at once that you're not a runaway schoolboy,' Fraulein Eva had said.

There was another item, one that was not on his official list. No matter how carefully he searched his pockets, and in the wet, flattened grass where he had landed, it was nowhere to be found.

At first, his head ached and he felt sick and shivery. In the grey light of a cold dawn he started on the food. It made him feel a little better. He was careful not to eat too much of it.

As the daylight grew he gazed in confusion at the extraordinary place he'd arrived at – a deep bowl-shaped meadow with nothing in it but last year's dead and matted grass. Then he saw that it was not bowl-shaped at all; it wound away into the distance, in both directions, banked high on each side.

His first task was to hide the parachute and flight overalls. With the shovel, he dug a shallow hole in the earth, and covered them over with long wet grass. That was easy. Then he climbed painfully to the top of one of the banks and looked cautiously about, taking in the wide grey flatness of the landscape.

At times during the long night he'd wondered if the Junkers had crashed. He was almost certain it had, but he was in a condition of shock, and his stunned mind couldn't focus on the idea of it. *If it has come down*, he thought, *is it my duty to find it and help the crew?*

But the crashed plane had already been found. A quarter of a mile away a policeman stood with a bicycle, and four or five others stood looking at the crumpled remains of the aircraft. It was upside down. An ambulance waited on the narrow track that ran alongside the riverbank. A boy – about his own age, or a little younger, he thought – stood staring at the scene from a distance with his hands thrust inside his trouser pockets.

That boy should be at school, he thought.

There was nothing Konrad could do. Operation Blackout had got off to an uncertain start. He was sorry for the crew, and sorry for the loss of the plane – but relieved that he was free to concentrate on his mission.

Then he saw the pillbox, close by and built into the grassy bank on the outside of the river. Exactly as promised. This was where the gelignite would be delivered. Konrad hoped desperately that it had not already arrived. He wanted time to think.

He'd learned about pillboxes at the training school. They'd been built in their hundreds at the start of the War when the British expected a German invasion. They were thick concrete bunkers, designed for observation mainly, but they had narrow embrasures from which a rifle or machine gun could be fired. But there had been no invasion and the pillboxes had never been put to use. They were already largely forgotten.

This, he thought oddly, is what it is like to have a British mother and a German father: one half of him could imagine creeping up on that pillbox with a machine gun; the other was inside, on his guard, expecting to be attacked at any minute.

Konrad approached the pillbox cautiously. The only sound was the soft, cold rustling of the wind. There was no sign of anyone inside.

It was hexagonal, with its back built into the old riverbank. There was a separate blast-wall outside the entrance. The concrete was raw and new, but grass had already grown back around its outside walls. There were two observation windows, horizontal and narrow.

Konrad stooped low and went inside. There was no one there, and no packs of explosives lay waiting. Nothing but a bare earth floor. On one wall someone had chalked *Come on, Adolf! What are you waiting for?*

Inside, Konrad sat on the floor with his back to the wall. A wave of dizziness and nausea swept over him – his instructors had said nothing about that, he thought bitterly. The bunker would protect him from the worst of the weather but there was nothing cosy about it. Cold concrete offered nothing in the way of comfort.

He went outside after a while and dug up wet clods of earth and grass with his shovel. He used these to stuff the windows, to stop the cold wind blowing in.

After that he felt weak and exhausted. He spread out his groundsheet so that he could lie down.

I must have a fire, he thought. The prospect of another long wintry night with no warmth was dispiriting.

When he'd gone back to Germany at the start of the War he'd joined the *Deutsches Jungvolk*. His parents had been unhappy because it was run by the Nazis. But he'd had no choice. No one was allowed not to join. Girls had their own organisation. But Konrad, who had been a boy scout in England, had enjoyed many of the activities – especially camping and foraging for food. He became skilled at getting a fire going.

He explored along the riverbanks, where hawthorns and elders grew. They were not big trees, but they had been growing there a long time and there was a litter of fallen branches from past years. He collected bundles of wood and stacked it in piles just inside the pillbox. None of it was dry, of course. So he made another collection of smaller twigs and strips of dead bark.

Finally he went back inside and ate some more food. Then he started work.

He lit one of the candles and held over it a tiny bundle of twigs, passing them back and forth in the heat of the tiny flame. He sat all afternoon doing that, patiently drying out small handfuls of damp twigs with a candle flame. Then he took a slightly larger bit of wood – you could hardly call it a log – and set about drying that.

His world had shrunk to the few inches of space between his face and the damp twigs steaming almost invisibly in the heat of the candle flame.

He stopped once and went outside. He'd become aware of voices shouting faintly in the distance, and of a vehicle being revved and shunted about. He saw at once that men had come to move the wrecked plane and take it away. A group of children watched from the road. One of them was the boy he'd seen that morning.

By the time he was satisfied that he had enough dry wood to start a small fire, darkness was falling. He placed his fire close to the open doorway, hoping the smoke would blow out, not in. The blast-wall was convenient – it would conceal the flames. Only someone who approached close by would see them.

With a candle he set alight a tiny bundle of the twigs he'd dried. They would burn for no more than about two minutes, and so he quickly laid a few strips of bark across them. He used his pocket knife to scrape small flakes of wax from one of the candles and scattered them among the flames. As the bark strips briefly flared, he built a small pyramid above and against the flames and sat back on his heels to watch, delicately shifting bits of wood to where they were most likely to catch.

He burned his fingers, he got smoke in his eyes, and the first two attempts failed. But at last he had a small fire, burning perfectly. It gave out only a little heat – but a great deal of comfort. Konrad felt pleased with himself.

But it needed constant attention. The branches were plentiful but they were not thick, and they burned away quickly. Konrad arranged his entire collection of wood inside the pillbox, stacking it in a wall around the flames so that it would dry out. Then he took off his shoes and socks and laid them close to the fire to dry out also. The grass in the riverbed was long and sodden, and he had not been provided with rubber boots.

His wristwatch told him it was eight o'clock – and he heard faintly across the fields the mournful sound of a distant church clock striking. He unwrapped all that was left of his rations. Enough, he thought, for something to eat now, and one more meal. Breakfast.

His mind kept returning to the German training school, with its comfortable bed in his private room, the regular meals, the kindly concern of the people there. He disciplined himself to think of other things.

With his groundsheet spread on the floor and the fire glowing comfortably, Konrad wrapped himself in the blanket and curled up. He lay, watching the flickering flames. He'd not slept at all the previous night, so now he was overcome with weariness. His eyes closed almost immediately.

He woke a couple of times in the night. The first time he saw the glowing remains of his fire, reddening and fading alternately as air passed over. The second time he awoke, the fire had gone out.

*

Next morning he felt stiff and sore and unwell. He ate the last of his food and cheered himself with the thought that the wood around the remains of his fire was good and dry now, and he would be able to start a new blaze much more easily.

But first he had to explore, and try to make sense of this winding grassy meadow that he'd found himself in. His wits had been astray the previous day, and it had taken a long time before he realised it had once been a river. His instructors in Germany had said nothing about an empty riverbed. He'd been shown an aerial photograph of the drop area. It was a fuzzy picture and he'd memorised it, but although it showed the old river, they had all assumed it was a broad, winding farm track.

As he'd been told, the landscape was entirely flat. Across the fields there was a small town, two or three miles away. There was no visible sign of an aerodrome, but he knew it was five or six miles away, due north. Further along the empty river he could see a wooden bridge and a few scattered cottages built nearby, nestling close to the bank. He walked cautiously on for almost a mile, approached the first of the houses, peered into the back scullery of one of them, and saw two dead rabbits hanging on hooks on the wall.

There was nobody about.

*

He knew how to prepare a rabbit for cooking. One of his tests in the *Jungvolk* had been to cook a rabbit over an open fire.

He'd passed – and had later done it again, several times.

This rabbit had already been gutted. Back at his pillbox, he took out his pocket knife and tried to hack off one of the legs. But the knife was not up to the job. And there was still the head to be taken off. After that it would have to be skinned.

Konrad had been brought up never to despair. Giving up was not part of his nature. He put the rabbit aside and set off back along the empty river to explore again. A miserable rain had set in, streaming bitterly across the sodden landscape. He pressed on doggedly, his shoes and socks already soaked again.

Where there were houses, he thought, there would be kitchens. And where there was a kitchen, there would be kitchen utensils.

The cottages he'd seen before had been on the side of the old river furthest from the distant town. But this time he saw there was a house on the near side, by the road. Above the grassy bank he could see the roof. There was smoke coming out of the chimney. Someone was at home.

He climbed the bank, but then he lost his footing and slid on his backside down the wet grass on the other side. There was a small garden at the side of the house, with a wooden gate, a mossy brick path, and a sodden water butt. Konrad crept towards a small window at the back of the house, peered cautiously in – and saw a woman with her hand raised, and a cleaver in it.

A butcher's cleaver.

-18-

Loopy Lavinia

He knew he hadn't made a sound, and she'd been looking the other way when he peeped in. So he was sure she hadn't seen him, or heard him.

'Come in!' she called in a high, wavering voice. 'Don't stand there at the door. Come in!'

So Konrad straightened like a soldier, opened the door, and stepped into the tiny kitchen.

She turned to face him, studying him oddly with her head on one side. She wore grey pyjama trousers, their bottoms tucked inside a pair of wellington boots. On the top half she wore a faded army battle-tunic with Royal Engineers shoulder-flashes. And on her head she wore what was more like a big woollen shopping bag than a hat. It hung down behind her, deep purple, apparently containing her hair.

'Shut the door quickly,' she said. 'We mustn't let him in!'

'Let who in?'

He heard himself saying the English words. The sounds of the words, and the tiny melody of the stress (let *who* in?), were deeply familiar. *His* words were correct and comforting to him, and spoken with a natural accent. But *hers* were startling.

'The devil,' she said calmly, as if he visited every morning. '*Satan* – he's always looking for a chance to get inside.'

Konrad stepped in and closed the door. 'I'm sorry –' he started to say.

But she interrupted him. 'What do you think? Onion? Or would garlic be better?'

'What for?' he murmured. He felt very uncertain of himself.

'My stew!' she said, as if it should have been obvious.

And then – to his amazement – they had a conversation about cooking. And all the time she was chopping up green leaves on a wooden board and adding them to a large pot already warming up on the range. She nodded her head emphatically whenever he made a suggestion that she agreed with. When he asked her why Satan was trying to make an entrance, she explained – with a good deal of detail – that she was under constant attack from the Great Enemy.

Konrad felt that a part of him was reawakening and unfolding again. This was the first time he'd spoken English to an English person for over two years. He'd spoken it in lessons at school, of course, and at the training college, but not in Britain. It was pleasant and reassuring; he felt that he was being recognised. I am *allowed* to be here, he thought. I belong here too.

He began to feel affectionate towards this dotty old lady.

Perhaps it was because he was lonely. 'What's your name?' he asked her.

She raised her chin and straightened her shoulders. 'I'm Lavinia,' she said. 'People call me Lavvy for short.'

There was another reason that Konrad felt grateful to her. Lavinia had not asked him a single question. She took him on trust.

She untwisted a screw of paper and tipped some white powder into the stew. 'Actually,' she added, as if she were sharing a secret, 'they call me *Loopy* Lavvy. But I don't mind – and they mean no harm. It's because they don't understand.'

'Do you live here alone?' he asked.

'Oh no!' she declared. 'I have a friend. She's *very* powerful in the fight against Satan.'

'Is she here now?'

'Of course! She's upstairs. But she's only visiting.'

Then, abruptly, Lavvy did question him. 'What do you want? Why did you come here?'

Since she was so direct in asking, he gave her a direct answer. 'Can I borrow your cleaver, please?' he said.

'But what do you want to cleave?'

'Meat,' he said.

She gave him a sly look, as if he'd been naughty. 'A rabbit?'

He nodded.

'Bring it back tomorrow,' she said, and handed him the cleaver. 'Have you got a chopping block?'

He shook his head. 'Take a log from my wood pile by the gate,' she said. 'You can burn the log afterwards – but please return my cleaver.'

As he turned to leave, he said, 'Why is Satan such a danger to you?'

She lowered her voice. 'Because of the wicked secret,' she said softly.

Outside, with his hand on the latch to push shut the door, he said, 'You have a secret?'

'I *am* the secret,' she whispered.

*

Konrad was relieved when his return journey was complete. The log was awkward to carry and the cleaver was too sharp to be careless with. Walking along the bed of the river was difficult because of the thick, tangled grass. But if he'd gone along the top of the bank he would have been visible for miles across the fields.

However, before he reached the pillbox, he climbed halfway up the bank and raised his head to peer over the top.

A man was walking along the road. There was no one else for miles around. The man did not look like a local farm worker, Konrad thought. He wore a raincoat, belted, and there seemed to be a dark suit underneath. He also wore a tie and a trilby.

He looked from side to side as if searching for something, and when he drew level with Konrad he seemed almost to look him in the eye. But he hadn't seen him, for he looked away at once, and his walking didn't falter.

But Konrad had observed that the walker seemed to have only one natural eye. The other was made of glass.

When the walker was at a safe distance, Konrad approached his pillbox. He half expected to find that the promised packages of gelignite had now been delivered. And there would be a message perhaps. But there was nothing.

How long would he have to wait before they made contact? And who was the walker in the raincoat? It was inconceivable that he'd walked by the pillbox without looking inside. What did it all mean?

It was growing dark when he placed the dead rabbit on the chopping block. With two swift and efficient blows he removed the front and back legs. A lighter blow disposed of the tail. The head took two attempts before he'd finally severed it. He threw the removed parts away into the darkness where some carrion-eating creature would find them and feast on them.

Finally he started on the difficult business of skinning the remains of the rabbit. But he'd done it before and he could do it again. The rabbit's previous owner had already cut open the belly and taken out the guts. Konrad peeled back the skin and rolled it free of all that was left of the back legs. He pulled it clear and – this was the hard part – turned the skin slowly inside out from one end of the rabbit to the other, until it came free.

He lit another fire, with less difficulty this time because the wood had dried during the night. He wished now that he'd asked Lavinia for a pan to fry the rabbit in. Or a roasting fork. And some salt would help too. But he would just have to manage without. Rabbit meat, roasted over an open fire, would provide essential nourishment, even if it tasted dull – and even if he burned his fingers during the cooking.

-19-

Abigail

Saturday morning was bright and sunny, almost like spring. Hannah was bright and sunny too – but she might not have felt so cheerful if she'd known how the day was going to end.

It was Mucker Bailey's fault, as you'll see.

She was clearing away the breakfast things when Abigail Murfitt turned up, standing on the doorstep looking excited, and a bit shy.

'What dyew want?' Mrs Pickens said. She sounded rude and unfriendly, but she wasn't. It was just her way. Mr Pickens just stared at Abigail, making it clear she wasn't welcome. Hannah knew what he was thinking – *nobody* was welcome.

But Abigail wasn't the sort of girl to be put off. 'I'm going to Ely this afternoon, on the bus,' she said. 'I thought Hannah might like to come with me.'

Might like? She'd absolutely *love* it! Apart from going to school, she hadn't been anywhere since she'd arrived from London. She was desperate to go somewhere! Anywhere!

She turned to Mrs Pickens, hoping she'd say yes. 'Hev ya got any money?' she asked.

Hannah still had the two shillings she'd brought with her. She raced upstairs to get it, and Mrs Pickens said, 'Doon't yew goo n spend all o that!'

Again, Hannah went out to the wooden bridge and saw Abigail off, only this time it was in brilliant sunshine. And she admitted to herself that those flat fields looked wonderful in the morning sun. Truly dazzling, as if heaven had opened up above them!

Or perhaps she was just in a good mood.

But when she went back inside, her cheerfulness received a jolt. Mrs Pickens had something to say.

'Come yew oover here,' she said. She was sitting at the kitchen table, slicing some leeks.

Was she getting a telling off? Had she done something wrong?

She sat down at the table. Mr Pickens stood in the background, like an executioner in the shadows.

'Now,' Mrs Pickens said. 'You know Molly Barnes.'

Hannah nodded.

'And you know she's Abigail's best friend.'

Yes, Hannah did know that. Everyone knew that.

'Did yew know she's gone and got measles?'

Hannah knew that too, and she knew it meant a whole month off school.

But what was Ollie's mum getting at? Was she trying to warn her that measles was serious, and that children sometimes died of it?

But that wasn't it. 'Abigail oon't be able to spend any time with Molly for the best part of a month,' she said. She opened her eyes wide in a peculiar way, as if there was more meaning than the words. And that extra meaning was in her look.

She sighed when she saw Hannah didn't understand it. 'Abigail's *lonely*,' she said.

Still Hannah didn't get it. 'When Molly gits better . . .'

'Oh, I see!' Hannah said. 'You mean Abigail will dump me as soon as she gets her friend back!'

Mrs Pickens nodded. They'd got there at last! 'I doon't want yew to git hurt,' she said. 'Yew just need to know what the situation is.'

'Females!' Mr Pickens muttered.

'Y'see,' Mrs Pickens went on, 'I *know* yew! If Abigail Murfitt is your best friend and then suddenly she een't no more, yew'll be miserable.'

Hannah thought how kind it was that Mrs Pickens was anxious about her, and she went round the table and gave her a hug. And she thanked her and promised she'd be on her guard.

But she's completely wrong about me, Hannah thought. *She doesn't know me at all!* Hannah didn't care if Abigail was only using her while Molly Barnes was ill. And she wouldn't mind if she turned back to Molly when the measles was over. Hannah didn't care how many friends Abigail had.

Hannah didn't *want* a really special friend. She'd felt like that ever since the War started, and that's how she liked it.

*

This is why.

After Hannah's mother died, her grandmother had taken her to live with her in London. She was fond of her gran, but nothing the old lady did could stop her crying. She wanted her mother to be alive again. She cried all the time.

One afternoon there was someone in her gran's front room. They stood, stiffly, facing each other, working out ages.

'I've been sent to play with you. I live next door. I'm eight.'

But Hannah didn't want to play with anyone, and she started to cry again.

'You should never let anyone see you cry,' the newcomer said. 'Except your best friend.'

Hannah was sniffling. 'But *you've* seen me cry.'

'Well, I'm going to be your best friend. So it doesn't matter.'

Hannah was six, and she believed that if a person says something with conviction it makes it true. (She didn't believe that any more.)

But they did become best friends. They were inseparable. They went to the same school too, though not the same class.

From that day the crying had stopped. It was a kind of magic, Hannah thought.

But at the start of the War her friend's family moved away. Hannah was miserable, *totally* miserable. But no one knew, not even her gran.

-20-

Visitors for Hannah

They had a lovely afternoon in Ely. Abigail was like a tour guide. She showed Hannah everything – the river, the cathedral, and Woolworths. And there was a church with a plaque in the wall commemorating five or six men who'd been hanged for rioting about a hundred years ago. They larked about in the churchyard pretending to be hanged, and making silly confessions about their crimes.

A passing woman stared at them disapprovingly, and they ran off giggling.

When they were walking past Molly's house on the way home, Hannah asked about the measles. Abigail looked glum. 'Yes,' she said. 'She's not allowed out for four whole weeks!'

'What about the evacuee boy who lives with her? Has he got measles too?'

'Adam? No. He's gone to Wales, to stay with some relations.'

'Is he coming back?'

Abigail shrugged. 'Nobody knows.'

When they got to Abigail's house, she went in for her bike and walked it all the way back to the Old Bank. Hannah told her there was no need, because she wouldn't mind going by herself. But Abigail said no, Hannah would have to get used to it in time but she was still a beginner.

'There's nothing here but nature,' Hannah said.

They were surprised when they got there to see a small car parked beside the wooden bridge. There was frost on its roof.

'You've got visitors,' Abigail whispered. 'Goody!' She was shamelessly nosy. And they hurried across the bridge to see who had come to call.

But when Hannah walked into the warm kitchen and saw who had arrived, her blood ran cold. She felt it rushing away from her face – and then flooding back again as her heart started to pound.

It was the man with the glass eye. Cycle-tops, or whatever he called himself. It was bad enough that he'd been asking around for her, but now he'd got right inside Mrs Pickens' kitchen. He stared grimly at Hannah with his one good eye.

He wasn't alone. Seated beside him at the big kitchen table was a woman – and Hannah knew at once what kind of woman she was, in a way that these country people wouldn't understand. It was the way she was dressed, and the tilt of her head, and the way she sat. She was the sort of person who had never in her life expected to sit down in a kitchen like that.

Ollie was there too, and his little sister. And Mucker Bailey. On the scrubbed wooden tabletop were some cups and saucers that didn't match, a cracked bowl of sugar, a bottle of milk, and three dead rabbits, slightly bloody. Mr Pickens sat down at the head of the table, and the woman made no attempt to hide her slight movement away from him. For once, Hannah sympathised with him. It was *his* table. Why shouldn't he sit there if he wanted to?

'Good thing yew two turned up,' Mrs Pickens said. 'These people want a word with yew, Hannah.'

Hannah didn't want any words with Cycle-tops. Absolutely not! But who was this woman? Was she *Mrs* Cycle-tops?

The woman spoke, absent-mindedly stirring her tea. 'My name is Mrs Lufton,' she said. 'I'm an Inspector of Evacuees.'

Hannah was puzzled. What had an Inspector of Evacuees got to do with the strange man she'd met in a bombed-out factory in London? It made no sense. But she kept quiet, and waited.

'When you met this gentleman in London, you picked up a piece of paper he accidentally dropped.'

But Hannah wasn't interested in that. 'How did he find out where I was?' she asked. She wanted to *understand*. She hated not knowing.

'*Hannah!*' Mrs Pickens said. 'Doon't be rewd!'

Mrs Lufton sighed and replaced the teacup which had been raised halfway to her mouth. 'He went to the evacuees' office and enquired. I came here with him – as part of my job as an inspector.'

'This bit o paper musta bin very important,' Mrs Pickens

said. She was suspicious, you could tell.

'It *is* important,' the woman said.

Then the one-eyed man spoke. For the first time. And Hannah remembered that unpleasant grating voice she'd heard on the night of that terrible air raid. 'It's to do with the war effort,' he said. He didn't exactly speak, he *croaked*.

Hannah was seized by a sudden desire to be done with all this. She didn't believe this woman was an inspector. And she didn't believe the paper had anything to do with the War Effort. But she wanted to be done with it. She wanted never to see Cycle-tops again!

'It's upstairs,' she said. 'I'll go and get it.'

When she came back down, Mrs Lufton was sipping her tea with her little finger sticking out. Mr Pickens was glaring at it as if he wanted to bite it off.

Hannah wanted to see the back of these two, for good. But she couldn't quite let go of the mystery. 'It's only a list of names and numbers,' she said as she handed it over to the woman.

They both looked at the paper and then briefly at each other. And Hannah saw at once that Cycle-tops was *relieved*. Immensely relieved! And it seemed to her then (Abigail thought so too, she said afterwards) that Mrs Lufton was his boss, and that he'd been in trouble because he'd lost that bit of paper.

When they stood up to go, Hannah remembered how big this man was. He had to stoop in that low-ceilinged room. He was like a troll in a cave. As he loomed over her, she studied his face for a few seconds, looking upwards.

How can you tell from someone's face what kind of person they are? What does a face tell you? Was he a *good* man, a *kind* man? He knew she was studying him, and she believed he knew what she was thinking. She wanted to understand him, and she wanted to know why he scared her so much.

But she was none the wiser for staring.

Ollie opened the door for them to leave. Mrs Lufton, who had drunk only half her tea, said, 'You're a sensible girl, not to have thrown the paper away.'

Her voice was totally insincere. Those kind words came out of her mouth as if they'd never travelled that way before.

But at least they were leaving. Then Mucker Bailey spoiled it. 'It wouldn't a mattered if she *had* thrown it away,' he said. 'She knows all them numbers by heart. She memorised em!'

They stopped at the door, turned back, and stared at Hannah. The woman's lips went tight and thin, and her eyes narrowed. But Cycle-tops went white with fury, and his one eye – *both* eyes actually – glared at her. Her blood froze.

What did it all mean?

But they left at last, and they heard the car drive away on the other side of the Old River.

'Can I have one of those rabbits?' Abigail said to Mucker.

'Yes, yew can. But the price as gone up. They're worth a pound each now!'

'Don't be daft!' Abigail said to him. 'My mum won't pay a

pound for one of them. She'll pay the usual price.'

'Worth a try,' Mucker said sadly.

'I wonder what happened to his eye,' Ollie said.

Mucker gave one of his ugly grins. 'He threw someone a glance, I expect,' he said. There was no response to this, so he added, 'And someone caught his eye.'

'*Yuck!*'

Hannah wasn't paying attention to any of that. The visitors had gone away, but she could still see their faces when they were told that she knew by heart the names and numbers on that slip of paper. *Furious*, apparently.

But why?

-21-

Hansel and the Witch

Konrad's day started badly.

He had eaten nothing since the last of the rabbit. His stomach hurt, his mouth was dry, and his head ached.

And he couldn't think clearly. His mind was a confusion of anxieties. When would someone deliver the explosives? Would the person who brought them also bring him some food? How would he transport the explosives and the other equipment to the building that he was supposed to blow up? He forced himself to concentrate on the map he'd memorised back at the training school. His target was about six miles away, he remembered. Along apparently empty country roads.

But would he actually do it?

Ought he instead to go at once to the British police and tell them everything? Would he be able to do that without being observed by hidden agents who would report back to German high command?

His father kept breaking into his thoughts. At the training school Konrad had been kept so occupied – and so tired – that he'd been able to keep these thoughts away. But now his father was with him a good deal of the time. He was not a spirit, nor a ghost. He did not advise him, or instruct him, or admonish him. He said nothing. He was just there, in Konrad's head. Stern and sad.

He spent the morning gathering wood under the stunted trees that grew on the riverbanks. Each time he did this he had to search further afield. It was hard work for someone who'd eaten nothing for more than a day. He stumbled in the long, wet grass, and scraped his head painfully as he stooped under the low branches. His movements were clumsy and inefficient.

But he did not give up. He made repeated journeys back to the pillbox, and when he'd gathered sufficient he stacked it inside the doorway, beside the dried wood left over from the previous night's fire. But if only he had something to cook! If only he'd learned how to catch rabbits as well as how to prepare them! He'd seen several on the banks, where the grass was shorter.

The thought of rabbits reminded him of the cleaver. It was time he returned it to its owner. In spite of his bodily weakness, he forced himself to set off towards the cottage where Lavinia lived. He couldn't bring himself to think of her as *Loopy Lavvy*. It was disrespectful and unkind.

When he reached her house he struck lucky. Lavvy was making an enormous stew, and she invited him to stay and have some. Perhaps it was because she was pleased to have her cleaver restored to her. Or perhaps she was just kind.

It took a long time, that stew! Konrad – far too polite to grumble – sat in the tiny kitchen as the day wore on and stretched into the afternoon. He did, however, ask if he could have a drink of water, and Lavvy also gave him a loaf of bread, a breadknife, and a chipped plate. 'Help yourself,' she said.

She looked the same as she'd looked before, except that her long grey hair hung down her back instead of being contained inside its woollen bag. It made her look witchlike as she stooped over the contents of the big iron stewpot cooking on the range. Konrad thought of Hansel and Gretel, but he put the idea out of his mind.

'There's some cheese in that cupboard,' she said. 'Help yourself.'

'Did you make this bread?' he asked. He was just being polite, just making conversation.

'No, I did not,' she snapped. 'I got it from the Co-op. *And* the cheese.' She sounded insulted, as if he'd accused her of being too stupid to go shopping.

She sat down, facing him across the small kitchen table. 'What's your name?'

'Barnaby Hamilton,' Konrad said promptly.

'What are you up to?'

'I've run away from my school.'

'Why?'

'I was unhappy there. It was a terrible place!'

'I've seen a man with a glass eye. Is his good eye looking for you?'

Konrad frowned. 'I don't think he's looking for me.' For a few brief moments he'd thought the glass-eyed man had come to make contact. But his hopes faded, for there was something about him – his clothes, the way he moved, his false eye – that made Konrad feel certain that he was not part of Operation Blackout.

'Well, who is he then? And who is he looking for? No one comes all the way down here for nothing!'

Konrad, with his mouth full of bread and cheese and recalling their previous conversation, said, 'Perhaps he's the devil.'

Lavvy showed no surprise, no irritation. 'No,' she said thoughtfully. 'He's not the devil. We would have known.'

She was quiet after that, and Konrad laid his head on his arms and fell unexpectedly asleep. When he woke, the afternoon outside was already darkening and a big bowl of thick stew had been placed in front of him. It was still hot. There was more bread too.

There was no sign of Lavinia. Perhaps she was upstairs, having her meal with her friend, Konrad thought. There was no sense in letting the stew grow cold, so he set about it at once.

He wondered briefly about that mysterious friend upstairs.

Could *she* be officially watching him? Could she be the one? It seemed unlikely.

When he'd finished eating, there was still no sign of Lavinia. His stomach was grumbling at the sudden arrival of so much food after so much emptiness.

He went to the bottom of the stairs and called up. 'I'm going now,' he shouted. 'Thanks for the stew! It was delicious!'

Few places are as silent as a silent house.

As Konrad was shutting the garden gate behind him, an upstairs window was thrown open. There she was, her face bobbing about as if unattached. Fairy tales and horror stories kept breaking in, he found.

As he laboured through the deep grass in the bed of the old river, Konrad became aware of an unfamiliar sound. Quickly he scrambled up the bank and raised his head a little so that he could look down into the narrow lane on the other side.

There was a small brown van – coming slowly back from the direction of his pillbox. It had no lights on in spite of the falling darkness. But just as it drew near, one of the occupants of the cab flicked on a cigarette lighter, and for a few seconds Konrad saw them clearly.

A man was driving, one-handed as he lit a cigarette. He had, Konrad was sure, *two* eyes. With him was a woman, smartly dressed, looking sour-tempered.

Were they something to do with his operation? If not, why had they been driving along this desolate lane that led nowhere?

Or was it possible that his German superiors had dropped him there and left him to get on with it?

At the back of his mind – he admitted it now to himself – he'd hoped that someone would arrive and take this responsibility from him. An adult. Someone who would make the decision, and carry out the job. But that wasn't going to happen, and he knew that really.

All his life, he'd had people around him. But now he felt abandoned, and totally alone.

-22-

A Watcher Watched

It had all started so well, Miss Feelgood thought crossly.

She'd left her car at Littleport, five miles from Great Deeping, and reserved a room in a hotel at Ely, five miles from Littleport. So no one at Littleport knew where she was staying. No one at Ely knew she had a car. And no one at Deeping would know either of those things. They would see only a stranger who arrived each day by train.

And – as planned – she called herself *Mrs Lufton*.

But then things started to go wrong. First, there was that tiresome child called Hannah Conway who knew that missing list was important and who would have to be disposed of because she had *learned its details by heart*.

Not by her, of course. Cyclops would have to do that. Then, later, *she* would have to deal with Cyclops. She had come prepared.

Hannah Conway wasn't her only difficulty. There was also the matter of the explosives. She was supposed to supervise their delivery into the proper hands. Well, where were they?

For three successive afternoons at four o'clock (as instructed) she'd waited outside Lloyd's bank, which seemed to her to be the oldest bank in Deeping. She wore (as agreed) a dark blue overcoat and a dark red hat with a feather. From where she stood she could also keep an eye on the only other bank in the town, in case she was wrong about their age.

She felt foolish standing on that corner. And very conspicuous – the one situation a woman in her job should avoid at all costs! And it was bitterly cold. The winter wind funnelled straight up a side street and focused itself exactly where she had to stand.

Nobody spoke to her, everybody noticed her. She loathed it.

On the third afternoon a small group of boys and girls walked past her on their way home from school. One of them was Hannah Conway. Miss Feelgood-Lufton huddled into a shop doorway and peered at a window display of men's boots and shoes.

The children passed by. As she stood on the pavement fidgeting with frustration, an old brown van pulled up in the street beside her. The driver got out and coolly looked her up and down, taking in her dark blue coat and dark red hat.

She blushed furiously. Then he spoke. 'I've bin driving up and down these ruddy streets since Sunday afternoon! You're supposed to be waiting at the Old Bank!'

Miss Feelgood-Lufton loathed being in the wrong. Mistakes

were foreign to her nature. It turned out, she found, that the Old Bank was not a bank at all, but a place, or a road, somewhere out in the country.

'Get in!' the man said. He was very bad-tempered.

And there were other things she disliked. He was unshaved and unwashed, and his clothes seemed to be almost solid with grey dust. She might not have minded riding with a mere labourer if he'd been working for the Nazi cause. But this one was just a small-time crook who was being paid to make an illegal delivery.

'Who are you?' she demanded.

'Spratt,' he snapped back at her. 'People call me Jack.'

'Your *code word*?' she said crossly.

'Oh, that! What was I was supposed to say?' He pondered as he negotiated the van around a tractor parked outside the library. 'Something to do with mirrors, I reckon.'

She prompted him, though it was against the rules. 'Going *through* one?' she suggested.

'Yeah! That's it! *Through the looking-glass.*'

He turned and grinned at her. Miss Feelgood-Lufton saw his teeth and shuddered with distaste.

Still, the job had to be done, the delivery had to be made. 'Where are you from?' she asked him.

'Up north,' he said.

'Why is this vehicle so *dusty*?'

'Because I work in a stone quarry,' he said. 'Where did

you *think* you were going to get gelignite from? Marks and Spencer's?'

As they approached a level crossing they overtook some of the children walking home from school, huddled and hunched against the wind.

Darkness was falling as Jack Spratt drove the van out of the town and into the countryside. 'This,' he said, 'is the Old Bank.'

This is where that girl . . . Miss Feelgood-Lufton thought. *This is where I came a few days ago!* But on that occasion it had been Cyclops who had been with her – and he hadn't mentioned the name of the place.

The coincidence made her uneasy. 'There should be a pillbox,' she said. 'Keep going.'

They passed the last of the scattered houses, and the lane beside the winding riverbank grew narrower and muddier as they went on. Finally it died out altogether and became a grassy track. There, tucked into the bank, was a concrete pillbox, new and raw.

Her courage failed her then. Miss Feelgood-Lufton shuddered. 'You go first,' she said.

Mr Spratt gave her a look of contempt. But he got out of the van and walked towards the pillbox. 'Who's going to be detonating this load? Not you, I reckon.'

'Certainly not me,' she snapped back. 'It's been arranged.'

*

When Konrad was certain the brown van was out of sight, he cautiously approached the pillbox. He switched on his torch and crept slowly inside.

Stacked on the ground against the back wall – as far away as they could be placed from the remains of his fire – were three sacks and a paper package. The sacks contained sticks of gelignite neatly packed inside a cardboard box, sixty in all; two reels of cable; and a plunger-detonator.

In the paper package there were some thick beef sandwiches, with mustard.

('What are *they* for?' Miss Feelgood-Lufton had said in amazement. 'The poor bugger will be half starved!' Jack Spratt had snapped at her. 'How do you think he can get anything to eat, stuck out here?' Even small-time crooks have generous impulses.)

Konrad set about lighting his fire, a small one, well clear of the explosives. Once he'd got it going nicely he would settle down, enjoy the sandwiches, and consider – on a full stomach – what he was going to do.

He felt immensely cheered. Partly because of the food, but mostly because the delivery made him feel connected again. There was, in spite of his doubts, an organisation out there, with people who were supporting him.

But it meant that Operation Blackout could not be put off much longer.

What Konrad didn't know was that there was a watcher

outside, crouched low under the leafless branches of an elder tree.

A one-eyed watcher.

But what the watcher didn't know was that there was another watcher watching him.

Konrad was being watched by a man with one eye. And *he* was being watched by a boy with two.

*

Hilda Pritt had been busy too. Not *watching* exactly, but searching.

She'd never been able to put out of her mind the thought that there might be a schoolboy, lost out there in that flat and desolate landscape. Lonely, scared, and possibly injured.

She had her duties to perform. She'd flown two flights out, and two flights back to the airfield. In between, whenever she had an hour or two to spare, she borrowed a bike and explored the empty side roads around Great Deeping.

So far, these trips had taken place in daylight. But she planned, as soon as she had the chance, to go out after dark. If there was a boy somewhere out there, he might let down his guard at night.

She was a fearless young woman, and she'd been brought up in the country. There was nothing in the countryside after dark to scare her. And who knew what she might find?

-23-

An Evening Out with Mucker Bailey

Betty was having her weekly bath, in the tub, in front of the fire – an all-over body wash, because she refused to sit down in the water. Mrs Pickens' patience was being stretched to the limit.

Abigail Murfitt had cycled over with some books. Hannah knew she had nobody else to spend her evenings with. But she didn't care. She was glad she'd come.

'I dunno why you spend so much o your time readin books!' Mrs Pickens said over her shoulder. She was on her knees, rubbing away at Betty. '*Especially* I dunno why yew wanna read the same book *twice*!'

She knew that when Hannah had finished *A Little Princess* she'd started it again. If she liked a book, she always read it twice. (She'd read *The Railway Children* five times.) And besides, there weren't any other books in the house. She'd asked her once if there were any books she could read and Mrs Pickens had said no, apart from *Pilgrim's Progress*. When she found that, it turned out to be an old prayer book. Everyone in that family was vague about books. Ollie sometimes brought home a comic, usually passed on to him by Mucker Bailey. But Hannah never saw him with a book.

'If yew don't stand still yew're gooin to git a *slap*!' Mrs Pickens said to Betty. 'I *mean* it!'

Betty stood in the tub, with her bottom stuck out behind and her tummy stuck out in front, and her lower lip stuck out like a scoop.

Ollie sat at the other side of the table, trying to mend an old rat trap that Mucker had given him. His dad was outside somewhere.

At times like that Hannah pretended she was a member of the family, and that she belonged there, with them. But it was just a game. She didn't belong, not really. She was just temporary, and all this could end at any moment. Something unexpected could happen. Or she could just decide to go.

All three of them heard the outside scullery door open and shut – and the next minute Mucker Bailey slipped into the kitchen. He stayed back in the shadows and jerked his head sideways at them. He wanted them to go out with him.

'Ma! We're just gooin outside for a bit.' And before Mrs Pickens had time to say no, they were out of the room. Abigail and Hannah grabbed their coats, Ollie wrapped a woollen scarf around his neck, and in no time they were outside, with Mucker. It was pitch dark out there.

They all heard a high, wailing voice from inside: '*I want to goo with them!*'

'Where we gooin?' Ollie said.

'I got suffin to show yew,' Mucker said. 'Git yer bike – and yew'll need yer cart for her.' (He meant Hannah.) And then he said to Abigail, 'Are yew comin an all?'

'You bet I am!' Abigail said. She was game for anything.

They went over the bridge to the other side of the empty river. Then the three of them followed Mucker along the narrow road beside the bank, past Lavvy's house, and the other one. He led the way, Abigail was behind him, and then Ollie, with Hannah in the wooden cart.

So she was at the back, with no one behind her. She rested her chin on her bare knees and tried not to think about it.

It was really cold. Not one of those bright frosty nights, with starlight. The sky was dead and blank, and the landscape empty of everything. It was as if the world had gone blind. Only the narrow lane was a paler shade of darkness, winding forever on, further and further into the fen.

So the houses along the Old Bank were not the end of everything, Hannah thought. They were heading beyond even them.

When they'd gone past the place where the plane had crashed, and where the lane turned into a farm track, Mucker stopped. 'We'll avter walk now,' he whispered.

He laid his bike against the bank and Hannah climbed out of Ollie's cart. 'Now!' Mucker said. 'Doon't make a sound!'

Abigail went to take hold of Hannah's hand. 'You haven't

got any gloves!' she whispered. 'Here! Wear one of mine!' She made Hannah wear her right-hand glove, and their two bare hands held each other warm inside Abigail's coat pocket.

Mucker led them silently along the track, where it bent round to the left, still hugging the Old Bank. Then he stopped and they huddled beside him, and stared. There was a small concrete building close against the riverbank. It was not like anything Hannah had ever seen before.

'Does someone live there?' she whispered.

Certainly someone had lit a fire. It was invisible from all directions because there was a wall that hid it from view. But from close up it was as bright as a small firework.

'Praps there's a soldier in there,' Ollie said.

'But why would a soldier be living out here?' Hannah couldn't make this new thing fit into anything she understood.

Ollie explained patiently. 'The army built this. In case there was an invasion.'

'That een't a soldier,' Mucker said quietly. 'I've seen who it is.'

Abigail gripped Hannah's hand tightly.

*

Konrad, with the sandwiches eaten, had leaned his back against the wall of the pillbox and allowed himself to doze.

But unexpectedly, sharply, he was awake again, and every

sense was focusing. He had heard something, the faint crackle of a footstep perhaps, or the soft sound of breathing.

Quickly he calculated. And quickly he concluded there was no escape. He was trapped. The only thing he could do was to be poised and ready for whatever was going to happen.

Kneeling and sitting were bad positions if you needed to move fast. And the roof was too low for him to stand up. So he got to his feet and crouched, staring all the time at the open entrance where his fire was quietly burning, with the blast-wall behind it.

He *knew* someone was outside. He felt surrounded.

A voice in the darkness called out. 'We're comin in!'

It was a boy's voice! But what did it mean? What nuisance was this? And how was he to deal with it?

It wasn't just one boy. There were two, one entering from each end of the blast-wall. *To block my escape,* he thought. The first one ducked and came in from one side, then the second from the other. They were followed by a couple of girls.

Girls? When the second entered, Konrad frowned.

'My name is Barnaby Hamilton,' he said quickly. 'Who are you?' He directed the question at Hannah.

But one of the boys said, 'Don't yew try that, mate! We live ere! Yew don't! So *we* ask the questions.'

*

Hannah stared in disbelief, taking everything in. *Has he been living in this place?* she thought.

It was warm, but there was no comfort. The walls were bare concrete, the floor was dry earth covered with a rubber sheet. Little Betty having her bath beside the fire seemed to belong to a faraway universe.

All three boys were squaring up to one another, on the edge of a fight. Hannah had seen it before, she knew the signs. But they couldn't stand up because the roof was so low. Somehow that made fighting impossible.

She sat down by the doorway, close to the fire. And that seemed to work like a signal – because everyone sat down then, with their backs to the wall, and their legs pulled up in front of them.

'Now!' said Mucker. 'What did yew say your name is?'

'Barnaby Hamilton.'

'Oh yeah? Well, who's Barnaby Hamilton?' Mucker said with a sneer.

Barnaby Hamilton? Hannah thought. 'Why are you here?' she asked him.

He looked directly at her. 'I've run away from my school,' he said quietly.

She took that in, and thought about it. 'Why?'

'It was a terrible school,' he said.

Then Abigail took over the questioning and asked him the name of the school. Hannah saw Ollie, staring anxiously.

And Mucker looking suspicious.

'Fraxton Hall,' he said. 'It's in Cheshire.'

'You've come a long way,' Abigail said.

'I wanted to get as far away as possible.'

'But why here?'

'It's remote. There's nothing here,' he said. Then he added bitterly, 'But it was a mistake.'

'Why, what do you mean?' Hannah asked him.

He looked her squarely in the eyes. 'I'm less likely to be seen round here. But there are fewer people and it's harder to get food.'

'How long have you been on the run?' Abigail asked him.

'Nearly two years.'

Ollie gasped. *Two years living like this!* he was thinking.

'You've survived all that time,' Abigail said.

'Obviously.'

Then Mucker interrupted. 'It was yew who stole my rabbit!' he said.

This was a sore point. 'I didn't steal it,' the boy said. 'I paid for it.'

'All the same . . .' Mucker was working himself into a rage.

Abigail put a stop to this growing quarrel. 'What was wrong with your school?' she said. 'Were you being bullied?'

'No, I wasn't. I can look after myself.' *That* was meant for the boys.

'I was going to have to leave anyway,' he said. 'My aunt died

– she paid the fees, and I didn't know where they were going to send me when the money stopped.'

'Have you got your ration books?' Abigail said.

'They're out of date.'

'How have you been finding food?' Abigail was brightening up and Hannah could see she was enjoying this. She liked the business of cross-examining. It felt a bit like being a policeman, or a detective. So she went on and on, and Ollie and Mucker just let her get on with it. She was making a story out of the boy's adventures, building it up with every detail.

There was a gradual change in the atmosphere. Everyone grew a little more relaxed and the threat of a fight receded. Ollie leaned across and put a fresh log on the embers of the fire.

Then Mucker changed everything. 'I doon't believe a word on it,' he said. 'Thas a load o bollocks!' He spat into the fire.

They stared at him, all of them.

'Yew was on that plane that crashed a few days agoo,' he said.

Abigail was silenced completely. So was Hannah. And the story they'd been building about Barnaby Hamilton began to collapse.

'Yew're a German spy!'

Konrad straightened his back, as if braced.

'An I'll tell yew suffin else,' Mucker said. 'We een't the oonly ones who've seen yew. Someone else as bin watchin yew! A bloke with a glass eye! So what dyew think o *that*?'

-24-

Mrs Lufton Gets a Letter

When she came in from work and examined the letter lying on the doormat, Mrs Lufton immediately recognised the handwriting on the envelope. Anxiously she tore it open, and anxiously she read the contents.

There was no *Dear Mrs Lufton*, no *Dear Anybody*. Typical of its writer, she thought crossly. All the underlinings had been neatly done, with a ruler.

I have had a frustrating time. The delivery was three days late, and the driver was rude and uncooperative. However, everything was done in the end. Fortunately, it is not my job to put the material to use. Someone is being parachuted in to do that. He wasn't at the scene.

On that other little matter, nothing has gone right. That girl is a bigger danger to us than we thought. It turns out that she has <u>learned the list by heart</u> – which means that she knows it's important. She will have to go. She might do nothing, and forget all about it in time. But I am not prepared to take that chance. Not to deal with her would put us all <u>at risk</u>.

Cyclops is here, of course, but he is useless — a clumsy thug with <u>no brain</u>. He says he's already made one attempt, and failed. I am sure he is <u>lying</u>. I will decide later what to do about him.

I have been using your name down here. Now don't fly into one of your panics. There is no danger to you if you ensure that you are <u>seen by lots of people</u>. All you need is an alibi.

After I have dealt with the girl, I will just disappear and the police will come looking for you because I've been using your name. But you will be able to prove to them that you were somewhere else all the time.

I can't be bothered to wrap all this up in coded language. Codes can always be broken anyway. <u>So burn this at once. NOW.</u>

That woman thinks she's so clever! Mrs Lufton thought angrily. *So clever that she never even thought of using our code. Anyone could have got hold of that letter and read it!*

Nevertheless, she did as the letter instructed. Then she phoned her sister down in Devon and asked if she could stay for a few days. 'I need a break from the bombing,' she said.

Mrs Lufton had a kindly face, with soft, wrinkled skin. Babies and small toddlers always wanted to stroke her cheeks. But her heart was as hard as cheddar. Not with cruelty but with indifference. With *not caring*.

She gave not a moment's thought to Hannah Conway's approaching fate.

-25-

Doubts and Dilemmas

Konrad did some rapid calculations and concluded that he had to tell them the truth. He had no choice.

His name was Konrad Friedmann. And he'd been sent there because of his cousin Adolf.

Cousin Adolf? they all thought. *Adolf who?*

No one knew anyone called *Adolf*! There were no Adolfs in Great Deeping. There were probably no more than half a dozen in the whole country. The only Adolf any of them had ever heard of was Adolf Hitler. The most hated and feared man in the world. Was this boy . . . ?

Hannah had one of her moments of clarity. This happened sometimes – moments when she seemed to see right into what other people were thinking. She knew from his face that Ollie was disbelieving and scared, still working it out. She glanced at Mucker – and saw his wide-open eyes shining in the candlelight. Mucker was *excited*.

And Abigail? She was eyeing Konrad with a quiet gravity, working it out. Adolf Hitler was a depraved and evil madman. Abigail had seen him on newsreels at the cinema, countless times, ranting and strutting. They all had. And this boy was *related to him*? Could it be true? If it was, was the boy a monster like his relative? Was it *safe* to be near him?

But Hannah wanted to be clear. 'So if you blow up that building your mother and sister will be safe.'

'That is correct.'

'And if you don't, they'll be shot?'

'Yes.'

'Would they really do that?' Abigail's neat face was puckered up with shock and disbelief. She – like Hannah – was thinking that nothing like that would happen in Britain.

Ollie found his tongue at last. 'Woss in those bags?' he said.

The boy glanced behind him. 'Sticks of gelignite.'

'*What?*'

'How did yew git hold o them?' Mucker demanded.

'I found them here.'

'*Found* them?'

'Someone delivered them.' Konrad was growing impatient.

'Are they safe?' Being sandwiched between a burning fire and some sacks of gelignite made them nervous.

He had a haughty look on his face then, as if safety was too trivial to worry about. And, Hannah supposed, for him it was.

'Well,' Mucker said, 'what are yew gonna dew then?'

So far, he'd managed to make them feel that he was a grown-up person and they were just kids. Ollie – who was older than Konrad – felt as if he was about eight. But when Konrad was asked that question his haughtiness vanished.

'You've got to go to the police,' Abigail said.

'I know,' he said. 'But I can't.'

And that was his difficulty, precisely summed up.

'I keep putting it off, in case I get a better idea.'

He sounded more like one of them when he said that, more human. They talked his difficulty over and over and through and through, analysing every detail, considering every angle, trying to find a way out. There surely *was* a way out! They were young, they believed in happy endings.

But Mucker Bailey said, 'Yew're wastin your time, gooin on and on about it. Yew *got* to tell the police, cos if yew doon't, *we will*!'

Abigail turned on him. 'Mucker Bailey, why can't you keep your mouth shut?'

'I doon't care what yew say, Abigail Murfitt! All that stuff about his father – how do we know thas trew? He's a *German*, een't he? And Germans hev to be locked up.'

'I am British.'

'No, you een't. Your dad worked in the German High Command, and you're related to the Führer – and then yew try to tell us yew're British? Wodyew take us for?'

Hannah had never heard words said with such hatred. She didn't like Mucker Bailey at that moment, with his scoffing and his sneering.

But Konrad insisted. 'My mother is British. Her parents

were British. And I spent the first ten years of my life in England.'

'Yeah! But then yew went back!'

'We went back,' Konrad said quietly, 'because the British were going to lock us up if a war started.'

'I doon't believe a word of what yew say,' Mucker said. 'And I'm gooin straight into Deeping. *Now!* To the police station.'

Then something weird happened. In the entrance to the pillbox a pale face appeared. They saw there was a young woman there, in a dark uniform, crouching on the other side of the glowing embers of the fire, and pressing her hat down on her head as she stooped.

It was creepy. None of them had heard anyone approaching. But Abigail cried out, 'Miss Pritt!' – and Hannah could tell she was pleased to see her. Abigail started up, forgot the low roof, and banged her head on it. '*Ow!*'

The newcomer stepped awkwardly around the fire and came in, crouching. There was hardly any room for a sixth person so they all had to draw in their legs to make space. 'I say! It's beastly cramped in here,' she said. 'Hello, Abigail. It *is* Abigail, isn't it? Did you hurt your head?'

She took out a big torch and shone it on their faces, one by one. It was dazzling in the candlelight.

Hannah was mystified. Who was this person? And how did she know Abigail?

Miss Pritt knelt on the floor and faced Konrad. 'I think this belongs to you,' she said, and held something out towards him.

It was a white prayer book, with ivory covers. Hannah had once owned one like it, but it got lost in the bombing. Hilda opened the book and read out what was written on the flyleaf. *'To my beloved son, Konrad, on your tenth birthday, from your proud father, Helmut Friedmann.'*

Mucker took the prayer book from Hilda. 'Hev yew bin listening?' he demanded.

'Yes, of course!' she said. 'I heard everything.'

'Where did this come from, this ole book?'

'It was found in the plane that crashed a few days ago.'

Then they all knew – even Mucker Bailey – that Konrad's story must be true. The second story, not the first.

'He's *still* a German,' Mucker said. 'An he's *still* a spy. An he come here to blow suffin up! We can't just *let* him!'

'Gosh, no!' Hilda said. 'Of course we can't. But we need time to plan what to do.'

'We doon't need to plan nothin,' Mucker said. 'It don't take no planning for one of us to goo t the police station.'

Hilda looked at Mucker as if she'd just spotted a new species of garden slug. Abigail told Hannah later that she was quick-thinking and always knew what to do in a crisis. But to Hannah she seemed as worried and doubtful as the rest of them.

'Which building are you supposed to blow up?' she said to Konrad.

He hesitated for a moment, as well he might. 'There's an

intelligence block on the airfield. Near the perimeter fence, on the south side, exactly a quarter of a mile from the main entrance. Something to do with codebreaking.'

Hilda Pritt looked startled. Hannah saw it clearly. 'I know the building,' Hilda said slowly. 'It's a *big* building! It's not just some kind of *hut*.'

'I know it's not a hut,' Konrad said.

Hilda thought for a moment and then, unexpectedly, she turned to Hannah and said, 'You're wondering who I am. And how Abigail knows me.'

Hannah nodded. 'I *was* wondering that.'

'Abigail and her friends were involved in a little something, a few months ago. I lent a helping hand, that's all. It was terrific fun!'

She moved briskly on and asked Konrad if he could manage to survive another night in the pillbox.

He held his chin a little higher. 'Of course I can.'

'I've got a couple of days off,' Hilda said. 'What we need is a Council of War! And time to make a plan. Anyway, there are some things I need to find out. So why don't we meet tomorrow afternoon in Auntie Marge's tea-shop? After school.'

But Mucker objected. 'He'll scarper in the night,' he said.

'Do you promise,' Hilda said to Konrad, 'not to run away?'

'Of course.' He sounded posh, Hannah thought. As pompous as a peacock.

'And not to try blowing things up?'

He nodded.

'You are on parole,' Hilda said. 'You know what that means?'

Of course he knew what it meant. So Hilda turned to the others. 'Not a word to anyone about this,' she said, 'until after tomorrow. He promises not to *do* anything, and in return you all promise not to *say* anything. It's a dangerous and difficult situation. Until it's settled one way or the other, *keep your mouths shut!*'

She stared at Ollie. He nodded emphatically. Then at Hannah, who agreed at once. Mucker said he was willing to wait a day – *only one day, mind!* – before telling the police.

Finally Abigail, who just stared back at Hilda.

'Ah,' Hilda said. 'I forgot. You'll tell your friend Molly – and nothing I can say will make you not.'

'Molly can keep a secret,' Abigail said quietly. Hilda had to be satisfied with that.

She gave Konrad the prayer book. 'You can have this too,' she said, and handed him a bar of thick chocolate. 'Make it last till breakfast. And don't forget – if you have to speak to anyone, your name is Barnaby Hamilton.'

Abigail opened her eyes wide at the sight of the chocolate. Hilda saw it and said, 'Yes I *know*! I eat a lot of it on long flights.'

Then she said something they had all thought. 'Do you know, it had never occurred to me that Hitler had a *family*. Suddenly, a few years ago, he was just *there*, intent upon throwing the world into war.' She stared at them, thinking it out. 'I never thought of him having uncles and aunts and cousins.'

There was a general movement then as everyone scrambled to get out into the night. Konrad came outside too. It was a relief to stand up straight.

'Where is this tea-shop, please?' Konrad asked.

Abigail explained. 'It's in the high street. It's the only tea-shop in town, so you're bound to find it.'

'What about my clothes?' Konrad asked. 'I've been living rough. Are they smart enough?'

'They're no wuss n mine,' Mucker said. 'Nobody minds me – so yew'll be all right!'

'Are we very late?' Abigail said into the darkness.

Hilda wore a luminous wristwatch. 'It's half past eight,' she said.

'Crikey! I've got to get home!' Abigail said.

'Will you get into trouble?' Hannah asked her.

'No. But I've got to write to Molly. I write her a letter every day to tell her what's been happening. Tonight's one will be about twenty pages long!'

She cycled off ahead, followed by Hilda Pritt on a bike she'd borrowed from someone at the airfield.

As Hannah sat in Ollie's wooden cart, she thought about Abigail at home, writing pages of news to deliver next day to Molly Barnes. That was real friendship.

*

When he was little, Konrad's mother had told him that the most important people in his life made a chain of friendship that would always hold him, and help him, and sustain him. Whenever he was frightened he used to think about that.

But when they'd moved to Germany and the War had started, he forgot about it. Chains of friendship meant nothing. They could get broken.

Chains of command were the order of the day. Especially if you were related to the Führer.

-26-

Invisible Action

When streets were dark, houses were shut, and even the pubs had closed, the man with the glass eye went out. He had found somewhere to stay on the far side of town. He borrowed a bike and went in search of a phone box.

Cyclops wanted to speak to his boss. She had given him the telephone number of the hotel where she was staying.

A man's voice answered. 'I need to speak to Mrs Lufton, please,' Cyclops said. He had been told to ask for *Lufton*, not Feelgood.

The receptionist was bad-tempered. 'What time of the night do you call this?'

'It's important,' Cyclops said.

'We don't have phones in the bedrooms,' the receptionist said. 'This is not one of them fancy London places.'

Cyclops insisted, and the man at the other end put down the phone. But he took his time, and the permitted four minutes were almost over when he picked up the receiver and spoke. 'She's not there.'

'Are you sure?'

'Listen! I hammered on the door hard enough to wake everyone else in the building. She's not there!'

Ten minutes later Cyclops phoned the number a second time and asked the man in the hotel to try again. He was even more bad-tempered this time, and again he came back to say that Mrs Lufton was not in her room. Or not answering her door. 'And don't ring me no more!'

Cyclops stood for a while in the telephone box, deep in thoughts of wickedness, his one good eye flickering from side to side. He liked to know where his boss was. He preferred to know what she was up to.

When he stepped outside, a light mist had come down, feathering the dark and empty streets with wavering layers of paleness. He remounted his bike and set off.

He went beyond the town, beyond the railway line, beyond the real river with water flowing in it, and along the narrow lane that led across the flat and featureless fields to the Old Bank itself; and finally to the wooden bridge that crossed the other river – the one with no water flowing in it.

Beyond everything. To the very back of beyond.

At the wooden bridge he stopped. He hid the bike behind a mountainous hump of brambles, and walked quietly across. He stepped slowly, deliberately, glancing from side to side, casting his single eye on everything around him.

Down the other side of the bridge he went, softly into Mrs Pickens' frozen vegetable garden, and softly towards the front door. Here he stopped, and stood for five full minutes, timing himself by his luminous wristwatch. The door had heavy bolts on the inside. He'd noticed them on his last visit, with his boss.

He wished he knew where she was.

The back door was less likely to be bolted. These country people rarely locked their houses at night. They trusted their neighbours, and they had nothing worth stealing anyway.

He went stealthily round the side of the house. He was good at this. Any foraging night-time animal that happened to be there – a rat, perhaps, or a weasel – would probably not have noticed his movements. And in no time he reached the back door.

Here he stood, motionless, for another five minutes, timed by his watch. His senses were alert. He had done this before, many times. He was trained and disciplined in the skills of invisible action.

Silently he raised the latch on the back door. Silently he pushed open the door. He took out a small torch and shone it into the wash house. He stepped inside and quietly latched the door behind him. Here, he found an upturned tub, sat down on it, and made himself wait for fifteen minutes. He shone the torch around him and memorised the meagre contents and layout of the wash house.

An old song came into his thoughts.

Oh, please don't burn our wash house down,
Father will pay the rent.

Oh, please don't burn our wash house down,
For all our money is spent.

All the time he listened. We all know how to focus our eyes, but he had taught himself to focus his ears as well, to attend so closely to hearing that the sound of a mouse washing its whiskers, or a night spider walking across the scullery table, would have been distinct and audible to him.

He stood, pushed open the inside door and peered into the darkness of the big kitchen. Again, he shone his torch around him.

He stepped inside and crossed to the door at the foot of the stairs. With the slow and deliberate care of a person threading a needle he lifted the latch and opened the door. He placed his left foot on the bottom step.

But there was a sound, a tiny scraping of metal. Cyclops recognised it at once. Someone had lifted the latch on the outside wash house door. Silently he moved to the distant corner of the room, and crouched in the shadows between the big range and an old straight-backed armchair.

Stillness is often the surest form of concealment.

He heard cautious movements in the wash house. Someone was taking off an overcoat or mac, and hanging it up. Then rubber boots were quietly pulled off. Finally the latch on the inner door was lifted and the door pushed carefully open.

Someone had been out. But who? And why?

From the shadows he watched as the figure crossed the

kitchen. She was small, wearing a boy's shirt. Her bare legs and feet were pale in the darkness, her face too. She had in her hand what seemed to be an empty pie dish. One of those white enamel dishes that everyone had.

She opened the larder door and quietly placed the dish on a shelf.

Cyclops waited, taking tiny inaudible breaths.

Then she walked softly across to the stairs door and was gone. A little later, there was the slightest sound of a movement in the bedroom above his head. In his mind Cyclops imagined her hugging herself small in the feeble warmth of the bedclothes, pressing her cold feet together.

Cyclops sat down on a chair by the dying remains of the fire. Above him, Mr and Mrs Pickens were asleep in their room, and the brother and sister in theirs. And in one of them the girl who had memorised the list. And who had crept out in the middle of the night with a pie dish.

There were sounds from time to time. Sleepers turned in their beds. Someone coughed once, twice. One of the sleepers – lost in some private dream-sorrow – sighed deeply.

Cyclops – a giant crouching in the shadows – sat for an hour, unmoving, attentive, listening. Hardly breathing.

Then he rose, crossed the kitchen, and went into the wash house, carefully shutting the door behind him.

In the wash house a row of nails had been hammered into the woodwork. Overcoats and raincoats were hung on them, humpy and still. One of them was the one the girl had worn. Cyclops unhooked it. He held it high with his left hand, and rummaged his right hand through the pockets.

Nothing! No clue. He hung the coat back on its nail, and slipped silently outside.

But he was in no hurry to go away. A thick, freezing fog had come down, damp and bone-chilling. Cyclops went back towards the bridge over the dummy river. At each corner of the house he stopped, stood still, and made himself wait for five minutes before moving on.

He heard the church clock striking two, distant and muffled in the thick fog.

There was a moon, pouring its pale light over a wide ocean of thick white mist that had flooded the flat landscape and drowned every tree, every building, every irregularity. On the bridge, his head and shoulders rose above the fog, like a sea-swimmer surfacing. Wisps and flakes and layered planes rose and slowly billowed above the drifting fog-tide. From time to time, a wave would rise tenderly free, floating above and then falling away into nothing , gentle and apologetic, covering all of him, then sinking slowly down again. *I mean no harm*, it seemed to say.

The tower of Ely Cathedral – about ten miles away, he guessed – was faintly visible, no more than a stump, a tiny smudge, in the pale distant obscurity.

Slowly the night passed. Every hour he walked carefully

around the house, listening and watching. His glass eye shone icily in the moonlight, but his one good eye was never for a moment distracted from its watching.

What it watched most was Hannah Conway's bedroom window. Once, briefly, he saw her curtain twitched aside, and a white face looked out across the ocean of fog.

Slowly the cold night passed. Four o'clock, five o'clock, six o'clock – hour after weary hour, until at long last the sky lightened in the   -east, the moon in the west grew paler, and the cold ocean of mist began to sink away. Above a house further along the Old Bank, a chimney began to smoke. Someone had lit a fire to begin the new day. A weak candlelight came on in Hannah Conway's bedroom.

In the growing daylight Cyclops climbed astride his borrowed bike and set off stiffly back to his lodgings on the other side of town.

*

Hannah went sleepily downstairs to light the fire. It had become her job. She was good at it, and no one else seemed to like doing it.

But before she left her room she peered out of her window. All that was left of the fog was a pale ghost-river drifting softly downstream in the rising sunlight.

She thought of her father, and wondered where he was.

-27-

Improvising

Konrad had eaten a quarter of Hilda Pritt's bar of chocolate for supper the previous night. He ate the rest for breakfast. It was pleasant, but not sustaining.

The empty hours until their meeting after school stretched interminably ahead. Another day in the pillbox with nothing but his thoughts for company would be unbearable.

Unpleasant thoughts. The gelignite had been delivered now, and his only excuse for not acting immediately was that he still had to find a way of transporting it. But he'd noticed the previous night that one of the boys had a bike with a wooden cart fixed to the back. He needed to think about that.

Hilda Pritt was another unpleasant thought. He knew she probably meant well. But he couldn't help thinking of her as a nuisance, a further complication. She had not been planned.

Never make an important decision on an empty stomach, Fraulein Eva had said to him. He was unexpectedly stirred by a sharp and vivid memory of Eva's physical self, trim, efficient and attractive. The others at the school had taught him skills –

but she had got inside his mind and shaped his thinking. *I will do as she would advise,* he said to himself.

I will play for time, he thought. He would explore the lie of the land. And find some food. She would approve of that. He imagined her giving him praise.

The morning was bright and sunny. Dazzling, in fact, but very cold. With his hands pushed into his pockets for warmth, and the collar of his coat pulled tight around his throat, he set off on the long walk into Great Deeping. It was time, he told himself, to test his training.

It was time to *be* Barnaby Hamilton.

He'd walked about half a mile when he saw Mucker Bailey standing firmly in the middle of the road. His legs were apart, his arms folded.

That boy! Konrad thought. Another complication.

'Where are yew gooin, *Barnaby Hamilton*?' he said. He was aggressive and determined.

'Into town,' Konrad said. Fraulein Eva had not prepared him for this kind of confrontation. She hadn't foreseen anything like it. But then, he thought, who *could* imagine anyone quite like Mucker Bailey? Luckily, Konrad had enough sense of his own to know that nothing was to be gained by having a row with this scruffy and unappealing schoolboy.

'Why aren't you at school?' he said.

'I goo t school when I feel like it,' Mucker said. 'And I don't feel like it today!'

'Why not?'

'*Why not!* I'll tell yew why. There's a bloody German with a load o dynamite, who plans to blow up a bit of our airfield – and yew ask me why I een't gooin t school!'

'Oh, I see. You're keeping watch on me,' Konrad said.

'Someone's got tew.'

'Well, you can relax. I have no plans to blow anything up today.'

'Where are yew gooin then?'

'Shopping. I need something to eat.'

Mucker thought for a moment. 'Hev you got some money left then, after spending a whole pound on my rabbit?'

'Yes.'

'Ration book?'

'No.'

'Well, yew can't git no food then.'

'Not all food is rationed,' Konrad pointed out.

'Oh yeah? What do yew know about it?'

'I know that bread isn't rationed. Nor potatoes.'

'*Taters!* Huh! There's millions o tons of taters all round yew! In the fields.'

'I know that,' Konrad said. 'I do not intend to steal potatoes from the fields.'

'Why not? *We* dew!'

'OK, but I'm right. And you know I am. About bread.'

'How did yew know that?'

'Because I'm half British.'

'You're half *German*! I wouldn't care if yew starved to death.'

Fraulein Eva came into Konrad's mind again, not for anything she'd said, but for her calmness, her imperturbability.

'If you want to keep watch on me,' he said, 'why don't you come with me?'

After a moment's hesitation, Mucker Bailey said, 'OK. I will!'

So they walked together, awkwardly, side by side but not close.

After a while Mucker spoke. 'That plane,' he said. 'The one yew came in.'

'What about it?'

'Well, the crew were all killed. How come yew weren't?'

'I'd jumped – before it crashed.'

'Lucky for yew!'

'Yes, it was.'

'With a parachute, I spose.'

'Of course.'

'Well, where is it then?'

'I buried it.'

'How did yew know how to make a parachute jump?'

'I was trained.'

'*Trained?*'

'Yes, trained.'

'How? Where was yew trained?'

So Konrad told Mucker Bailey about the school where he'd been taught so much. Not its name, of course. And not its location. In the telling, Mucker asked questions and Konrad filled in the details, and they walked a little closer together. Almost like friends.

Mucker probably didn't notice this change. Konrad did.

They arrived at last at the bridge that crossed the real river, the Great Ouse. The town began on the other side, where there was a level crossing. 'Thas where Abigail lives,' Mucker told Konrad.

Konrad spotted someone at an upstairs window in Abigail's house, a woman, watching them as they walked past. Abigail's mother, almost certainly, wondering about this unknown boy walking into town with Mucker Bailey.

And as they walked the length of King George Street, Konrad felt that every person they passed was eyeing him with suspicion. He knew he was probably imagining it but it was hard to control.

He'd not expected to feel like this. But he realised now that walking along an ordinary street in an English town in war-time – on his way to the shops with Mucker Bailey – was very different from walking to the shops *before* the War, with his best friend.

There were dangers everywhere. Three soldiers in uniform, with kitbags and rifles, came out of a stationery shop. One of them gazed intently at the two boys. An RAF jeep pulled up outside the post office and the driver jumped out, glancing at Konrad as he did so.

An old lady at an upstairs window shook her fist at him. When he looked back, she wasn't there at all and he thought he'd imagined it.

And there was a policeman walking slowly along the high street towards them.

There seemed to be nothing and no one in war-time Great Deeping to make Konrad feel welcome there. He felt exiled. There was an invisible line, a boundary of some sort, and he was now on the *other* side of it. He was half German, with a stash of dynamite hidden away – and it felt as if everyone in the street knew that fact. Or suspected it.

When they reached the Co-op in the high street, Konrad braced himself. 'This is my first public performance playing the part of a boy called Barnaby Hamilton,' he said quietly.

'I'm gooin in with yew!' Mucker said. 'I'm performin the part of a boy called Mucker Bailey!'

So the two of them shopped for food. Konrad asked for:

- Potatoes (big ones that could be cooked in his fire).
- Cheese (*That een't rationed yet!*), eggs (*nor een't they!*)
- Sausages (*everyone reckons they will be soon*)
- Some biscuits (mixed varieties),
- A loaf of bread, but not butter (*that's bin rationed since the start*).

The shopkeeper loaded the whole lot into two brown-paper bags and Konrad handed over the money. Mucker watched him carefully for signs of uncertainty, but there were none. Konrad managed the whole deal.

As they left the shop, he felt immensely satisfied. Fraulein Eva would have been proud of him! He *liked* being his English self again, and his anxieties faded a little.

But outside they faced an unexpected difficulty.

The police sergeant stood on the opposite side of the street, watching intently. As soon as they emerged from the Co-op he crossed the road towards them.

'Mucker Bailey, why aren't you at school?'

This was a familiar situation for Mucker. He had years of experience. 'I een't well enough,' he said.

Sergeant Bly was sceptical. 'You look well enough to me.'

'Ah, thas as maybe! I was sick in the night. And I'm still a bit poorly.'

'You spend more days feeling poorly than you do at school.'

Mucker grinned. 'Yeah. I dew!'

'And who is this?' the sergeant said, turning to Konrad.

Konrad was ready for this, and his reply was instantaneous. 'My name is Hamilton. Barnaby Hamilton. I have my identity card.'

But as he put his hand into his inside jacket pocket, he realised that Sergeant Bly was looking curiously at him. Had he made a mistake?

'I'll tell you something,' Sergeant Bly said at last. 'There are probably around three hundred kids in and around this town.'

What is he getting at? Konrad wondered.

'And I can guarantee that none of them carry their identity cards around with them. They're tucked behind clocks, or at the backs of cupboards, or used as bookmarks – but they are never – *never!* – carried about in pockets. They *should* be, but they never are.'

Fraulein Eva had failed to anticipate this. She and her staff had spent hours researching and making his fake identity card – but none of them had understood that most people in Britain just put them in a safe place and forgot about them.

And they certainly never offered them to a policeman before they were asked.

So now Sergeant Bly's interest was aroused. 'You don't live here,' he said to Konrad. 'So where are you from?'

In the briefest fraction of a second Konrad understood something else that Fraulein Eva had got wrong. If he said he'd run away from a boarding school, this policeman would immediately take him in charge. No policeman could ignore such a thing. He would investigate it.

But Mucker Bailey saved the day. 'He's my cousin,' he said. 'He's stayin at my house.'

Sergeant Bly stared at Mucker in surprise. 'Your cousin?' he said. 'I didn't know you had any cousins.'

'Yew don't know everything,' Mucker said.

'Maybe not. But I went to school with your mother and I know she didn't have any brothers or sisters.'

'Ah,' Mucker said in triumph, 'but you didn't go to school with my pa – cos he went to school in Downham! And he has a sister.'

'A sister.'

'Yes. And she's my aunt – and . . .'

Konrad knew that Mucker almost said the wrong name at that point. But he corrected himself after only the briefest hesitation.

'. . . and *Barnaby* is her boy, my cousin. And *she's* got the flu, which is why *he's* come to stay with *us*. Until *she* gits *better!*' Certain words were emphasised, like sharp little jabs of triumph. He didn't actually say '*so there!*' But he might as well have done. 'So if yew doon't mind, we'd like to git off hum! These bags are heavy!'

Mucker didn't wait for permission. He simply turned away and set off, and Konrad was glad to follow.

He was relieved of course. But also angry – with himself for having almost been caught out, and with Fraulein Eva, for her failure to imagine her plans being tested in action.

And with England for not being what it used to be.

But the more he thought about Fraulein Eva, the less severe he was inclined to be. For there was something else she said once. *It's my job to prepare for everything we can anticipate,* she said. *But from the very moment you land in England, you will have to improvise! Remember that!*

On their way back along King George Street, Konrad thanked Mucker for his help.

Mucker was ungracious. 'That doon't make no difference though,' he said. 'I still think yew should be locked up. And thas what I intend to say when we meet that Pritt-y woman this arternoon for tea!'

-28-

Little Green

Over near the airfield there was a tiny village called Little Green. It was called that because there was a village green – a *little* one – with houses built along each side. It had a tiny church, a shop and a pub. There is a bus every two hours to and from Great Deeping. Most of the passengers were airfield staff from the base.

Since the start of the War, life had become a lot more interesting for the people of Little Green.

In one of the cottages lived an old lady called Edith Pritt. She was Hilda Pritt's grandmother, known to everyone in the village as Edie. She was very old and rather frail, but in her prime she had been a tall, strong woman. She still had that look of strength about her, and because she was tall she swayed a little as she walked, like a tower about to topple. But she never toppled.

She came outside that morning because the overnight fog had melted away and the February sun was shining with a warm promise of spring. Her front garden was small, just a patch of grass with some leafless rosebushes and three beehives. Outside the gate stood a wooden table with a basket, and a notice saying, *EGGS FREE. HELP YOURSELF.* In the summer there would be jars of honey, but those would have to be paid for.

Hilda Pritt was very fond of her grandmother. When she was a schoolgirl, she'd spent holidays at Little Green. These days, when she flew a plane to the airfield she usually flew another one out again the same day. But if she was delayed for a night – or even a few hours – she always went to visit her grandmother.

So old Mrs Pritt was not surprised to see her granddaughter, on a borrowed bike, skidding to a stop outside her garden gate. They didn't hug or kiss, those two. Nothing like that – and a passer-by would not have known that either of them cared much about the other.

'I say, Gran!' Hilda said. 'What a glorious morning!'

'My bees are out already, some of them,' Mrs Pritt said. 'Have you just flown in?'

'Ah! Well, no!' Hilda said. 'This visit is a bit different. Thing is, I need you to do me a favour.'

Hilda never beat around the bush.

'Oh, you do, do you! What favour?'

'Can you put someone up for a few nights? A lodger? I'll pay for his keep.'

'What kind of lodger?'

'A boy.'

Granny Pritt pulled a knowing face. 'Will you be here too,' she asked, 'with this *boy*?'

'You really are an old shocker!' Hilda said. 'But you've got the wrong end of the stick. He's a *school*boy.'

Mrs Pritt swayed a little and steadied herself with her hand on the gatepost. 'A schoolboy?' she said.

'Yes. Look here, Granny, if you don't want to do it, I'll think of something else. But this is a *no-questions-asked* sort of situation.'

'Hush-hush?'

'Yes, *jolly* hush-hush!'

'How long will he be here?'

'Three or four days, a week at the most.'

'Will I have to feed him?'

'Afraid so. And he'll be awfully hungry. He's had a rather rough time. He'll need a bath too.'

'Has he got a name?' There was a hint of sarcasm in Edith Pritt's voice.

'Of course he has! He's called Barnaby Hamilton.'

'I'm finding it very difficult not to be inquisitive,' the old lady said. 'But I'll help – as long as you promise to tell me afterwards what it's all about. Now, come on through and say hello to the fowls.'

A brick-floored passage led straight through from the front door and out into the even warmer sunshine in the back garden, where Hilda admired her grandmother's eighteen chickens.

As they stood in the sunshine Mrs Pritt said, 'He'll have to sleep in the little back bedroom. Better have a look and see what you think.'

The little bedroom was perfect, Hilda thought. Certainly better than a pillbox. 'I say! What's all this?'

Facing the window were a comfortable armchair, a small table, and a pair of binoculars.

Hilda laughed at her grandmother. 'I believe you've been spying!' she said.

'I spend quite a lot of time watching the comings and goings of the airfield.'

'You wicked old woman! They'll have you locked up!'

'It's not against the law to look. I like watching the planes taking off, and coming in to land. *If* they come back, that is. There was one this morning that almost didn't make it.'

'I know. It was a Wellington. The pilot lost an arm. Awfully decent chap.' Hilda, adjusting the binoculars, peered over the perimeter fence and swept her vision across the airfield. Then she focused. 'What's that building over there?' she said, pointing to a brick building that looked like an office block. It was the one she'd asked the commanding officer about.

'Ah!' her grandmother said. 'I can't tell you because I don't know. But I do know they've stopped using it. About two months ago, four big RAF trucks were parked outside and everything in that building was taken out and loaded up. There used to be people coming and going, all day every day – but not any more. It's abandoned, I reckon.'

'I think it must be,' Hilda said, knowing already that it was.

-29-

Tea at Auntie Marge's

The next day Ollie had a bad cold and was too ill to go to school. And because Ollie wasn't going, Betty persuaded her mum that she should stay at home too. Mrs Pickens was a pushover where school was concerned.

But when Ollie explained that they were supposed to have tea at Auntie Marge's tea-shop in the afternoon, he got a sharp reply. 'If yew're too ill t goo to school, then yew're too ill to be gadding about at tea-shops!' she said. 'Anyway, *why* are you having tea there? And who with?'

'It's that pilot woman,' Ollie said. 'Miss Pritt.'

Mrs Pickens scowled. '*Who?*'

'She's a friend of Abigail's,' Ollie said.

'What's she got to do wi yew?'

Ollie was hopeless at explaining, so Hannah said, 'We just happened to be there when they were talking about it.' It was true, in a way.

'So yew got invited as well?' Mrs Pickens was suspicious.

'Yes,' Hannah said. 'And Mucker Bailey.'

'*Mucker?* I doon't believe it! Auntie Marge will have a heart

180

attack if she sees *im* gooin into her precious tea-shop!'

It was the first time Hannah had walked to school on her own. She could have used Ollie's bike with the cart attached, but she preferred to walk. She left the house at around eight o'clock and set off towards the distant town. There was no sign of Mucker, so she supposed it was one of his illegal days off.

The overnight fog had cleared, there was a hazy blue sky, and she could feel the warm sun on her back. She had an unfamiliar feeling – it was the first time for months that she was looking forward to the day. Those dark London nights seemed a long way off, as if they belonged to a different world.

But London wasn't a different world, just a different place in the same war. She heard the growing roar of three twin-engined bombers approaching low, coming in to land. They flew right over her head. One of them had only one working engine, and the other propeller swung uselessly as the plane passed overhead. Part of the plane's tail end had been damaged too, and she could see right through the rear end of the fuselage. There was just a skeleton there, with the aircraft's skin torn off. The other two planes flew one on each side, as if they were encouraging it to get home safely.

Mucker Bailey had taught her the names of the aircraft. These were Wellingtons. Mucker would be somewhere around, gazing up at them. Wetting himself probably.

She crossed the railway line at the edge of town and Abigail came out of her house to meet her. Hannah liked that, and they walked together, talking in low voices about Konrad.

When they got to the house where Molly Barnes lived, Hannah waited outside while Abigail went in. 'You can come too,' she said. But Hannah was shy. She hardly knew Molly, and she didn't know her mum at all.

'Is she any better?' she asked when Abigail came out.

Abigail shook her head. 'The doctor's coming later.'

*

That afternoon when school was finished, the two of them went to Auntie Marge's tea-room. It was an upstairs café, above a hardware shop. Konrad was in the street, waiting for someone to go in with.

They all felt shy. However, Abigail had been to the tea-room before. Lots of times. So she led them up the stairs.

Halfway up, something strange happened. They met a lady coming down, dressed in the weirdest clothes anyone could imagine. She wore a striped football sock on her head. Hannah saw it clearly. There was nothing funny about this. It was *scary*. And she wore a cloak, like a witch. As they passed her, she flattened herself against the wall, pulled a face, and held up her hands with her fingers fluttering as if trying to ward off some evil thing. She smelled of garlic, too.

She glared at Konrad as if he had done something especially

bad. You would have thought her eyes were going to pop out of her head as he edged by her on the stairs.

Then she clattered hurriedly down the stairs and out into the street.

'That's Loopy Lavvy,' Abigail said. 'She's all right really.'

The tea-room was spacious, with an open fireplace. A few people were already there, having tea. There was an alcove, apart from the rest of the room. Hilda had established herself there at a table where they could talk without being overheard. Mucker Bailey had already arrived and was with her.

To be fair, he had scrubbed himself up and made an effort. There was not much he could do about his clothes. You could see his shirt collar was worn, and the cuffs of his jacket were frayed. But he'd blackened his shoes, his socks were held up with rubber bands, and he'd wetted his hair and combed it flat.

'Now!' Hilda said. 'What are we all going to have? If the newspapers are right, sugar will be rationed soon – so let's make the most of the sweet stuff while we still can!'

Mucker seemed subdued. When Auntie Marge asked him if he'd like a menu, he asked her if it had currants in it. That was sorted out, and he spent a long time studying the treats that were on offer – so long that Hannah started to wonder if he could read at all.

Auntie Marge looked at him as if he'd brought in a bad smell. But Hannah couldn't smell anything except Lifebuoy soap.

'I say,' Hilda said to Auntie Marge. 'Could you manage to let this lad have something cooked?'

'He looks pretty well-fed to me.'

'No, not that boy. *This* one!'

'I stop serving cooked dinners at two o'clock.'

'Trouble *is*, you see, he's had nothing at all since yesterday. I'm sure you could manage something simple. Eggs on toast, perhaps?'

Good old Hilda! Hannah thought. Auntie Marge sniffed, but she went off to see what she could do. Hannah felt an odd rush of affection for Hilda, as if she'd known her all her life. She was beginning to understand why Abigail admired her.

Eventually, they were all settled with their chosen cakes and drinks. Konrad had to wait for his, but it was worth it – three slices of toast, two poached eggs, some baked beans and a sausage. Hannah had a fruit scone, with raspberry jam. Abigail had a thick slice of chocolate cake.

Mucker kept eyeing Konrad's meal. He said nothing, but Hannah knew it made him feel hungry, just to see it.

'Now,' Hilda said. 'To business! Barnaby, I have found somewhere you can stay.'

Hannah and Abigail maintained expressionless faces when Hilda said *Barnaby*. But not Mucker. He smirked knowingly. Anyone watching would have seen.

'The police station,' he said. 'In a cell! That's where he should be.'

Hannah should have felt angry with him. But she didn't. She felt warm and friendly towards him – this stupid, stubborn boy who wouldn't change his mind and always said what was in it.

'He's a *German*,' he added in disgust.

'Dear boy!' Hilda said. 'Keep your voice down, do!'

And Hannah wanted to laugh out loud. She found it all so *funny*! What was wrong with her? Was she going mad? And Konrad didn't protest at any of this because he was desperately stuffing himself!

'What's the plan?' Abigail said. Lovely Abigail, neat, tidy Abigail, who liked things to work.

'Well . . . I say, this is *scrumptious*! . . . Where was I? Ah, yes! Barnaby, you can stay for a few days with my grandmother. She lives out in the country . . . near the airfield.'

Konrad paused in his eating and paid attention. Hannah watched him, waiting for his reaction. 'Thank you,' he said, but she could tell he wanted to know more.

'She will feed you properly, and you'll have your own bedroom. It won't be for long, just a few days probably.'

'But it doesn't solve Barnaby's problem,' Abigail said. 'What about *that*?'

Hilda chewed her lower lip. *She's not sure how much she should say,* Hannah thought. 'I have worked out a sort of plan,' Hilda said. 'But it's not a very good one and I might not be able to make it happen.'

'I've *told* yew what should appen!' Mucker said. His mouth was full of fruit cake and it was a disgusting moment. 'Yew should take im straight to the police! Woss this idea of yours, anyway?'

Hilda glared at him. 'Can you keep secrets?' she demanded.

'Course I can!'

'Good! So can I! And I'm keeping this one.'

Hannah, feeling hopeful, needed assurance. 'Are you on our side?' she asked Hilda.

'Golly, yes! Of course I am. But . . .'

'But what?'

'It's a complicated situation, and I haven't quite worked out a way through it.'

She turned back to Konrad. 'Has your plan got a name?' she asked. 'A codename of some sort?'

'No,' Konrad said. He could not bring himself to reveal that. He knew that keeping it secret made no sense since he had given away everything else. But still, the German part of him had to keep something back from the British. So he kept the codename to himself.

Changing the subject, he said in a low voice, 'What about the gelignite?'

Hilda admitted that was a problem. 'I can't take that to my grandmother's house,' she said. 'Obviously! I think that pillbox is the best place for it. For now.'

Mucker opened his mouth to complain, but she spoke first.

'And you, Mucker, are the best person to keep an eye on it.'

'All right,' he said slowly. 'But –'

'No buts! That's the plan. Someone will be put in charge of it, the Home Guard probably. But until then, it's your job. Barnaby, there's a bus to Little Green in half an hour . . .'

And that's how their tea party came to an end. Hilda paid, and they all trooped down the stairs and out into the street.

Hannah watched Konrad go off with Hilda Pritt, wondering if he would be able to keep up his Barnaby Hamilton act. Then she felt unexpectedly left out. She was glad that Abigail was with her.

-30-

Confidential Report

In the room where Cyclops was staying there was an old typewriter. He put a sheet of paper into it and began to type.

Hannah Marion Conway.

Born: August 21st 1930, Southampton.

Mother: Died September 2nd, 1936.

Father: Currently Captain in the Royal Navy, commanding HMS Sweetheart. A Destroyer. Exemplary record.

Residence: Since 1936, HMC lived with her paternal grandmother, Harriet Susan Conway.
September 1940: refused to be evacuated and stayed in London to care for her grandmother.
Mrs Conway killed by enemy bombing December 2nd 1940. HMC moved in with a Mrs Ritchie.
Mrs Ritchie bombed out 29th December 1940.
HMC disappeared for approx. two to three weeks.

Thought to be living rough.

Subsequently turned up at Great Deeping. Now living as an evacuee at the house of Mr and Mrs Harry Pickens, The Old Bank, Great Deeping.

Character: Brave. Intelligent. Wilful and determined. Stubborn. Very interested in people. Likes to understand what they think and why they do what they do. Makes friends easily. Gets on well with local children. Gets on well with host family, but has not made the Pickenses into surrogate parents. Secretive. There's something she's not telling.

Risk Level: * * * HIGH * * *.

Cyclops was a careful typist and made no mistakes. When he'd finished he folded the paper and put it in an envelope. He sealed it and hid it carefully away.

-31-

Journey in the Dark

Hannah was unlucky that evening.

There was no electricity in the Pickens' house. No gas either. They used coal for cooking on a range, candles and oil lamps for light, and a battery accumulator to power their wireless set.

Mrs Pickens loved her wireless. It was switched on most of the day.

The accumulator powered the wireless for around a week – and then it had to be taken into Mackender's cycle shop in Great Deeping to be recharged. They had two accumulators. One was in use at home with the other being charged at the shop, turn and turn about. Each recharging cost sixpence.

Ollie fetched and delivered the accumulators every week. They were made of thick glass, filled with acid and very heavy. You couldn't go all that way carrying one in your hand. So Ollie always went on his bike, with the accumulator in the cart.

But Ollie had a cold, and Mr Pickens had been working on the land all day. So, when Hannah got home after the tea party with Hilda Pritt, guess who was expected to take the accumulator to the cycle shop?

She didn't make a fuss. If you move in with a family, you have to take your share of jobs. She'd always known there would come a time when she would have to make that journey, on her own, after dark.

Everywhere was quiet when she set off. As she pushed down on the pedals, she peered into the darkness across the flat fields towards where the distant river bridge should be. She wished Abigail was standing on it, flashing her torch.

The bike had a cycle lamp, but there was a piece of tissue paper stuck to the inside of the glass to weaken the light, because of blackout regulations. It threw a faint dimness on the front mudguard, and it half lit a bit of the road about the size of a tea tray. Its main effect was to make the surrounding darkness seem darker.

She stopped once and stood astride the bike, twisting round and looking behind her. Just to check that no one was following her. In London, she'd never felt scared like that, even at night, after dark. But she pressed on, and in time she reached the river bridge and swooped down the far side towards the level crossing. The gates were open, each with its dim red light glowing as she rattled across the tracks.

No light was visible in Abigail's house as she cycled past. Nor anywhere else.

There were a few people in the streets. Solitary voices called out 'G'night!' from one side of the darkness to the other. The town was closing down for a war-time winter's night.

But not Mr Mackender's cycle shop. That stayed open all evening. Hannah parked the bike beside the shop window and lugged the accumulator out of the cart, and into the shop. It was warm and bright in there, with a comforting smell of oil and grease and rubber tyres. There was something safe and pre-war about it. She paid the sixpence and took away the recharged accumulator. It bumped uncomfortably against the side of her leg, and she worried about the acid as she heaved it up and into the wooden cart.

On her way back, everything went well until she'd crossed the railway and left the town behind. Never in her life had she known such a lonely silence. She turned into the lane that ran beside the Old Bank, and thought to herself, *The last leg, not far to go now.*

On the right-hand side of the narrow road the bare, level fields stretched away unseen. On the other, the steep, grassy bank rose to four times her height. Part of it broke free and formed a separate shape that stepped into the road and blocked her way.

She knew straight away who it was. There was instant recognition. He stood in front of her – tall, leaning over her, big hands gripping the handlebars of her bike.

They were together again, in the dark, face to face. Like before.

'Hannah Conway,' he said.

'What do you want?' She was standing now, astride

the bike. She tried to make her voice sound as if she wasn't scared.

'We meet again.'

'Let me past! I'm nearly home, and I'm *tired*!'

'That list,' he said. For a moment she thought she'd seen a tiny gleam of reflected light in the glass eye. But where did it come from, that reflection? The cycle lamp was too feeble, and was directed downwards, shining faintly on his shoes and the bottoms of his trouser legs. The crazy idea came into her mind that the glass eye had a tiny light source of its own.

'I gave it back to you.'

He bent his head down close to hers, and said quietly, 'But you learned it by heart. You shouldn't have done that.'

She tried – she honestly did try – to understand him, to look into his face and work out what was in him. But how can you tell? How can anyone ever tell?

Why did he keep coming back into her life? There was such *pressure* in him, all focused on her. She could feel it.

Her gran came into her thoughts then. Right up to her illness, she'd protected Hannah from everything – bullying on the way home from school (once), a teacher who had it in for her (once), her fear of the Nazis (hundreds of times). And she'd made it all right every time her dad went back to sea.

But her gran had gone now, and she was on her own.

'Let me go,' she said, '*Now!*'

But the menace of the man! He still gripped the handlebars,

with his face pushed down and close to hers. She didn't flinch.

'*Did* you learn it by heart?'

'Why does it matter? I've forgotten it now.' The rest of the world had crept away and left the two of them, alone, in a vast and indifferent silence.

'Prove it!'

But that was silly. He *knew* it was silly. It's easy to prove you do remember something, but how can you prove you don't?

'I have to get home,' she said, and she raised herself back on to the saddle.

'No!' he said. 'I haven't finished.'

She was in despair then, and she thought she was done for. But the Old Bank changed its shape again – and turned into Ollie Pickens standing up high, looking down from the top. Dear old Ollie, who liked rounding up lost and frightened people.

He called down, doubtfully, into the dark, 'Hannah?'

'*Ollie! I'm here!*'

Cycle-tops straightened and stepped back from the bike. She sensed his fury, his frustration. But she pushed past him and pressed down on the pedals. Ollie slid on his heels down the bank to where she stood.

'I'm warning you . . .' Cycle-tops said.

But Hannah had no intention of staying to hear his warning. Feeling immensely grateful to Ollie, she set off on the bike, and he jogged along beside her.

'What about your cold?'

'I wanted to make sure yew were all right,' he said. 'So I come out t look for yer. What did *he* want?'

-32-

The Entrance Exam

Thursday was a special day. Miss Twisleton, their teacher, had told them about it the week before. Some of them were going to take the County Entrance Examination.

If they failed it, they would have to spend the rest of their schooldays in the same class, with her. Someone had questioned this. 'But that means we'll ha to learn the same things oover and oover again, miss.'

'Most of you *need* to be taught the same things over and over again,' Miss Twisleton retorted.

But any boy or girl who passed would get a scholarship. The boys would go to the Grammar School at Soham and the girls would go to the High School at Ely. There wouldn't be many who passed, Miss Twisleton warned them.

She had already chosen which of them should take the exam, and their parents had been written to. 'The examination will take place at Ely,' she'd said. 'You must all bring sixpence for the bus fare.'

One boy had only threepence. 'Then you'll have to walk home,' Miss Twisleton said. But they knew she was teasing him.

So on Thursday morning they stood in the sunny playground while Miss Twisleton fiddled about with her list of names.

Abigail was one of them. 'What about Molly?' she asked.

Miss Twisleton reassured her. 'Molly Barnes is being allowed to take the exam at home because she's ill.'

Abigail knew that already, but she liked to check that everything was working properly.

'She might cheat,' someone said.

'No, she won't. She's being supervised by the vicar. He had measles when he was a boy and can't catch it again.'

She went through her list a second time. 'Hannah, go back inside the classroom and bring Billy Gale out here.'

So Hannah did that, and Miss Twisleton said to Billy, 'I put you on the list to go, so why did you stay inside?'

'My pa oon't let me goo t the grammar school anyway, miss. So woss the point?'

Miss Twisleton was flummoxed. '*Education* is the point,' she said.

'When I leave orff school, I'll goo t work on the land. I already know everything a landworker has t know, so woss the point o learnin anything else?'

Miss Twisleton made no attempt to persuade him that he should take the exam. Hannah felt angry with him, and with her. He was being an idiot, and she should have tried harder.

Then Miss Twisleton spotted Mucker Bailey standing in the group, and she came over all sarcastic. '*So!*' she said. '*Cyril*

Bailey! You've decided to honour us with your presence today, I see! *Well, well!*'

Mucker grinned. He didn't care about sarcasm. Or perhaps he didn't know she was being sarcastic. 'Yes, miss. But I never knew nuffin about all this.'

'Of course you didn't! You weren't at school on the day I told the class about it.'

'That was one o my days off,' he said cheerfully.

'And you want to take the examination?' Miss Twisleton asked.

'Course I dew!'

'But *why?*'

'I een't never bin t Ely.'

'But I didn't write to your parents about this.'

'They wouldn't ha read it if yew ad.'

'I'm absolutely certain they wouldn't!' Miss Twisleton said. 'That's why I didn't bother.'

There should have been fifteen of them in the group, six evacuees and nine local kids. But Billy Gale wasn't going, so Mucker was allowed to take his place.

'Have you got your sixpence?' Miss Twisleton said.

Mucker shook his head and grinned. 'I never have no money,' he said cheerfully.

'Well then, you can't come with us.'

But Mucker could be stubborn when he chose. 'I doon't see why I shouldn't,' he said. 'Just cos I een't got no money.'

'There is also,' Miss Twisleton pointed out, 'the small fact that you hardly ever bother to come to school!'

But for some reason she relented. 'All right. You may come. I'll pay your bus fare.'

'An I'll git yew a nice rabbit for the weekend,' Mucker said.

She ignored that. 'Line up at the bus stop,' she said to them.

So they stood tidily at the bus stop, outside the school gate. Abigail stood with Hannah. She knew that was only because Molly Barnes wasn't there, but she didn't mind.

She didn't mind anything that morning! The sun was warm and they were all going on the bus to Ely. Besides, although she liked Miss Twisleton, she didn't want to go on being taught by her for the rest of the War. She'd once told the whole class that Hong Kong was the capital of China, and Hannah knew it wasn't. She'd been quite nasty to her when she said so.

At Littleport, another group of children was waiting near the church, and the two teachers sat together on the bus and chatted.

Hannah sat with Abigail, and behind them was Mucker Bailey, by himself because no one wanted to sit next to him. Abigail suddenly turned round and knelt up on the seat, facing him. She grabbed Mucker's left wrist and inspected his fingers.

'You said you were going to stop biting your nails!' she said to him.

Everyone around turned to watch.

'I *am*! I've started,' he said.

'Well, I can't see much improvement,' Abigail said back. She grabbed his other hand and they all saw that four of the nails were bitten down as usual – but the nail on his forefinger had grown into a decent shape and had been trimmed with scissors.

'I'm dewin one finger at a time,' Mucker said. And when everyone laughed, he went on. 'I dunno what yew find so funny! When my ma wanted to stop smoking, thas ow she did it. She useter smoke fifty fags a day. So she cut down one fag a week, an after a year she didn't smoke none at all! She een't never had one since! And thas what I'm dewing – one nail every month.'

'That'll take you till Christmas!' someone pointed out.

Mucker changed the subject. 'Ollie says yew've ad another visit from your one-eyed friend,' he said to Hannah. 'Wodyew say his name was?'

'Cycle-tops,' she said. 'Something like that. I didn't hear properly what he said.'

'That was probly Cyclops,' Mucker said. 'He was a one-eyed giant.'

Everyone stared. How did Mucker know that?

'I read books!' he said. 'From time t time.' No one believed him.

At Ely, Miss Twisleton told them all to line up in pairs to walk through the city. 'And if you don't behave properly,' she said, 'I'll make you hold hands!'

The girls looked contemptuous and the boys groaned. But she was in a good temper, and so were they.

'We've made a vow,' Abigail said quietly as they walked. 'Molly and me.'

'What vow?'

'If one of us gets the scholarship and the other doesn't, we'll both stay at school in Deeping.'

Hannah could see why they might promise that. But she thought they'd be wrong to do it.

'There are a couple of boys,' Abigail said. 'A year older than us – Micky Sparkes and Toby Myers. They were best friends – I mean *really* best friends. Then Micky passed the exam and Toby didn't.'

'Did they fall out?'

'Toby says Micky's turned into a snob because he goes to a posh school. And Micky says Toby's jealous because he doesn't. They don't even speak to each other now. And their *families* don't speak to each other any more either.'

Hannah didn't reply to that. When her best friend went away there had been no choices at all, for either of them.

*

The room where they took the examination was huge, like a church, with high windows and coloured glass. It was cold, in spite of the sun outside. There were lots of desks, arranged in rows. Each one had some paper, a white inkwell, a single small square of blotting paper, a pen and pencil, and a ruler.

Hannah hoped she would get a table near Abigail, but she was in a different row, at the back. The children sitting near her all came from different schools in the county. They all looked very clever.

There was a tall man in a black gown in charge. He looked very stern, the sort you wouldn't want to argue with. He patrolled silently up and down between the rows of desks, looking for cheats.

A tiny hair got caught between the prongs of her pen nib, and it dragged and smeared blue ink over her writing. It was a terrible mess, and her fingers got covered in ink too as she tried to pull out the hair. But the stern man in the gown was not so bad after all. He saw what was happening and gave her a fresh pen with a brand new nib. 'I'd start that page again if I were you,' he said.

She looked around from time to time. She could see Mucker Bailey three rows away. He never seemed to be doing much. But she daren't look anywhere too hard in case she was accused of copying.

There were three tests. The first was Arithmetic, the second was Verbal Reasoning. Then they had to write a composition on *My Home*.

Hannah wrote:

Home is where you are loved. My first home was in a big house because my father is a captain in the Royal Navy and he is quite rich. But he was away most of the time so there was only half the love.

My mother died ~~at the age of six~~ when I was six. So I went to live with my grandmother in London. She was quite poor and her house was smaller. But she loved me and it was a good home.

Then she was killed in the Blitz and the house was bombed. I was pulled out of the rubble. I lived for a short time with a lady called Mrs Ritchie. She was very poor and her house was even smaller than my gran's. She didn't love me but she was kind.

Then that house got bombed too.

For three weeks I had no home at all. I lived in the streets during the day and in air-raid shelters at night. People were kind to me sometimes, but no one loved me. I was HOMELESS. You ~~can't~~ cannot get much lower than that.

Now I am an evacuee and I live in a house surrounded by miles and miles of mud. I do not understand why they live in such a place. Their house is comfortable but they do not love me. I don't think they care much about each other either.

Evacuees have to live in other people's homes . . .

She wondered which of the other candidates were evacuees, like her. It made her angry, that title. Really angry. Had the examiners given it any thought at all? Why didn't people *think*?

But being angry helped her to write. Her pen raced along the lines, and words came into her head so fast she could hardly get them down. At the end she wrote, *This is not a made-up story.*

*

The trip ended badly for Hannah.

On their way back to the bus stop, she saw Cyclops approaching the doorway of the Lamb Hotel on the opposite side of the street. The woman who'd said she was an Inspector of Evacuees was with him. Hannah grabbed Abigail.

'*Look!*'

The woman had spotted Hannah. Then – as clearly as if they had been close beside them – Hannah and Abigail saw her giving an order to the one-eyed man. She was gripping his arm fiercely. *Go on!* she seemed to say. *Do it!* And Cyclops made a gesture that meant, *But what for? What can we do here?*

The woman was insisting. So Cyclops, looking nervous and reluctant, beckoned across the street for Hannah to go over to him.

Hannah felt embarrassment, not fear. Miss Twisleton had seen everything and was hurrying back. 'Do you know that revolting man?' she asked.

Illogically, Hannah felt a need to defend Cyclops, a desire

for fairness. 'He's not revolting,' she said. 'He's just lost an eye.' (*Why did I say that?* she thought afterwards. *I hate him, and he scares me!*)

'Do you know him?' Miss Twisleton asked her.

'Yes,' Hannah said.

'Does Mrs Pickens know him?'

'He came to see me at their house.'

They walked on. Looking back, they saw Miss Feelgood stalking up the steps into the hotel, looking furious. She also looked as if she'd made up her mind about something. They could see her resolution from the expression on her face.

Mucker had seen it too. 'She doon't look too pleased,' he muttered. 'Hannah, yew need to watch out!'

-33-

Watching, Observing, Spying

Konrad allowed himself a short holiday.

On the first night at Mrs Pritt's house he ate a satisfying supper, went early to bed, and slept deeply. Next morning, he consumed a large breakfast. This was to be expected when a boy had been living rough for several days and nights.

He'd awoken feeling happier than he'd felt since the War started. But his dilemma was still with him, immovable, like an unshakable monster clutching his back.

He helped Mrs Pritt with the washing up, and afterwards they walked slowly across the green to the village shop, where he was introduced as her great-nephew. On their way back across the green carrying her shopping basket, he enjoyed the cool early spring sunlight shining through the tall, leafless trees.

Mrs Pritt's back garden was entirely given over to chickens. A brick path went down the length of the garden, and there was a hen house on one side of the path with nesting boxes and a large open chicken run on the other. A tunnel under the path connected the two, and Konrad watched like a delighted three-year-old as the hens ducked their heads, disappeared into the tunnel, walked underneath him, and reappeared on the other side.

The open run had four sides. One was the wall of the next-door neighbour's house; two were made of wire mesh, the sort that you could buy in any hardware shop; the fourth was the perimeter fence of the airfield.

'Is that allowed?' he asked.

'The air force have had several years to complain,' Mrs Pritt said. 'And so far they haven't.'

After dinner, she went upstairs for her afternoon nap. And that was the end of Konrad's holiday. A morning would be sufficient, he'd told himself. It was time to start work. He went to his bedroom and turned his attention to the binoculars, and the airfield.

As he sat there watching, Konrad's German half was spying and his British half was the victim of spying. But it wasn't as simple as that, for he also found that his German self was *irritated* by the foolish, trusting British for being so casual about security. What *idiots* they were! They shouldn't have *allowed* anyone to sit at a bedroom window and watch their every move with binoculars! One part of him was annoyed that the other part was able to do what he wanted to do.

A chilling thought occurred to him. His German instructors had told him they would know if he successfully blew up the codebreaking building. Or if he didn't. But they'd never told him *how* they would know. Was there a German spy at that very moment watching the airfield, exactly as he was doing himself?

Or watching *him* perhaps?

But if there was a spy, why hadn't he contacted Konrad? And, anyway, how did he communicate with Germany? Konrad was beginning to lose faith in the idea that Britain was full of highly efficient German agents. Where *were* they?

However, as the afternoon wore on, all thoughts of spying died away. He became neither British nor German. He was just the person he was, absorbed by the activities of that vast place.

At the Waldbrand Training School they had shown him a map of the airfield, and he'd memorised it. He quickly located himself on the map that he carried in his head. The airfield was almost a mile across, with a perimeter fence all around it, topped with impenetrable coils of barbed wire. Konrad observed:

three massive hard runways, intersecting, and a grass one;

three enormous hangars, with four Wellington bombers standing outside;

a couple of brand new four-engined bombers, with people standing around, looking at them with interest (he had been taught to recognise all British aircraft, but these were new to him);

the watch-tower, with balconies, and high windows reflecting the low afternoon sun;

a cluster of buildings, like a small village (one of them –

built like a hotel – was probably the officers' mess, he thought);

a brick church;

a water tower;

a fuel-dump, grassed over, far away on the most distant side of the airfield;

small groups of anti-aircraft guns;

servicemen everywhere, working, chatting, and some sitting outside in the sun (pilots probably, he thought);

long trains, loaded with bombs, being towed by tractors towards the aircraft.

This was not just a place. It was a village, a community, where people lived and worked.

He saw what he supposed must be his crashed plane, dumped close to the perimeter fence. He studied it coolly, and moved his binoculars round to locate the brick building that he was supposed to blow up. It was quite close, about half a mile away from Mrs Pritt's cottage. He studied it carefully for a long time.

His hopes began to rise for it was clear that there was no activity, no sign of life. Hilda Pritt was probably right: the building was abandoned and disused. So why shouldn't it be blown up? But almost immediately he felt dispirited again, remembering Hilda's uncertainty.

He felt very alone, with no support from German agents, and assisted only by a young British woman who wasn't even a proper member of the RAF.

And there she was! A distant jeep sped across the airfield towards the building. Through the binoculars he saw that Hilda Pritt was in the passenger seat, and was being driven by a senior officer. There was no one with them. They stopped outside the building, and went inside.

All the time he watched.

When they came out, Hilda seemed to be remonstrating with the officer as they walked to the jeep. Magnified, they seemed to be alarmingly close, so that it seemed impossible that he couldn't hear what they were saying.

What Konrad saw next, however, was so laughably ordinary, so commonplace, and so plain *daft*, that it distracted him. In the long grass at the edge of the airfield just behind Mrs Pritt's back garden, there was a brown hen, one foot lifted thoughtfully and her head on one side as she peered intently at the ground, with one eye.

Through the binoculars the hen was so close that he felt as if he could reach out and stroke her feathers.

Then he saw another, white. And a third, a soft grey speckled one. He counted eleven of Mrs Pritt's chickens trespassing on War Department land.

For some time there had been sounds downstairs. The old lady had finished her afternoon nap and was working in the kitchen. Konrad went down to tell her that some of her chickens had escaped.

'I know,' she said. 'They do it every day. But what can I do?

I've told the people on the base there's a hole in their fence – *repeatedly!'*

Three times she'd reported the matter, she told him. She'd written a letter to the commanding officer, she'd phoned reception at headquarters, and only a couple of weeks before she'd walked to the main gate and talked to the guards on duty there.

But nobody had come to repair the fence, and still the chickens wandered freely.

'Will they be safe?'

'Oh, yes,' she said. 'They'll come in when it begins to get dark.'

'What about foxes?' he said.

'There are no foxes on an airfield,' she replied. 'There's no cover for them. And besides, the RAF wouldn't allow foxes.'

'Only chickens!' he said.

They both laughed and the conversation moved to other things. But already Konrad had the beginnings of an idea, a chicken-brained idea.

Or a fox-brained one perhaps. Cunning.

-34-

Three Military Conversations

Private Charlie Brewster of the Home Guard lifts himself, rearranges the old sack under his behind, and eases himself down into a slightly more comfortable position. 'Can I have a fag?' he says into the darkness of the pillbox.

'What, with all them explosives sitting right beside us! Course yew can't!'

Charlie has not been called up for the army because farm workers are exempt. The country has to grow all the food it can. His companion is Corporal Cecil Gotobed, owner of the only shoe shop in Great Deeping, who fought in World War I and is too old to fight in this one.

Time passes, and Charlie whines, 'How much longer?'

Corporal Gotobed looks at his luminous pocket watch. 'Another hour and ten minutes,' he says. They are to be relieved at nine o'clock.

'Why couldn't they just take the gelignite away?' Charlie grumbles.

'Don't ask me,' Cecil Gotobed says. 'I don't make the decisions.'

It is a particularly dark night, with no moon and no stars. It's quiet too, and very still. Nevertheless, Charlie thinks he has caught the faintest of sounds, as if the night itself is fidgeting slightly.

'Listen!' he whispers.

The two men strain their ears. They hear nothing – nothing at all – but in the square of slightly paler darkness where the doorway is, there is a faint oval luminosity.

A face, peering in.

Charlie freezes with terror. But Corporal Gotobed switches on his torch. 'Mucker Bailey!' he says angrily. 'What the hell are yew doing, creeping up on us like that?'

Mucker ducks his head and enters the pillbox, where he sits down with his back to the wall. 'I offen come ere,' he says.

'Don't give me that! Why would you want to come here?'

'I come ere sometimes,' Mucker says, 'to read in peace.'

'Get away! *Can* you read? Your father never could! Nor your ma.'

Mucker ignores this comment. 'I spoose yew're guardin them bombs,' he says.

'How do you know about them?'

'I helped to find em.'

That was news to the two men. 'Well, you need to keep your mouth shut,' the Corporal says. 'That's supposed to be kept secret. And we're supposed to be guarding it in secret.'

'If yew're spoosed t be secret, yew shouldn't ha left your

bikes outside – leanin against the pillbox in full view!'

He's grinning. They can't see the grin, but they can hear it in his voice. 'I fell oover one on em. Thas why yew heard me comin.'

'Who else knows about these explosives?'

'Who doesn't?' Mucker says. 'I'm surprised yew haven't had another visitor.'

'*Another* visitor? Who would want to be out here on a night like this?'

Then Mucker tells them about the man with one eye, who has been seen prowling about – and who seems to have a particular interest in the Pickens' evacuee girl.

They talk about explosives and security, and spies and saboteurs, and food rationing and evacuees. And Charlie Brewster finds that the last hour of his guard duty passes much faster, and much more pleasantly, than he'd expected.

*

At the Waldbrand Training College there is a conversation at high table after the students have left the dining room.

The Commandant has returned that day from a meeting in Berlin. Fraulein Eva leans across the table towards him and says quietly, 'How did you get on at your meeting?'

The Commandant puts down his wine glass and says thoughtfully, 'I heard something which will be of interest to all of you, I think. About young Friedmann.'

'Good news, I hope?' Fraulein Eva says.

'I think so. I was talking to an Obergruppenführer in the SS. He had news of Operation Blackout. You will be pleased to hear that young Friedmann arrived safely in England.'

'But we heard that the plane crashed.'

'True. But young Konrad parachuted out *before* the crash. He is alive and fit. Our training served him well.'

'And the gelignite?'

'Delivered to the right place,' the Commandant says in triumph. 'And the boy has located it!'

'Did the Obergruppenführer say if the mission has been accomplished?'

The Commandant's face clouds a little. 'Our knowledge is incomplete. Apparently, there is only one agent sending us information. Until we hear from him we must assume that the building has not yet been destroyed.'

'And the Führer? Is *he* aware of this?'

The Commandant considers his reply carefully. 'He is taking a strong interest in this business. So far, the boy's mother has not been harmed, but she is still under surveillance. The Führer is growing impatient.'

Their faces are grave.

'Young Konrad had better get on with it!'

'Indeed yes,' Fraulein Eva murmurs.

*

In the basement of a famous hotel in London, six men are seated around a candlelit table. Three of them are in uniform, and three in civilian clothes.

They are in the basement because an air raid is going on above, and they are in candlelight because the electricity went off soon after the bombing started. The basement is cold and uncomfortable. But there's a War on and they're used to this kind of thing.

These six work for separate branches of the War Department. Once a fortnight they meet to consider 'unusual situations'. The meetings are often disagreeable.

One of the men in civvies is in charge. 'Gentlemen,' he says, 'we have one more matter to discuss. It is the matter of the boy, Konrad Friedmann. I explained the situation at our last meeting.'

'Has he been located?'

'He has been found. And the explosives have been delivered.'

'I hope,' one of the army men says, 'that the person who supplied the explosives has been arrested?' His tone is sarcastic.

'He has not been arrested. He is being watched. It is our intention that he should lead us to the head of the whole operation. These people are dangerous.'

'And the boy? Where is he?'

'He is being cared for. He is quite well – but there is a difficulty.'

The others wait.

'I told you last time who the boy is. We now know that his mother and young sister will be shot if young Konrad Friedmann fails to blow up the building on the airfield.'

Silence, complete silence in the cold and shadowy room. People who run wars hate this kind of dilemma.

There is a question. 'He has been instructed to commit an act of sabotage – or his mother and sister will be executed. Is that correct?'

'Precisely.'

'What goes on in this building?'

'Nothing, absolutely nothing. There *was* a codebreaking group working there until a few weeks ago.'

'But they've been closed down?'

'No. *Not* closed down. Relocated.'

'To Bletchley Park,' someone says softly – and the others are embarrassed and say nothing because Bletchley Park is, probably, the biggest secret of the War. They never mention its name, even to each other. Never!

'There is nothing in this building. No staff, no equipment. It's all gone. It has been suggested that we should allow it to be blown up.'

There is an outburst then. What? Destroy RAF premises on an airfield? It would be an outrageous act of sabotage!

The staff officer in the RAF speaks. 'Trouble is,' he says, 'there's a young ATA pilot, and she has taken the boy's side.'

One of the men splutters with rage. 'What the hell has it got to do with her?'

'She is the one who found young Friedmann.'

'And she thinks the building should be blown up?'

'Yes.'

'We cannot allow ourselves to be influenced by a sentimental young woman with a soft spot for a German schoolboy!'

'Quite!' someone says.

'Hear hear!' someone else murmurs.

'Those in favour of destroying the building?'

'I'm astonished that you're asking us to vote on what would be a serious act of treason! *We cannot allow it!*'

'But we *can* allow it. That's the point! If we give our approval, it would not be a criminal act of sabotage, it would be an authorised demolition.'

'I would never give my support to such a proposal!'

'I understand your disapproval. But I would like to know what everyone at the meeting thinks. Is there anyone in favour?'

One hand is raised.

'Those against?'

Four hands.

'I forgot to say,' the chairman says, 'that the boy's mother is English. We'll take the vote again.'

They fall silent as they consider whether a full English life is more valuable than an empty English building. But when the vote is repeated, the result is the same: four against one.

'I suppose,' one of them says slowly, 'that that young woman wouldn't be tempted to blow up the building herself?'

'Surely not! She must know she'd be court-martialled!'

'Not court-martialled, I think, because she's not in the RAF. But she *would* be tried for treason.'

On that ominous note the meeting breaks up, and its members set off upstairs to see if the hotel bar has been hit by enemy action.

Two days later the person who'd mentioned Bletchley Park is posted to a military base in a remote part of Scotland and given a job that has nothing to do with security.

-35-

All that Squit

One night there was a row.

'Thas all very well yew takin zaminations,' Mrs Pickens said, 'but who dyew think is gooin to *pay* for everything if yew pass?'

'It's a *scholarship*,' Hannah said. 'There won't be anything to pay.'

'Thas what yew think! That scholarship won't pay for no school uniforms! And special clothes for yew to play hockey in.'

'Hockey!' said Mr Pickens in a sneering way that Hannah hated. She *liked* hockey.

'We een't got no money to pay for all that stuff,' Mrs Pickens said. 'An there'll be other things. Pa'll have t work a whole extra day's overtime just to buy a bloody hockey stick! Then there'll be the boots an all!'

'My dad will pay. He can afford it.'

'I daresay he can. But where *is* he? Yew keep gooin on about him – but he een't showed up. He don't even know where yew are!'

That was true. Until he got Hannah's letters, he wouldn't know what had happened to her.

She was alone and fatherless.

'If I pass,' she said slowly, 'I won't be starting at the high school until September. By then, my dad will have got my letters – and he'll arrange the money. He earns a lot of money – he's a ship's captain.'

Mr Pickens' face darkened. 'Bully for him.'

'I dunno why yew wanna go to a school like that,' Mrs Pickens said. 'Ollie never wanted tew.'

Poor Ollie! Hannah knew that Miss Twisleton had not selected him to take the exam two years previously. Ollie had told her. But it was no use expecting him to stand up for her. He was a big, soft-hearted boy, and very loyal, but he had no fight in him, especially against his mum and dad.

'Well, I do want to,' she said.

'But *why?*'

Hannah was upset by her. She'd been really kind to her since she arrived at the Old Bank. But in this argument she ganged up with Mr Pickens.

'Because I want a proper education,' Hannah said. And of course that led to another argument.

'Woss wrong with the local school?'

'Nothing's wrong with it, but . . .' She hated it when her sentences petered out like that. But what could she have said?

'Yew'll git all high an mighty, like that Abigail Murfitt and Molly Barnes.'

Hannah was truly amazed. She thought Mrs Pickens liked Abigail. That happens in arguments: people say things that take you by surprise. 'Abigail's not high and mighty!' Hannah said. She didn't know much about Molly Barnes, but she didn't think she was either.

'Course she is! They all look down on us! They think we're no better n *pig muck* cos we live out here.'

'Who's *they*? *Who* thinks you're no better than pig muck?' But when Hannah said *pig muck*, it came out posh, though she hadn't meant it to.

Mrs Pickens couldn't answer Hannah's question. 'All on em,' she said vaguely. 'Besides, what's so special about a good education?'

She said *a good education* as if it was a bad smell.

'I want to read good books, and know about history,' Hannah said. 'And science and art.' But she knew it sounded feeble and vague. It was hard to stand up for something when she didn't yet know what it was.

'I can't be doin with all that arty-farty stuff,' Mrs Pickens said. 'Thas a load o squit!'

Then Mr Pickens had his say. His voice got louder and louder as he spoke, and spit sprayed out of his mouth as he shouted the last few words. 'There een't no time in life for readin and thinkin and all that stuff. Yew'll find out soon enough. So why waste time and money gittin used tew it? If gooin t that school will help yew git a good job, that'd be all right. But that *won't*! Specially for a girl! That'll just fill your head with *bloody nonsense*!'

Hannah concentrated her attention on him. 'My dad always told me to do the best I could at school, and to go to the best school I could get into.' She thought that would shut him up. Surely he couldn't argue with her dad.

But he did. 'Your dad spends all his life at sea! Woss he know about life here?' He didn't mean *here in Britain*. He meant *here, in this house, on the Old Bank*.

'Dew yew listen to me!' he said. 'The people in Deeping only half understand what thas like down here. And the people of Ely, well, they're even wuss! They're all just snobs.' He was shouting again, and he hadn't finished. 'And as for Londoners like yew, well, yew doon't know anything! What yew need is a few weeks slavin away out on them bloody fields, not pussy-footin about at posh schools.'

That's another thing about arguments: they go where you'd never expect them to go. Who would have thought that a quarrel about schools would end up as a shouting match about working on the land?

Then Hannah broke another of her dad's rules. She lost her temper, and she shouted back at him. But she lost it *slowly*, *deliberately*, allowing herself to get angrier and angrier as she spoke. 'There's something wrong with you. You don't like the *high school*, you don't like *Abigail Murfitt*, you don't like *Ely*, you don't like *Londoners*, you don't like *books*. And you certainly *don't like me!*'

She didn't know where that all came from. But it came out with the words all clear and in the proper order, as if she'd been thinking about it and getting it ready for weeks. Everyone went quiet and she knew she'd been very rude. She'd known it as she said it – but sometimes you just have to say what's in your head.

Then she added a bit more for good measure. 'Is there anything you *do* like?' she shouted at him.

She thought he was going to hit her. And Mrs Pickens' face was red and angry. She was itching to give her a walloping. But Hannah went over to the stairs and up to her bedroom. Perhaps there was a bit of fear in that, but mostly it was anger. She was angry with them for their stupidity, but she was angry with herself too – not because she'd said those things, but because she'd failed to make them understand.

As she left, Mrs Pickens had said, 'If yew want people to *like* yew, yew have to *be likeable*.'

She'd touched a sore point. Hannah had often thought she was *not* especially likeable.

*

She didn't sleep that night.

A small part of her wondered if they were right. *Would* she become a snob if she got educated? *Was* she dislikeable? Why was it so hard to explain what you believed in without making people angry?

Ollie came up with some milk and a couple of biscuits. 'Are they still cross?' she asked him, but he just shrugged and pulled a face. Poor Ollie! He didn't care who'd been right and who'd been wrong, he just wanted everything to be friendly again.

She lay awake most of the night, going through in her mind what they'd said, what she'd said – and, most of all – what she *wished* she'd said. She still wanted them to see why they were wrong, but her thoughts kept going back to the last thing she'd shouted: that there was nothing in their lives that they *liked*. And that Mr Pickens especially disliked *her*.

Everything was so *muddled*. How could she have known that Mrs Pickens secretly resented Abigail? She was fairly sure Abigail had never done anything to deserve it. And how could she have known that Mr Pickens hated working on the land? And hated her dad because he didn't! Where did all that anger come from?

She buried her head in her pillow, longing passionately for her father. He was never muddled. Everything he did and everything he said was clear and straightforward. He thought what he wanted to say, then he said it. He thought what should be done, and then he did it, as simply as possible and without fuss.

But where was he? Was he still alive even? The three people in her life she loved and needed were all gone. Four, if you included her mother. Her gran was dead, her dad was somewhere in the mid-Atlantic, and her best friend couldn't help her.

She remembered the goodbye letter pushed through the letterbox in the middle of the night, shortly before War broke out. It was the clearest, shortest letter you could imagine. In three sentences it explained why the family had to go away, immediately. There'd been no muddle there either.

She'd memorised that too. With bitterness in her heart.

She lay awake all night, until she heard – faintly, from another bedroom – Mr Pickens' alarm clock go off at six.

Her anger and confusion sorted itself out. She knew what she had to do.

*

She got dressed and went downstairs, early. Mr Pickens had already left for work, and Mrs Pickens didn't speak to her as she went through the kitchen. Hannah went outside and up onto the bridge.

In the pale early-morning daylight she could see for miles around. Mr Pickens was already at work, a solitary figure in the middle of a vast flat field. There was no one else in the world.

When she got there, she reckoned it was about two hundred

yards across, and rows of strawberry plants were planted at about a yard apart, or less. They looked grey and shabby after the winter.

There was a cold bitter wind that morning, and the sky was bleak.

When she was level with the row Mr Pickens was working on, she waited. He was hoeing, taking a slow step at a time, pushing the hoe through the soil in front of him to slice off any weeds, and then taking another step. His boots were encrusted with earth. After a few steps he stopped and rubbed the blade of the hoe clean with his finger and thumb.

He didn't hurry himself, but after what seemed like an age he reached where Hannah was standing. He looked directly at her, scowling as usual. His eyes were watering in the cold wind.

'I've come to say I'm sorry. I shouldn't have spoken to you like that.'

'Did *she* send yew out to say that?'

Hannah shook her head. The truth was that she did *not* think she was wrong. Definitely not. *He* was the one who was wrong, and he should have apologised too. However, she left it at that.

'Hev yer done yer sums?'

This confused her for a couple of seconds, but then she understood what he meant, and she nodded. 'How long is this field?' she asked him.

'About a quarter of a mile, I reckon.'

A quarter of a mile. And two hundred rows. That was around fifty miles of hoeing.

'My ole ma,' he said, 'she useter dew it on her hands and knees. Farmer, he wouldn't let her use a hoe.'

She crawled along each row? Hannah thought. *Two hundred of them?*

'In all weathers,' he added.

'Why don't you get another job?'

'*What* other job?'

'There must be something.'

He thought for a moment. 'Who dya think our house blongs tew?'

'You?'

He shook his head. 'That blongs to the farmer I work for,' he said. 'If I git another job, we'll git thrown out – all on us.'

'He must be a horrible man,' she said.

'No, he een't. He's a good man, if ya want to know. But he's just a farmer. Thas what farmers dew. Wasps sting and rats bite – and farmers throw yew out o yer house if yew change jobs. It's the law. Always has bin, always will be.'

That was it. A short conversation in which a lot got said. He turned to begin on the next row, and Hannah set off back to the house.

-36-

Breaking In

The plan was simple – to break into the intelligence building and check that it really was disused and empty. Konrad needed to be clear about that.

There were many things that he had promised Hilda Pritt he would *not* do, but she hadn't thought to include trespassing in her list. So his conscience was untroubled.

When the old lady had gone to bed and everywhere was quiet, he got up and dressed himself. He already knew that both the front and back doors were securely bolted, and it would be impossible to open them quietly. It would have to be his bedroom window.

Despite his parachute training, he couldn't simply jump to the ground. It was a tiny window and he wouldn't be able to stand on it and launch himself cleanly. So he eased himself out, feet first, and hung there, clinging to the sill with his fingertips. If the old lady had been in the kitchen at that moment – which was directly under his bedroom – she would have seen his body stretched out from top to bottom of the window.

His feet were only a short distance from the ground. He

let go, and landed neatly. He moved quietly down the garden, reached the chicken run, and let himself into it. The birds were all safely inside the hen house on the other side of the path. For a moment or two he stood motionless at the end of the pen, peering through the perimeter fence.

There was a great deal of activity on the airfield that night. Engines were roaring in the distance, and there were lights too, small and faint, half a mile away in the region of the hangars. The airfield was alive and busy, humming with purpose.

Konrad groped about in the dark until he found the hole that Mrs Pritt's chickens used when they went trespassing.

There was hard, flattened earth on the inside and long grass on the other. He risked a brief flash of his torch, so that he could bend some of the wire and make the hole big enough for his shoulders to get through. The wire – long buried in the soil – had begun to rust, and was easy to handle. He took a deep breath, pushed himself head first into the hole, wriggled his upper body awkwardly through, clawed forward with his hands and elbows until his legs and feet were through too, and finally rose to a crouch on the other side.

He breathed deeply. Success!

He turned to the right and began his walk along the inside of the perimeter, which would lead him round to where the disused intelligence building stood. When he drew near to the main gate, he moved more cautiously, crouching, and making frequent stops. There was a guard room beside the gate, and two RAF men stood on duty, motionless, with their rifle butts resting on the ground. Their bayonets were fixed. There would be more men inside.

He waited. Minutes passed, and still he waited. Patience was one of Konrad's most useful characteristics. Almost half an hour went by, and still he waited. A local taxi drew up outside the gate, and three men in uniform got out. There was some cheerful shouting as they paid the driver and called out goodbyes.

As the taxi reversed to leave, and everyone's attention was distracted by the returning airmen, Konrad slipped across the road.

There was nothing else to delay him, and he quickly found himself approaching the intelligence building.

Despite the darkness, there was much that he could see: that it was a plain brick office block with square windows; that if the windows had blinds or shutters, no one had closed them; that there was no light inside; and that there was no upper floor. The place had an abandoned and forlorn look about it. He went all round it, and found that there were only two entrances, one at the front and another at the back. He didn't bother to try the doors. An instinct told him a window would be easier.

At that moment, there was a series of deafening roars from across the airfield, but Konrad ignored the noise and concentrated on the task in hand. In no time at all he found a cracked windowpane, out of sight, at the back of the building. With his hand wrapped inside his handkerchief, he pushed at the glass, hard, until a bit of the pane fell inside with a soft, tinkling crash. The rest of the glass he was able to pull free of the crumbling putty that held it. Then he reached inside and pulled open the window handle. The window was stiff, and it groaned as he wrenched it open. But the sound of a creaking window was tiny in the great vibrating thunder of the airfield.

In no time at all, he was inside. He pulled out his torch, and began his inspection.

*

There was excitement on the airfield that night.

Twelve brand new, freshly delivered Halifax bombers were flying their first mission. The crews had been briefed, the planes were taxiing into position, and groups of onlookers – who on most nights would have stayed inside – had come out to watch.

There were always a few watchers when a squadron set off on a mission. But that night everyone was there.

The biggest group had gathered around Hilda Pritt, for she had more experience of flying the new bombers than anyone else. She had not flown on a mission, of course. That was not allowed. But she'd been delivering Halifaxes to airfields all over the country for the last few weeks. Like all the pilots in the ATA she was expected to fly any plane to any destination. Five of the twelve new aircraft had been flown in by Hilda.

So the men off-duty, trainees, even canteen staff, stood close to her – partly because they liked her, and partly because she began to talk through the procedures as the aircraft prepared for takeoff.

Hilda knew exactly what was happening in each cockpit. She knew when the pilot would be checking the crew members – the engineer, the navigator, the wireless operator, and the tail-end-Charlie at the rear, each one answering in turn. Their voices would be low and casual, as if asking for someone to *pass the brown sauce, please*. Hilda could hear them in her mind.

She went through the procedure, saying the words aloud.

Stand by for taxiing. Fuel cocks on. Then she altered her voice as if she were reading two parts in a play. *Standing by. Fuel cocks on.*

Start port outer. Start port inner. Starboard inner . . . Then in the other voice, *Port outer started. Port inner started . . .*

The pilot's voice: *Close bomb doors.*

The reply: *Bomb doors closed.*

Fuel boosters fully on. Flaps twenty degrees down.

Each order was acknowledged. The navigation lights were flashed. *Chocks away*, said Hilda.

Chocks away, came the reply.

The listeners standing around her were getting a running commentary. Hilda's imagined pilot called control for permission to take off.

Stand by for take off.

Ready for take off, would come the answer.

The pilot of the lead plane released the brakes and slowly opened the throttles.

One after the other, the planes roared across the airfield into the darkness, and as each aircraft reached around 120 mph, the pilot eased it off the ground.

Brakes on. Wheels up.

And the reply: *Brakes on. Wheels coming up.*

Finally: *Wheels locked. Brakes off.*

The towering sky-space over Great Deeping was filled with aircraft, stacked one above the other, each carrying seven or eight tons of bombs, until all twelve had been launched and they could assemble in the positions agreed at the briefing. The noise was tremendous, a great shuddering thunder on one unrelenting note.

'Hilda,' one of the bystanders shouted. 'How much training did you have for flying Halifaxes?'

'None at all, old chap! I just read the manual.' He thought she was pulling his leg. But she wasn't.

The last of the twelve rose into the night at the edge of the airfield. As the sound of the planes was fading, Hilda saw a distant light, faint, instantly extinguished. It seemed to come from the empty intelligence building. Had the last plane carelessly left its landing light on, so that it reflected in one of the windows of the building as it flew over?

But that was unlikely. Hilda said nothing, but as the groups of onlookers slowly dispersed and returned to the buildings, and the sound of the bombers faded in the eastern darkness, she grabbed a bike that someone had leaned against the wall of a hangar. Nobody noticed her setting off – not round the perimeter road, but straight along the edge of the silent runway.

*

Konrad had switched on his torch and begun to explore the building.

A wide corridor ran straight from front to back, and another crossed it at right angles. There were three big office spaces, a common room, and several smaller rooms. There were two lavatories, and a store cupboard. All were empty, apart from a few shabby and broken bits of furniture – a desk or two, a table, a sagging armchair. There was nothing – not the tiniest clue – that would have told anyone what this building had been used for – except for a large rolled-up picture lying on the floor half hidden by a broken chair. It was an aerial photograph of a railway station in Berlin.

There were a few items still fixed to the walls: a cleaning rota, a picture of the footballer Stanley Matthews, a photograph of a cricket team, and a newspaper cartoon making fun of Hitler.

There is no reason why this place should not be blown up, Konrad thought. That was what he'd wanted to settle, one way or the other. Now he knew.

The roar of planes from across the airfield changed. The first of them had taken off, its path directly over the intelligence building. The noise as it lifted its great weight off the runway was deafening, frightening. One after the other they came, twelve in all, powering heavily into the night sky, each seeming for a moment or two to be sitting on the very roof of the building.

British planes, Konrad thought, *going to bomb German people.*

The last of the planes passed overhead and the quietness of the night was restored. As he stood in the pitch-black darkness of one of the smaller offices, he heard a sound. Someone was unlocking the main door at the front.

Security? he wondered.

He listened attentively to the sound of cautious footsteps proceeding along the passage, towards him.

They stopped. He waited, letting out a silent breath.

Then a voice. '*Konrad? Konrad!* If you're here, come out at once and stop wasting my blinking time!'

In truth, neither of them was especially scared. He had suspected the intruder might be Hilda, and she was fairly sure that if anyone was in the building it would be Konrad.

Nevertheless, she was not too pleased. And when he called

out to her and went to meet her in the corridor, she let her anger fly.

'I say, what kind of idiotic caper is this?'

'I wanted to –'

'I don't care what you wanted. I trusted you to stay safe with my grandmother! *Not* to start trespassing on airfields!'

'I know, but –'

'But *nothing*!' she snapped. 'Do you have any idea what might have happened if anyone else had seen you – and not me?'

Konrad shook his head.

'No, of course you don't!'

Konrad was surprised. He'd had no idea she had such steeliness in her. She went on for several minutes and he stood mutely, in the dark, hoping it wouldn't go on for much longer.

'How did you get out without my grandmother knowing?'

'Out the window. Then through a gap in the fence. In the chicken run.'

He sensed that she found this funny. And eventually she said, 'What were you looking for?'

'I wanted to find out if this place was really unoccupied.'

She nodded thoughtfully. 'Well, as you can see, it *is*. But I don't think it will do you any good.'

'What do you mean?'

They walked slowly along the passage towards the main entrance, side by side, as colleagues must have walked there many times when the place had been a working office.

'I've been trying to persuade the bosses that the place should be blown up. To save your mother and sister.'

'But?'

'No official reply yet,' she said. 'But I don't think they're going to agree.'

They stopped walking and stood there, side by side, in the shadows. He didn't waste any words. He didn't go on about justice and fairness, and how much he loved his mother and his sister. If Hilda couldn't persuade the authorities, he knew that nothing he might say would help.

But there was another idea, which he'd kept at the back of his mind. Now it came to the front – and he was suddenly afraid that Hilda might somehow be able to see it inside his head. It was a *huge* idea, a *dangerous* idea. An idea that would turn him into a genuine German saboteur against the stupid, *stupid* British! And it was exactly what he'd been sent there to do.

He changed the subject. 'How did you know I was here?'

'You flashed your torch, you bally idiot!' she said. She was no longer angry. In fact, she was thinking how strange it was that she was talking to someone related to the Führer. How *could* he be? How could this young boy be related to the wickedest man in the world, hated and feared and despised by everybody?

This youngster was a scamp, just like her younger brother

when he was that age! An *intelligent* scamp, but still just a scamp. With a terrible dilemma.

'Now! You got into the airbase on your own, and you're jolly well going to have to get back out on your own!'

'I'll be all right,' he said. 'By the way, how did you get in here?'

'I visited this place with the captain,' she said. 'I pocketed the key after locking up. He didn't notice. It all comes down to low cunning in the end.'

-37-
A Nice Cup of Tea

Make no mistake. Have no illusions about Miss Feelgood.

Cyclops might have been a murderous and brutal thug, but Miss Feelgood was a calculating and ruthless criminal. If *he* was in the second division of criminality, *she* was at the top among the champions and cup winners.

If anything stood in her way, Stephanie Feelgood always removed it without hesitation. And if the obstacle had to be destroyed, she would do it with efficiency and refinement. It made no difference if the thing that stood in her way was a person.

She'd learned early in life that if she made her plans carefully and acted swiftly, she could always get away with it. She made no mistakes. Mistakes were foreign to her nature.

She had discovered this about herself when she was ten. She'd always hated cats, and when new neighbours moved into the next-door flat she was irritated to distraction by their cat, which made itself comfortable in her bedroom, slept on her bed, and curled up on her dressing table among her things.

Once she'd made up her mind, she didn't hesitate. She

scooped up the wretched animal, carried it lovingly on to Battersea Bridge after dark, and threw it into the Thames.

Now, whenever she thought about Cyclops, she was gripped by a similar fury. He should have disposed of Hannah Conway ages ago. Furthermore, he knew too much, and he was not reliable. Her fury hardened itself into a decision: she would deal with him at once, now. Afterwards – as soon as she had disposed of the girl too – she would go back to London, resume her proper name, and no one would be any the wiser.

Miss Feelgood made her preparations with the minimum of fuss. As soon as she was ready, she instructed Cyclops to meet her for afternoon tea at Auntie Marge's.

He was a big man, but nevertheless he sidled unobtrusively into the tea-room like a small one, with a shifty and ironic look in his face, and his one living eye taking in everything and everyone who was there.

She had chosen a table close to the fire. As they drank their tea, Miss Feelgood talked to him in a low and relentless voice, listing his many shortcomings and failures. 'And the result of your dilly-dallying is that she is still here with that knowledge in her head. And when she decides to tell someone about our list, we'll all be exposed.'

'I just need more time,' he said.

'More time? You've had enough time! *And keep your voice down!* Besides, you draw attention to yourself, which is dangerous in our line of work. It's that eye of yours.'

'Not much I can do about that.'

'Go and buy us a couple of those nice-looking buns. My treat. They'll go nicely with our second cup of tea.' *He must have a second cup,* Miss Feelgood said to herself. She had an immense and ecstatic feeling of power.

She opened her purse and found a shilling.

While he stood at the counter, she checked that no one was watching her. Then she quickly took a small screw of paper from her purse, unfolded it, and dropped some powder into the teapot.

Why not into his cup? Because strychnine powder would leave a scum floating on the surface, which he would notice. So she took the lid off the pot and stirred the contents as if to improve the brewing of the tea. Finally, with her usual delicate and careful precision, she threw the little screw of blue paper into the fire.

Cyclops came back with the buns, and picked up the teapot. 'Allow me,' he said politely, and poured them both a second cup.

I must take care not to drink, Miss Feelgood reminded herself.

At that moment her attention was drawn to one of the other occupants of the tea-room, who had risen to her feet and begun – in complete silence – to *dance*. Quietly and with a delightful gracefulness, a tall, middle-aged lady a few tables away from Miss Feelgood was jigging and jogging to a gentle melody that only she could hear.

She was dressed strangely, with a long purple woollen skirt that went almost down to her ankles. Under it, you could see that she wore wellington boots. Now, as she gathered up her other garments, she dipped and ducked and swayed and swung to the imagined music in her head.

Miss Feelgood couldn't tear her eyes away. Everyone else in the tea-room was watching too. It was mesmerising.

All in complete silence.

The strange dancer already wore on her head what looked like a rugby sock, striped in blue and red. On top of it she placed a bowler hat. Finally, unhurriedly, she took a yellow crocheted scarf of enormous length and – throwing out her arms – she flung one end round her neck. Then the other. Then – because of its great length – these actions were repeated a number of times.

All her movements were sweetly and elegantly hypnotic to watch. And everything was done to the unheard music.

One of the other customers leaned across to Miss Feelgood and said quietly, 'That's Lavinia. *Loopy Lavvy* some people call her. She means no harm, poor thing.' She smiled affectionately. 'She dances like that in church on Sundays – jigging about in her pew during the hymn-singing.'

Lavinia turned then, and saw that everyone had been

watching her. Unembarrassed, she laughed good-humouredly, saying, 'I expect you think I'm mad.'

'Not at all,' murmured Miss Feelgood.

'It's my way of keeping Satan at a distance. He can't stand happiness, you see. And dancing makes me happy.'

'Well, if it helps . . .'

'He is everywhere this afternoon, dodging about all over the place as I walked in. But, *today* . . .' She lowered her voice, sharing a secret. 'Today I have *support*!'

The other tea-drinkers, who were already familiar with Lavvy's struggles with Satan, were interested to hear about her support. This was a new development.

Still swaying and dipping in her own private rhythm, she picked up a fat leather bag and stood it on her tea table. Then she unzipped it just a few inches.

Immediately the handsome head of a cat appeared, staring indignantly around.

'Where did that come from?' someone said.

'He came into my life some time ago,' Lavvy announced. 'He is *especially* strong in the struggle against Satan.'

'Why?'

'He has the power of the Holy Trinity!' Lavvy declared. 'He has *three legs*!'

Miss Feelgood was totally absorbed by this strange drama. Unconsciously, her right hand moved towards her teacup, two fingers and a thumb gripped the handle, and her little finger stuck out like a small signal of her superiority. She did what she had done a hundred thousand times. Absentmindedly, thoughtlessly, she raised the cup to her lips.

Distracted, Miss Feelgood drank.

When she replaced the cup on its saucer, the white chink of china against china brought her back to her senses – and she realised what she'd done. Her face drained as white as a sheet and she kicked her chair back from the table. In the one and a half seconds it took for Miss Feelgood and the chair to fall backwards to the floor, a single thought possessed her mind as her body threshed about and she gasped for breath. *It's not fair!* she cried inwardly. *I never make mistakes!*

Less than a minute after she came to rest on the wooden floorboards, she was dead.

Cyclops stared for a few stunned seconds at his untasted cup of tea. Then he rushed off hurriedly, saying he would get help. The other customers in the tea-room rose from their chairs and crowded anxiously over the prostrate form of Miss Feelgood stretched out upon the floor.

'A heart attack,' murmured one.

'A seizure,' said another.

'Send for a doctor,' said a third.

'I think it's too late for that,' the first speaker said.

Auntie Marge – realising that her tea-shop was going to be the centre of some attention and wanting it to look its best – hurried over with a tray and cleared away the things from

Miss Feelgood's table and took them away to be washed up. Including the teapot.

Meanwhile, Lavvy performed a deep curtsey. 'I *told* you Satan was here!' she said.

-38-

Konrad is Given his Freedom

No sensible person could expect an energetic schoolboy to stay cooped up in a cottage for days on end with only a very old lady for company. It was against nature.

Konrad explained this to Hilda when she came to visit her grandmother. *Was she, or wasn't she,* he said, *going to allow him to go out by himself?*

Hilda sympathised. It was agreed that Konrad could go out whenever he liked, provided he told Mrs Pritt in advance where he was going. They even managed to borrow a bike for him, from a young woman who lived on the other side of the green and whose husband was in the army.

It was, Konrad thought, satisfactory. But something else troubled him. 'How long will I be staying here?' he asked Hilda. 'What is going to happen to me? After I . . . ?'

After *what?* Mrs Pritt wondered. But no one asked. And Hilda didn't explain.

'The authorities will find a boarding school for you to go to.'

'But I haven't any money.'

'You will be the responsibility of the War Department. They will pay your fees.'

'Is there still no decision about –' he glanced at Hilda's grandmother, unsure how much she'd been told – 'about my task?'

Hilda looked uncomfortable. 'There *is* now a definite decision,' she said sadly. 'We heard this morning. I'm afraid the answer is no.'

The British authorities had not given permission for the empty security building to be blown up. Konrad turned away and stared out of the window, seeing nothing. He'd been prepared for this, of course. But it seemed cruel beyond everything.

Hilda, perhaps hoping to distract him, said, 'Someone will be coming down from the War Department to question you. Soon. It's called debriefing.'

Konrad knew what a debriefing was. 'I had expected that to happen as soon as I was found,' he said. He was shocked at British inefficiency.

'Me too,' Hilda said. 'I think generals and air commodores find it hard to think that a schoolboy can know anything useful, or do anything important.'

Well, they're wrong! Konrad said to himself. *And they will learn their mistake.*

It was not in his nature to sit back and do nothing.

-39-

Teatime in Devon

When the front doorbell rang, Miss Louisa Weston hurried anxiously into the hall. Two visitors were standing on her doorstep – a young policeman, and a WVS woman.

'Miss Weston?' the policeman asked. 'Miss *Louisa* Weston?'

She was almost overwhelmed by terror. A policeman at the door always meant trouble, or bad news, or both. 'Yes,' she said. 'I am. What's . . . ?'

They had such grave faces that her heart sank into her boots. 'Am I right in thinking that you have a sister? A Mrs Lufton? Mrs Rosemary Lufton?'

'Yes, I do. But what's this about?'

'Miss Weston, may we come in?'

'Yes, but please tell me . . .'

'It would be better to talk inside,' the WVS woman said. 'Honestly it would!'

So Miss Weston, trembling, held open the door and they stepped into the shadowy hall. They clearly expected to be invited into the lounge but Miss Weston's impatience was stronger than her good manners. 'Now,' she said desperately.

'Tell me why you're here. *Please!*'

But still they didn't. 'You might like to sit down,' the policeman said.

That was the last straw for Miss Weston. '*Tell me why you're here!*' she almost screamed. '*NOW!*'

He took a deep breath. 'We have some rather bad news for you, I'm afraid. Well, *very* bad news, actually.'

Miss Weston braced herself. What could it be?

'It's about your sister – Mrs Lufton, Mrs Rosemary Lufton. She was taken ill yesterday and – well, I'm sorry to have to tell you that she is dead.'

What with the War, the young WVS woman had been present on a lot of occasions when bad news had been broken. Really bad news sometimes. She thought she'd seen every possible kind of reaction. But not this one – for Miss Weston gave a funny little scream, a small hoot of dismay. Almost a *laugh*.

'She was visiting a town in Cambridgeshire. On the border with Norfolk, in fact. She was there as part of her work.'

'Almost in Norfolk?' Miss Weston repeated. 'Part of her work.'

Shock, the WVS woman thought to herself. That was normal, she could handle that. 'We think she had a stroke. Or a heart attack.'

'A stroke,' Miss Weston repeated, looking from one face to the other and back again.

'I'm afraid so. She died instantly. Your sister is dead, Miss Weston.'

'No she's not!' Miss Weston whispered, as if it were a secret. 'She's here! In my lounge! She's staying with me for a few days.'

Now it was their turn to be confused.

'Rosemary!' Miss Weston called out as she turned towards the lounge door. 'Rosemary, they think you're dead!'

Mrs Lufton (the *real* Mrs Lufton) had been listening to every word, her heart thumping with the fear of immediate arrest on a charge of treason. Her mind had raced in just a few seconds from this living moment (with a trim little cucumber sandwich on a tea plate) to the one where she would be standing in a grim, dark place (with a noose around her neck).

But she recovered her composure (outwardly at least) and when her sister came into the room followed by the visitors she looked up innocently. 'I am Mrs Lufton,' she said.

Then it all came out – that a woman calling herself Mrs Lufton, and pretending to do Mrs Lufton's job of inspecting evacuees, had died suddenly in a tea-room somewhere in East Anglia.

'A case of impersonation,' the policeman said. 'It must be!'

'Did this woman have any papers on her person?' Mrs Lufton asked. She was beginning to feel a great surge of joy and triumph that that hateful Miss Feelgood was apparently dead. But it was too soon to give way to gloating. There might still be danger for herself.

'I don't know all the details,' the policeman said. 'May I use your phone, Miss Weston?'

While he was in the hall telephoning the police station, the other three went over this astonishing story again and again – making no progress with it. But when he returned he was able to tell them that the dead woman had nothing on her at all that gave any indication of her real identity.

Oh good! Mrs Lufton thought. And that was when she allowed herself to admit how much better her life would be without that arrogant Miss Feelgood in it. Why, she might even be allowed to take over the running of the organisation – *she herself,* Mrs Lufton!

And her sister (bless her innocent heart!) had never in all her life had the slightest idea of the wickedness that lurked in Mrs Lufton's generous and womanly bosom.

-40-

'Suffer the Little Children'

After school one afternoon, Hannah was surprised to find Mr Pickens waiting at the school gate. He'd come on Ollie's bike, which was leaning against the wall, with the cart fixed behind it.

Ollie was there, with Betty; Abigail too. Even Mucker was there that day. He'd started coming to school more often since the scholarship exam. But Mr Pickens ignored them all; they might as well not have been there. He jerked his head at Hannah, and indicated the cart. 'Get on,' he said.

She didn't want to go with him. And she wasn't going to ride in that cart! The night she arrived at Great Deeping she'd been in no state to care. Besides, it had been dark. But she had no intention of travelling through the town in that contraption on a fine afternoon in March when everyone could see her.

But Mr Pickens took her school bag and put that in the cart. Betty wailed that she wanted to ride in it, but he took no notice. There was a small metal luggage rack fixed over the rear mudguard of the bike, and an old cushion had been tied on it with string. Hannah realised she was expected to sit on that.

So she climbed astride it. But *why*? She couldn't bring herself to hold on by putting her arms around him; so instead she clipped her fingertips under the back of his saddle.

He cycled steadily through the town. He probably didn't know – or perhaps he didn't care – that behind him Hannah was wriggling about to find a comfortable position, and hardly managing to hold on. If she'd been about five, she might have found it fun. But she just felt embarrassed. And uncomfortable. The cart rattled and bumped along behind.

He didn't cycle straight home. He turned into the centre of the town, and along a road that led behind the church, to where a new cemetery had been started. He stopped the bike and dismounted. He held it for Hannah to climb off.

He leaned the bike against the wall and set off into the cemetery. Was she supposed to go too? She was puzzled, but she followed him along the pathway between the graves.

He said nothing, not a word. He led her to a far corner where all the graves were smaller. *Dead children*, she thought. Some had small stone rectangles to mark the grave, some had no more than a small hump, as if the child lying there had been tucked up in a grassy bed.

It was a very sad place.

At the foot of one of these, Mr Pickens stopped, and she stood beside him. There was a headstone. The lettering was fresh and clear.

Small details she had seen, incidents she had noted – they all fell into place. It was like a tumbled jigsaw puzzle magically forming itself into a clear picture before her eyes.

Mr and Mrs Pickens had had a daughter – another daughter – who was, or would have been if she'd lived, the same age as Hannah. And almost exactly a year after she'd died Hannah had turned up at their house. Now she understood why there had been an empty bedroom, with a bed, neatly waiting. And how Mrs Pickens had found clothes for her to wear.

They walked back along the path between the graves in silence.

You might have heard people say that *words failed them*. That's what happened to Hannah, literally. No words came into her mind, or into her mouth. But she tucked her hand in the crook of his arm, and he slowed his walk to match hers. When they got back to his bike, he said, 'You cn walk hum if yew'd rather. That seat must be a bit rough on yer backside!'

But not for the world would she have abandoned him at that moment. So she climbed aboard and made herself sit still as they cycled through the town. She still couldn't bring herself to put her arms around him. She held on to the tail of his jacket instead.

'Where yew bin?' Mrs Pickens demanded.

'I took her to see Eleanor.'

'Ah!' Mrs Pickens said. She ducked her head over a saucepan of potatoes she was holding, and Ollie and Betty stared at their dad.

Mr Pickens was not transformed into a cheerful and kindly man, always especially nice to Hannah. But he was less fierce and angry after that. And he stopped glaring at her.

Later she asked Ollie what his sister died of. 'Measles,' he said.

-41-
Making Plans

'*What?*' people said in amazement.

'*Where?*' they asked.

'In Auntie Marge's tea-room,' they were told.

'When?'

'Yestiddy afternoon.'

'You're pulling my leg!'

'I'm not!'

'How?'

'He had a bottle of arsenic. And he poured the whole lot in her tea!'

'Never!'

'An while she was dyin on the floor he stood there with his foot on her throat!'

'He never!'

'He did! An she took *fifteen minutes* to kick the bucket!'

'Loopy Lavvy was there an all! *She* probly did it, with one of her spells.'

'Don't be daft.'

'I een't bein daft! She had a three-legged cat! In her shopping bag! You can't tell me thas *normal.*'

So the story of what had happened in Auntie Marge's tea-room spread around the town, and reached the school the following morning, at playtime. They all stopped what they were doing and gathered in groups to share the delight of it. (Except the infants, who weren't interested. And a group of boys who never stopped playing football. *Never!* Even when the bell went they continued passing the ball to and fro all the way to the main entrance.)

Later, Hannah and Ollie and Mucker – with Konrad, who'd cycled over to meet them after school – mooched along the old river and found themselves a sheltered spot. They sat on the grassy bank facing the warm afternoon sun.

Since there was no one to hear them, they worked out their plan.

Two plans, actually.

Two because Abigail had seen a film about a gang of bank robbers who planned to break into a famous bank in New York and get away with the biggest sum of money ever stolen. When they'd planned it down to the last detail, they swore they would never mention it, *not even to each other*. For the sake of absolute secrecy.

Then they invented a second plan, a dummy plan about a robbery at a different bank. This one they *did* talk about. Not too openly of course, because it would make people suspicious. But word got out, and the police set a trap. But while the police were watching one bank, the robbers were busy at the other. They broke in and got away with millions of dollars.

'That's what we should do,' Abigail said.

Mucker pulled a face. 'What? Break into a bank?'

'No. We should work out two plans. The proper one, and a different one as well so that everyone thinks *that's* the thing we're working on.'

The others agreed, and that's what they did. They made *two* plans. One of them was legal. The other was illegal. Not only illegal but dangerous.

And when they started to make the second plan – the serious one – Mucker immediately became enthusiastic and efficient.

'I shall need wire cutters,' Konrad said to him.

Mucker said quietly, 'I cn git wire cutters.'

'*Strong* ones.'

'I cn git strong ones,' Mucker said.

Hannah was surprised. The boy who'd wanted to report Konrad to the police had unexpectedly turned into his right-hand man.

They worked out the illicit plan – down to the tiniest detail. And then they *shut it down completely*. None of them would say a word about it. Until Saturday.

But the other plan was a different matter. In Mucker Bailey's kitchen they sat and made arrangements, huddled around the table – Ollie, Hannah, Abigail, and Mucker himself. When Mrs Bailey came into the room, they fell quiet and waited until she'd gone. But they allowed her to overhear references to *Loopy Lavvy's cat*, and to something that was going to happen *next Saturday morning*. Abigail was heard talking about *a cat basket*.

Mucker's mum was no fool. 'They're up t sumfin!' she said to Ollie's mum. 'Whatever it is, thas gooin t happen on Satturdy. I reckon they're gooin to steal Lavvy's cat.'

Mrs Pickens objected. 'She een't got a cat.'

'Yes she hev! She took it out and showed everybody in Marge's tea-room.'

'Took it out of what?'

'Out of a shopping bag.'

'Sounds daft to me. All on it!'

'Praps that *is* daft. But that oon't dew no harm to keep an eye on em on Satturdy.'

So that's what they did – Mr and Mrs Pickens, and Mrs Bailey. They didn't share their suspicions with Abigail's mother because she lived too far away, on the far side of the river. Nor was Mucker's dad involved. He didn't care what his son got up to.

*

The next day something entirely different distracted everyone.

From time to time, letters would arrive at the Old Bank, reminding the people there that there was a world beyond their knowledge, further away than Great Deeping, further even than Ely.

This time, they were official letters with the results of the scholarship examination. Hannah had passed. So had Abigail and Molly Barnes.

But the most amazing thing was that Mucker Bailey had also passed. *Mucker!* 'Can you imagine Mucker in a grammar school uniform?' Abigail said to Hannah.

'I een't never bin t Soham,' Mucker said.

But Hannah felt sad for Ollie. No grammar school for him. He seemed not to mind, but you never know what people are thinking. She'd been wrong so many times.

Their heads were full that windy week in March.

There was so much happening, and so many changes were coming. In school playtimes, walking to and from the Old Bank, between meals and on cycle rides to Little Deeping, they whispered and planned and puzzled themselves crazy – about exams and results, high schools and grammar schools, and three-legged cats.

And all the time, there was their *other* plan, fully worked out and never mentioned. An experienced teacher would have known something was cooking. There were shared glances and knowing looks. There are ways of saying nothing that make it clear there is something being said.

But Mr and Mrs Pickens didn't pick up the signs. Abigail's mum would probably have suspected something. But she never saw all of them together.

-42-

Visitors in Gudvanger Strasse

Frau Friedmann, looking out of the window of her apartment in Gudvanger Strasse, saw a long grey car pull up in the street below. She straightened her shoulders, stiffened her back.

A uniformed driver leaped out of the car, marched briskly around to the other side, and opened the door. A high-ranking officer in the Gestapo stepped out of the car. Two more got out from the other side.

The driver saluted. The three officers ignored him and approached the front door. There were three wide round military hats immediately below Frau Friedmann's window. If she'd had a bomb, she could have dropped it straight on to their heads. It was a foolish thought.

She heard voices in the hall below, footsteps on the stairs, her own heartbeat. When they were admitted to the room, she faced them, braced for whatever was about to come.

'Good afternoon, Frau Friedmann!'

She bowed her head briefly and stayed silent.

'I hope you are well?'

'Thank you,' she said.

The officer looked coolly round the room. He was different from the others. She hadn't met this one before.

She couldn't bring herself to wait any longer. 'Is there any news of my son?'

'Yes. He has arrived.'

Frau Friedmann knew that already. She'd been told last time.

'And he has made contact,' the officer said. 'But he has not carried out his mission – yet.'

'What *is* his mission?' She'd asked before and had been told nothing.

She was not told this time either. 'Where is your daughter, Frau Friedmann?'

'Upstairs, in her room.'

'Call her down, please.' Then, seeing the hesitation, he added, '*At once!*'

'You're not going to take . . .?'

'I wish to see your daughter.'

Frau Friedmann went out into the passage and called upstairs.

They heard soft footsteps approaching. The door was pushed quietly open and a young girl walked in. She looked anxiously at the three men. She was frightened. They were between her and her mother so that she was forced to stand apart.

'You are Natalie Friedmann?'

'Yes, sir.' Her voice was low, almost inaudible.

'How old are you?'

'Eight, sir. It was my birthday last week.'

'Are you well?' In spite of himself, the officer spoke gently to this slight, fair-haired girl with soft blue eyes.

'Yes. But I don't like it when the British drop bombs,' she said.

The officer's clipped and arrogant manner wavered. The discipline of fear which he – and thousands of others – had been taught, slipped a little. He spoke softly. 'We will put a stop to that,' he said.

'May I offer you some tea?' Frau Friedmann said. She wished to change the subject.

He stared at her. 'Of course!' he said, smiling. 'You are English. *Afternoon tea!* Before the War, I had tea at Grantchester. And in London, at the Ritz. But no, we have no time for tea. I came to tell you that there is some *doubt* . . .' he emphasised the word, '. . . as to whether your son intends to complete his mission.'

'Then there is nothing for it,' Frau Friedmann said. 'We must wait and see.'

'Precisely! I'm glad you understand. May I remind you that you are still under surveillance, Frau Friedmann. *Heil Hitler!*'

He saluted. The others saluted too. Then, with a click of their heels, they about-turned and left.

-43-

The First Plan

On Saturday morning, they knocked on Loopy Lavvy's back door. Just Abigail and Hannah.

Lavvy opened it, and stared at them, grinning, and saying how nice it was to have visitors so early in the morning. (*Early?* It was around eleven!)

She'd only just got up. She was wearing an ancient dressing gown and her bare feet stuck out at the bottom.

But she was friendly enough and invited them into her kitchen. Konrad had warned them what to expect. While Abigail was explaining about the cat, Hannah looked around at the clutter – the hanging herbs and dried plants, and the pots and tins with strange labels on them. And the cleaver.

Lavvy didn't seem to mind that she was being asked to give back the cat. 'So he belongs to Molly Barnes, you say?' She peered closely at Abigail as she spoke.

'No. Molly has an evacuee called Adam – and she belongs to him. They're both from London.'

Lavvy frowned. 'Molly Barnes is not from London.'

'*No!* The evacuee and the cat are from London. And it's a *she*, by the way, not a *he*.'

Lavvy led them upstairs. There was no carpet, just the wooden steps – and not much space to put your feet because there were flat boxes all the way up, with potatoes laid out. They were brown and dry, with small sprouts sticking out of them. 'They're my seed,' Lavvy said.

They didn't look like any seeds Hannah had ever seen.

'That'll soon be Easter. Good Christians always plant their seed potatoes at Easter.'

At the top of the stairs was a landing with two doors. Lavvy probably slept in the room on the right. She certainly couldn't have slept in the other one. When the door was opened they were almost overwhelmed by the sweet smell of apples. It was Lavvy's storeroom, and there were apples on every possible surface, wrapped in newspaper.

On an old armchair there was a cat, sitting upright with her single front leg firmly in place, and watching them with an interested look in her eye, as if she knew something was going to happen.

Hannah was expecting a hideously deformed animal, with a stump. But there was nothing deformed about this cat. She was trim and neat, and she had managed somehow to sit with her one front leg centrally in front of her, for balance.

'He's a very special cat,' Lavvy said. 'Did you know that?'

Again, Abigail said, 'He's a *she*. Her name's Tibby.'

Lavvy ignored that. She picked up the cat and handed her carefully to Abigail. 'How are you going to get him home? Would you like to borrow my big bag?'

'I've got a basket on the back of my bike,' Abigail said.

'With a lid?' Lavvy asked.

'Yes.'

Lavvy stared. 'Just like Toto,' she said.

Then it was the girls' turn to stare. Neither of them knew what she meant.

'In the film,' Lavvy said. '*The Wizard of Oz.*'

Then they understood. Toto, in a bicycle basket! It had not occurred to Hannah that Lavvy might do such a normal thing as go to the pictures.

'That Wicked Witch,' Lavvy said. 'She was a real bad 'un! She gave me the creeps. I saw that picture five times!'

They talked a bit about the film. Hannah had seen it with her gran, and Abigail had seen it with Molly. 'That's a powerful story,' Lavvy said. 'But the wickedness was defeated in the end!'

Hannah had started to think that Lavvy wasn't so very loopy after all. But then she went a bit weird again. 'That story should be in the Bible,' she said. 'I told the vicar so – and he promised to speak to the bishop about it. They're going to put Dorothy and the Wizard into the Old Testament!'

They'd expected a fuss. But Lavvy was not upset about handing over the cat. And in no time Hannah and Abigail were cycling back along the lane beside the Old Bank.

They were full of their cleverness.

They saw as they approached the bridge over the empty river that Mucker's mum and Ollie's mum were blocking their way. One big and sturdy, the other lean and wiry. Both with their arms folded.

'Abigail Murfitt! Woss in that basket on the back o your bike?'

Abigail looked innocently surprised. 'In my basket?' she said.

'*Yes*, in your bloody basket!'

'A cat,' Abigail said.

'Whose cat?'

'Ours.' Then she corrected herself. 'Well, she belongs to Mollie'e evacuee. And Lavvy had got her.'

'I *see*! And how, may I ask, did yew get hold o this cat?'

'We asked for it.'

Mr Pickens was watching from three fields away, where he stood beside two huge shire horses. He could not work out what was happening.

Mrs Bailey turned to Hannah. 'Is this trew? You *talked* to Lavvy?'

'Yes,' Hannah said. 'We knocked on the door and she answered it. Then we talked.'

'Did yew goo inside?' That was Mrs Pickens, who had already begun to understand that they'd got the wrong end of the stick. 'Woss her house like? Inside?'

Mr Pickens saw from a distance that the two women stepped aside, and the girls continued on their way to Great Deeping. *Them and their daft suspicions!* he thought. He also noticed Mucker Bailey walking along the lane. He was too far away to see that Mucker was carrying a pair of wire-cutters.

*

Afterwards Hannah thought a lot about Loopy Lavvy, and she reckoned she had a pretty good life. She went to bed when she liked, cooked her meals when she liked, wore what she liked, and did what she wanted when she wanted to do it. There was no one to order her about.

I wouldn't mind living like that, Hannah thought.

So that was the first plan, the legal one. Now they had to deal with Konrad's. The illegal one.

-44-

What Can Happen When People Care Too Much About Football

During the hours of darkness, two Home Guard men were always on duty at the pillbox. In the daytime, there was only one – and that Saturday morning Private Charlie Brewster arrived for his allotted four hours. But there was a problem.

One of the many things that kept going all through the War was football, even though the youngest and fittest players were almost all away in the armed forces. Charlie played for Deeping Town. He was their striker – their only player under thirty-five, in fact. That Saturday afternoon they faced Soham Rangers in the semi-final of the local cup. It was vital that he should be at the ground on time.

It happens with all organisations. Rules are relaxed, understandings take over. It's human nature. Charlie would leave the pillbox half an hour early, and Corporal Gotobed (a kindly man) would say nothing about it. What harm could that possibly do? Who in the world – in such a remote and empty spot – was likely to go anywhere near the pillbox in the thirty or forty minutes that it would be unguarded? This had happened the previous Saturday too, and nothing had gone wrong.

Very little that happened along the Old Bank passed without Mucker Bailey taking note of it. So they were all expecting it to happen again.

It was the day of the semi-final. *Of course it will happen again!* they thought.

They were right. It did.

Five children hurried along the lane to the pillbox, remote, lonely, and unguarded. Adults were safely occupied elsewhere, catching up on the time they'd wasted with their foolish suspicions. The children were safe. Miles from anywhere. Deep in the fens.

Ollie had his cart fixed to the back of his bike, and in it was a sack containing a rusty square tin box, a couple of big ancient buckets, round like reels of cable, and an old wooden box roughly the same size as a detonator.

In no time at all, the contents of the sacks were swapped over.

Abigail was doubtful. She didn't think anyone would be deceived. 'Noo one een't going to have a close look,' Mucker said. 'They're tew scared!'

When they got back to the waterless river, Mucker took charge and hid the cart in the long grass under the bridge. When Corporal Gotobed cycled slowly past on his way to the pillbox, the children stood there in a group, watching.

'Not gooin t watch the football then?' Mucker shouted at him.

'I'm tew old for football,' the corporal called back. 'Cricket's my game, come summer.'

He cycled slowly past, thinking perhaps about his batting average, and unaware that he was on his way to stand guard over three sacks of rubbish.

-45-

The Illegal Plan

There were five of them, but only four bikes. So Ollie jogged along beside them as far as the town. The plan was that he was going to the pictures. He would be their alibi. His job was to tell them about the film and they'd be able to talk about it, to prove they'd seen it. He had considered five tickets as further proof but he gave up that idea. That sum was beyond his reach.

Konrad was in charge. He chose Hannah to ride the bike with the cart fixed to it.

'Better her than me,' Mucker Bailey said. 'Hannah, dew yew make sure yew doon't go oover tew many bumps! We doon't wanna git blown up afore we even git there!'

Konrad reassured him: bumping would *not* make the gelignite go off. 'Gelignite has to be detonated,' he said. He was irritable, understandably.

Abigail was quiet. Hannah thought she might be having regrets about her part in this. Or perhaps Molly Barnes' measles had turned into pneumonia. Hannah knew that happened sometimes.

Pedalling about with sixty sticks of gelignite tested their

determination. And despite Konrad's reassurance, every time the cartload bumped they half expected the whole lot to blow up.

'If yew have time to *expect* it,' Mucker said, 'then that een't happened!'

'What do you mean?' Abigail said.

'Yew wouldn't have time to *expect* it to blow up. Yew'd be strawberry jam!'

It was Saturday night, with darkness setting in early. Most people in Great Deeping had shut themselves indoors for the night. But there were a few cinema-goers in the empty streets, arm in arm, or hand in hand, huddling close in the blackout.

They saw Charlie Brewster with a couple of his mates heading towards the Spade and Beckett. They didn't look very happy, so probably Soham Rangers had knocked them out of the cup.

They said goodbye to Ollie. He was secretly relieved to be free of this dangerous business. Hannah could tell.

Then they cycled quietly through the darkening streets and out into the Fens on the other side of town.

*

The night was raw and black, and a cold east wind blew from Germany across the unprotected land.

There aren't many hills in the Fens, luckily, but there were bridges with steep slopes. Going up, Hannah felt the weight of the cart dragging against her strength. Going down was worse, because the drag turned into a pressure, pushing the bike too fast for safety.

They didn't say much. What had seemed exciting when they planned it was not exciting at all as they put it into action. It was a grim business. It took nearly an hour of their precious time just to get where they needed to be.

When they were almost at Little Green, Konrad stopped them beside a wide field with a five-barred gate. He pushed it open and they wheeled their bikes into the field and across the grass. Twenty or thirty shadowy cows loomed close, enormous in the darkness. But they lumbered away, and no one knew that Hannah had almost screamed.

When they reached the perimeter fence of the airfield, they left their bikes and approached the wire, peering through. 'That's it,' Konrad said softly.

The doomed building was silent and empty. The whole world had fallen quiet. It was hard to believe that half a mile away was the heart of a big airfield.

It was almost half past seven. If their cinema plan was to work, they had to be away from there by about nine-thirty, and home soon after ten. If they were later than that, there would be explaining to do.

'Wire cutters,' Konrad said softly.

He expected Mucker to hand the cutters to him, but

Mucker set about the job himself. They were massive, with big handles. 'Where d'yew want the hole?' he said to Konrad.

'There,' Konrad said. Their eyes were accustomed to the dark, and on the other side of the fence they could see the outline of a window in the back wall.

Mucker knelt down and burrowed in the long grass at the base of the perimeter fence. They crouched around him, huddled. Eventually, they heard a snap. From that moment they were criminals and there was no going back. What they'd begun could not be undone.

Steadily, strand by strand, Mucker was snipping his way upwards in a straight line. When he reached above head height, he turned the angle of his body and cut sideways, and then sideways again in the other direction.

When he'd finished, there was a jagged T-shaped cut in the wire. He dropped the cutters on the grass, grabbed the severed edge and bent it back. It was immensely strong – but so was Mucker. At the bottom he had to rip the wire out of the ground where it had been buried. Then he bent away the other edge.

The T-shape had turned into an open doorway.

-46-

Ollie at the Pictures

If Ollie had paid tenpence and sat in the children's seats, this would not have happened. But he was older than the others, and on his own; so he'd paid the full shilling and sat with the courting couples in the back row.

There was a news bulletin that gave him the creeps because it showed the Führer shouting at a vast, cheering crowd, surrounded by ranks of soldiers and tall flags with swastikas. He was raising and lowering his right hand, clenched, as if he was beating a child into the ground. Was Konrad, Ollie thought, *really* related to this man? It seemed impossible!

The gangway was on Ollie's right, and a man had pushed past him and taken the seat next to him, on his left.

He was a large man. A silent man. In the darkness of the cinema Ollie had paid him no attention. But then this man settled his arm around Ollie's shoulders. And in the flickering shadows of the cinema Ollie turned – and saw who it was.

No one had seen anything of the one-eyed man since that woman had died in Auntie Marge's tea-room. Ollie knew that Hannah hoped she'd seen the last of him. But he'd come back!

And here he was! Sitting in the next seat, *with his arm around Ollie's shoulders.*

Cyclops leaned sideways, close, like a companion. 'Where is she?' he whispered.

'Who?' Ollie asked. But he knew (of course he knew!) who this man was. And he knew it was Hannah he was asking about.

'*Tell me!* Where *is* she?'

'I dunno.' Ollie couldn't think of anything else to say.

'Why are you here by yourself? Why didn't they come to the pictures with you? *What are they up to?*' He was insistent. Ollie felt as if the words were being hammered physically into his head.

Then the lights went up. Before the War, usherettes would appear selling ice creams and sweets. All that had stopped now, but still the lights always came on for five minutes before the main film. Ollie muttered something about needing the toilet, and hurried out.

All the way out – into the dark street.

Cyclops followed more slowly. It seemed that he'd taken Ollie at his word, for the first place he went searching was the toilet. And this gave Ollie the few moments he needed to get away.

Ollie was no fighter. He knew – they *all* knew – why he'd been chosen to go to the pictures that night. But he was loyal, a rounder-up by nature, someone who liked to know his flock was safe.

So he knew he had to find the others and warn them. Especially, he had to warn Hannah that this man – whoever he was, and for whatever reason – was still hunting her. *Still,* even now!

But how could he get to Little Green? His trusty bike and cart were with the others. There were no buses at that hour.

Ollie set off on foot, out of the town and along the dark and empty road that led to Little Green. He looked back from time to time, hoping that perhaps some returning airman might stop and give him a lift. But he realised he couldn't risk it. If a car stopped beside him it might be driven by Cyclops. A couple of cars did drive by, but Ollie dived into the long dead grass at the roadside and lay flat.

He'd always been worried about their plan. Now it seemed crazy, absolute madness. And *dangerous* beyond anything he could imagine.

He was no longer sure whether he wanted to warn them about Cyclops, or to stop them completely.

He stood still for a couple of moments, ears cocked and attentive. And as he was debating with himself he heard – unmistakably – footsteps in the darkness back along the empty road.

A terrible possibility occurred to him then. *I am leading him to them!* he thought. *I am taking him straight to Hannah.*

But then a second thought came into his head. A comforting

one. *He will be outnumbered. There are five of us, and only one of him.*

Ollie walked on through the dark. And in his head he repeated the words over and over, with a rhythm that matched his steps.

There's one of him and five of us!
There's one of him and five of us!
Left right, left right.
One of him and five of us!

-47-

Wiring Up

So how do you lay sixty charges of gelignite? How do you make sure that all sixty go off together?

'How,' Hannah said to Konrad, 'do we connect everything up?'

'Carefully,' he said. Which didn't help.

'Then we stand well clear,' Mucker added.

First, sixty sticks of gelignite had to be properly placed inside the building.

There was the window that Konrad had broken into. It was still open, and he climbed inside. Hannah passed him the box of gelignite sticks, a smaller box of blaster caps, and one of the reels of wire. Mucker had also brought four pairs of pliers and some rolls of insulating tape. Then the others climbed inside too.

They had torches, but they had to be used carefully. If they shone them towards the windows, the light would be seen on the airfield.

Konrad gave them a quick lesson on placing the sticks. You couldn't just scatter them about. In mines or quarries, holes would be drilled in the rock and a stick of explosive pushed into each hole. They couldn't do that, but Konrad had seen on his first visit that there were round holes in the walls, close to the floor, where the central-heating pipes had been taken out.

So they crept about in the feeble light of their torches, searching out those holes and firmly pushing a stick of gelignite into each one. Before, Abigail and Hannah hadn't wanted to touch any of them, but there they were – as cool as cucumbers – stuffing them into those holes! *They're perfectly safe*, Konrad kept telling them, *unless they're detonated.*

Then a blaster cap had to be pushed into each stick of explosive. Konrad did this, all sixty of them, and they passed the caps to him, one by one, moving in a huddled group from one empty room to another in the light of Abigail's torch. The blaster caps were about two inches long, and connected to each one was a length of wire. These had to be unfurled and laid out on the floor.

All this made sense to Hannah. And she knew that, somehow, each blaster cap had to be wired up with all the others, and then connected to the detonator – which they'd left outside, standing in the grass.

So far, they'd made quick progress. But from that time everything seemed to take ages. The wires fixed to the caps were not always long enough, and extra lengths had to be added so that they reached into the main passage. This was a slow business, but Abigail and Hannah worked together and they quickly got the hang of it. Lengths of wire were snipped off with pliers, and then the two strands had to be stripped of their covering, twisted together – separately – and insulated with tape.

'Are you all right?' Hannah whispered to Abigail.

She shook her head. 'There's something *wrong*.' That's all she would say.

'How's Molly?' Hannah asked her. 'Has the pneumonia come on?'

But it wasn't that. Molly was expected to be better in a day or two – so what was troubling Abigail?

'There's something wrong *here*,' she said. She wouldn't look at Hannah.

After what seemed like hours all the wiring was connected. All sixty sticks of gelignite had blaster caps connected to them, and each of the caps was connected to a strand of wire leading to the main blasting cable laid out along the central passage. Three lots of twenty were connected in a line, and those three lines were joined to the leading wire.

It was complicated, and only Konrad understood it. He seemed to have been taught well at his German training school. Mucker knew nothing about the circuit, but his fingers were nimble and strong. With two or three quick twists of the wire, a swift wrapping of insulation tape, each join was made in an instant.

After that they got on faster. The lead wire didn't reach the window. It wasn't long enough. So Mucker went back into the field for the second reel, and that was connected up. Then they all climbed out, taking the reel with them, and hurried away from the building, unwinding the cable as they went.

But when the whole cable was unwound, they still felt dangerously close. Mucker had anticipated this. He'd brought with him a third reel. He'd found it in his grandad's shed, he said. It was older and grubbier than the other two. But just as effective. They connected it and unwound it to an even greater distance.

After that, there was nothing else to do except to connect the two strands of Mucker's cable to the terminals on the detonator.

Then one of them would have to push down the handle. That was all.

It was nine-twenty by Konrad's watch. They were on time. Just.

*

That was when Ollie arrived, breathless and hot with running all the way from Great Deeping.

They crowded round him anxiously.

'The one-eyed man!' he gasped out. 'He's on his way!'

'*What?*' Hannah stood there in despair, wondering if she was ever going to be free of this shadow-man who haunted her.

Ollie got his breath back, slowly, and managed to tell them the whole story.

'You think he's still after Hannah?' Abigail asked him.

'Dunno,' Ollie said. 'Praps he knows what we're dewin and wants t stop us.'

Abigail said to Ollie, 'Are you all right?'

Ollie just stared and said, '*He put his arm round me!*'

-48-
Cyclops

After Mrs So-Called-Lufton's death in the tea-rooms, Cyclops went underground for a few days. When it was clear there wasn't going to be a post-mortem, and that the police were not interested in the mysterious woman with a false identity who had apparently died of a heart attack, he resurfaced.

As darkness fell that Saturday evening, he'd seen all five children at the far end of the high street. Naturally, he had wondered what they were up to. But he was on foot, and they had bikes. He couldn't follow them.

So, when one of them left the group and walked into town, Cyclops followed him to the cinema. And *into* the cinema. And to the seat next to Ollie.

If Ollie had looked directly into the face of the man who had put his arm round him in the darkness of the cinema, he might have seen a miniature Führer, flickering madly upside down, coldly reflected in a glassy eyeball.

But Ollie hadn't looked him in the eye. And when he abruptly left his seat and raced out, Cyclops got up and followed him. He was not deceived by the boy's trick of going to the toilet, but he pretended to be.

Cyclops was anxious, and angry. *Those bloody kids! Surely they wouldn't . . .*

He followed Ollie at a distance through the streets of the town and out into the country. Cyclops knew where he was heading. He'd become familiar with the road to Little Green and its airfield.

He knew that Ollie would lead him to Hannah. And then perhaps this business could be finally settled.

But when Ollie turned into a field bordering the perimeter fence, Cyclops stopped and considered.

Cyclops never did what you'd expect him to do. He was true to form that night. Instead of following Ollie into the field, he continued along the road into the village.

-49-

Operation Blackout

Konrad made them check every room in the building one more time, to ensure there was no one inside. When everything was ready, the five of them stood around the detonator, hesitating, hoping they would be far enough away when the building went up.

After all their planning and hard work, would they finish it off? *Dare they do it?*

But they'd left it too late, for in that moment of suspended action they saw someone approaching them. Hilda Pritt came up to them in the dark – a different Hilda, frightened, angry, and feeling let down. She was like an avenging goddess. Transformed, utterly transformed.

Our torches! they thought. She'd seen their lights – and now she'd seen the cable running from inside the building to the detonator.

She might have shouted at them, giving sharp orders to dismantle the layout at once. But she didn't.

This was a new Hilda, fierce and determined, quietly and grimly spelling out the consequences of what they planned to do. She spoke slowly and deliberately, pausing after each utterance. There was no melodrama, just a cruel verbal clarity.

'Sabotage is collaborating with the enemy. It is a form of treason. The punishment for treason is death.

'– For a child, prison.

'– *All* of you.

'– Your families will be ashamed of you, and you'll be a disgrace to your country. You will be disowned by everyone. Even the other prisoners will despise you.'

Konrad drew himself up. 'My father would not be ashamed of me,' he said. 'If he were alive.'

'Then you should have planned it *by yourself*,' Hilda snapped, 'and not involved anyone else.'

Hannah tried to speak. 'But Hilda –'

Hilda lost her coolness. She was suddenly angry, and loud. 'Don't *But Hilda* me! You've already damaged RAF property! You have trespassed on RAF land. You have collaborated in a plot to blow up an RAF building.'

Then, directly to Konrad, 'And *you* are a German and your father was in the German High Command. How do you think *that* will sound in a British court-martial, you young idiot?'

Each sentence was a searchlight. She'd not used the word *traitors*, but she might as well have done.

There was some fidgeting, and a low mutter of grumbling – resentful, unsure what to do, and ready to give up. *It's too late,* they thought. *We're already in trouble, even if we stop now.*

Standing at a distance apart from them, hardly more than a shadow, a figure stood motionless, like a ghost doomed to haunt the edges of people's lives.

Only Hannah saw him. She couldn't see the eyes but she knew who he was. The bulk of his big, looming darkness was familiar. There was always a recognition.

Had he come to hurt her? Even now, when she was surrounded by friends? Or did he just want to stop them? Perhaps it was Hilda he wanted to stop? Hannah was confused. He had always confused her. She'd never understood what exactly he wanted. *Why* was he always there, wherever she went? *Why* did he keep turning up?

Then the answer came to her. *Of course!* He was there to make sure that the building really was blown up, so that he could report back to his Nazi bosses.

Konrad saw none of that. He was white-faced and hesitating, staring at Hilda.

Hannah knew what had to be done. She stepped forward to the detonator, grasped the handle firmly with both hands, and *pushed down hard.*

*

How does a detonator work? What happens?

   - When Hannah pushed down the plunger the muscular

energy in her upper body passed into the detonator.

~ The plunger's mechanism was forced into a rapid spinning motion as it was driven downwards inside a magneto, generating electricity.

~ Hannah's energy had now been converted into a powerful electric charge. But the charge was held back until the plunger reached the bottom, where it made contact with a brass spring.

~ Instantly the charge was transmitted along the cables to the sixty blasting caps inside the building. (This happened faster than you can blink.)

~ Inside each cap was a tiny, thin wire. The current passing through these fuses heated them up and made them incandescent. (This would happen before you could blink a second time – but only if the second blink followed immediately after the first.)

~ The sudden heat of the sixty fuses set off the explosive charges inside the blaster caps.

~ The exploding blaster caps detonated the sixty sticks of gelignite.

~ In each of the sticks of gelignite, solids were changed into gas, expanding rapidly.

~ The rapid expansion of gases fractured the solid brickwork surrounding the gelignite sticks, and the whole building erupted.

~ Hannah's original downward shove had passed into the

plunger, along the cable, into the explosives – and was finally dissipated upwards and outwards in the big night air.

*

Someone – was it Hilda? – cried out in horror. '*Hannah! No!*' (Afterwards, Hilda denied saying that. It must have been someone else.)

At first the plunger slid down easily, then Hannah felt a resistance. But she kept on pushing, as if she had to force the current manually along the wire.

On the other side of the perimeter fence, the security building erupted in a blinding fireball of flame and smoke. Debris was hurled upwards, and a monstrous, roaring crimson flame lashed in the darkness. Stars shining in the night sky trembled briefly in the boiling air. There was a huge *whoomph* as a shockwave blasted outwards, and was then sucked back. Then there was total blackness, and a cloud of dust and smoke rose into the sky, amid the muffled sounds of a broken building thudding into fragments on the soft grass.

The walls and roof were destroyed, utterly. Reduced to hardcore. Under the rubble the concrete floor remained more or less intact.

As an explosion, anyone who'd lived through the Blitz would regard it as a feeble affair. No enemy bombers droned endlessly overhead, no neighbouring buildings collapsed, no streets were on fire from end to end. No sticks of bombs fell jerkily from the sky. No houses crashed into chaos, one after the other. And there were no frightened people in the streets, shouting, screaming, running for safety, clutching one other. There were no ambulances, no fire engines. And hardly any *noise* at all.

None of that.

After the explosion the soft, clean quietness of the countryside was immediately restored. The stars held steady, and the dust and smoke drifted away. The event was wrapped about with tranquillity and stillness – of no more significance than the rosebush that Konrad had popped out of the ground at the end of his first lesson on explosives.

No. The real drama was where the people were, standing hushed and appalled.

'*What did you do that for?*' Hilda gasped. She was shocked and furious, utterly taken by surprise. It had never occurred to her that she wouldn't be able to stop them from carrying out their crazy plan.

Hannah was tired of secrets. She straightened and faced them. 'Because *someone* had to!' she shouted. 'And because *Konrad is my best friend!*'

-50-

Red Faces in the Dark

There was no time for explanations. With a great clamouring of noise, and a roaring and revving of vehicles, the RAF was coming, eager for action, and angry beyond belief. In spite of the blackout, a powerful spotlight was beamed at them from the roof of a truck as men armed with sten-guns and .303s scrambled through the hole in the fence.

'Nobody move!'

Group-Captain Rayburn was there, furious, shouting at everyone. Mucker Bailey's eyes lit up.

'Who did this?' the group-captain roared.

Cyclops – unseen by all of them except Hannah – stepped further back into the darkness. His disappearance went unnoticed because at that moment someone else came into view – a tall and rather stately figure, swaying slightly from side to side, as if a little drunk.

But she wasn't drunk, just old. And unsteady on her legs.

One of the armed guards swung round with his sten-gun aimed at her chest.

She was wearing a long, thick dressing gown, with the collar turned up. She pulled it tight across her throat. 'Put that ridiculous thing away,' she said to him sharply. Then she turned her attention to the group-captain and folded her arms. 'I did it,' she said.

'*You?*' Universal disbelief. No one believed her. Hilda stared at her grandmother.

'Of *course* the building had to be blown up!' Mrs Pritt said calmly. 'Of *course* we couldn't stand by and let this boy's family be shot! It's perfectly obvious – even to the meanest intelligence.'

'*Granny!*' Hilda cried. What are you doing here? How did you . . . ? What . . . ?'

'Madam! Do you know how serious it is to destroy military property? Especially in a time of war?'

'Don't be so pompous!' the old lady retorted. 'It was a cheaply built slum that nobody was using.'

'It makes no difference . . .' The group-captain took off his hat with one hand and pushed back his hair with the other. A sign of bewilderment. He tried again, 'Do you realise how serious –?'

She interrupted him. 'If you want to lock me up, I shan't mind,' she said calmly. 'Little Green can be *very boring*! You've *no idea!*'

Then everyone got even angrier and there were lots of red faces in the darkness. Hannah and Konrad, standing side by side, watched it all, slightly detached from everything around them.

'Take this . . . this *person* . . . and lock her up!'

'I say, steady on, sir,' Hilda said. 'You can't throw an old lady into the guardroom!'

'I most certainly *can*!'

'She's eighty-six!'

In the end nobody was locked up. Mrs Pritt was taken home. Armed military police were mounted at the front and back of her cottage (to the surprise of the villagers when they woke up next morning, already puzzled by the explosion).

The children were driven to some offices on the airfield where they were made to wait – which they did with that fatalistic misery children usually feel when punishment and exposure are about to fall on them. Hilda wasn't allowed to talk to them.

They didn't say much. Mucker and Ollie sat together, apart from the others. From time to time they glanced briefly at Hannah and Konrad, side by side, but silent.

Then Abigail – poor, unhappy Abigail – said quietly, 'You could have told me.'

And Hannah – amid the confusion in her head – felt ashamed, and wished she had.

There were midnight phone calls to people in London, very important people, including the military committee that had discussed Konrad and his mission. There was a rumour that Mr

Churchill at Number Ten Downing Street had been contacted, but no one really believed that. Decisions were made, orders were given. There were more red faces.

Someone phoned the police at Liverpool.

The group-captain remained red-faced for a very long time, but gradually he calmed down enough to realise that these children could not be kept all night from their worrying families. So they were driven to their homes in an RAF jeep – all except Konrad, who was not allowed to go back to Mrs Pritt's cottage.

There was a small medical room attached to the guardroom, with a bunk bed. Konrad spent the night there, with an armed guard outside the door.

*

Later, there were other red faces. The captain of the Home Guard was furious when it was found that he should have been told days before to move the gelignite from the pillbox. But someone had failed to give the order – and his men had been guarding it all that time, unnecessarily.

Corporal Gotobed and Private Brewster were a little red-faced too. They knew when the explosives had probably been smuggled out. But neither of them let on. Sometimes it's better that way.

-51-

Bad News for Captain Conway

An hour after midnight, Captain Dick Conway left the building in Liverpool. Cold rain swept across the wide blitzed areas of ruin along the docks, and the captain pulled up his greatcoat collar against the wind. A late train rumbled through the night on the overhead railway.

There was a car, and three men standing beside it. Two of them walked forward to meet him.

At that moment the air-raid sirens began their dismal warning. The ships in the newly arrived fleet that had not been sunk at sea by German U-boats were about to be targeted in port by German bombers.

'Captain Conway?'

The captain was cautious. 'Who is asking?' he said.

They were not in uniform. So he waited while they produced ID, and then shone his pocket torch on to the cards and studied them carefully. 'How can I help you?'

'We need to talk, sir. We'd like you to get in the car, please.'

*

The captain's ship had docked early that morning and he'd spent all day and most of the evening at Derby House, doing paperwork.

The Command Centre looked from the outside like a shop of some kind, or an office perhaps. But behind its innocent doors there was a labyrinth of underground rooms, bunkers, and tunnels. There was a mess, a games room, control rooms, rooms with bunk beds, and a medical clinic.

Captain Conway had spent an hour at the clinic, having his eyes tested. He'd known for some time that his sight was deteriorating. The news was not *very* bad, but nor was it good. He would not go blind, nothing like that. But his life at sea was over. The Navy wouldn't allow a man with poor eyesight to captain a ship. He would be given a desk job, in Liverpool probably.

He was philosophical about it. He believed misfortunes should be faced without fuss. If he had to work at a desk, he would just get on with it.

Besides, there were advantages. He would be able to find a place in the Liverpool area so that Hannah could come and live with him. It was time she had a normal home life.

Hannah had been much in his mind all those weeks at sea. While the convoy was assembling off Nova Scotia, he'd received a telegraph informing him of the death of his mother. But there'd been no mention of Hannah. Weeks later, as the fleet was approaching Liverpool, several sacks of mail were delivered to his ship.

Among the letters were two from Hannah. This was the first news he'd had of her since before Christmas.

It was late when he finished at Derby House. They offered him a bunk for the night, but he'd already rented a room in town. However, he did have a meal in the mess, and he reread Hannah's letters there. So when he set off into the darkness, she was very much in his thoughts.

*

'We'd like you to get in the car, please.'

Captain Conway didn't move. 'What's this about?'

'It's about your daughter.'

'Hannah? What's happened to Hannah? Is she all right? Has she been . . . ?'

'No, sir. Nothing like that. Please – we can talk more freely in the car.'

Hannah's dad climbed into the back of the car, with one of the men. The other got into the front, with the driver. The driver did not start the engine.

'There's been an incident,' the senior policeman said.

'What kind of incident?'

'Sabotage, sir.'

He waited for more.

'Your daughter was involved.'

'*Sabotage?* Hannah has been involved in *sabotage?*' It seemed madness to him. Impossible!

'We don't have the details, sir, but I can tell you that a building's been blown up. On an RAF airfield. In Norfolk.'

Captain Conway was dumbfounded. 'Hannah wouldn't . . . For god's sake, she's only ten!'

'It seems she got in with a bad crowd.'

'What do you mean?'

'Nazis, sir. Or Nazi sympathisers.'

'When did this happen?'

'About three hours ago.'

'My god, you chaps don't waste your time!'

'It's a serious matter, sir.'

'Who contacted you? The local police?'

'No. The police aren't involved. The authorities don't want this to become public.'

'I need to get down there,' Captain Conway said.

'We were sure you would say that. There's an overnight train to London in forty minutes, sir. We'll drive you to the station now. In the morning, you'll be able to catch an early train into Norfolk.'

Captain Conway was thinking, *Hannah! What the hell have you been up to?*

'You'll be met at Euston station, sir. Chap wearing a black overcoat, bowler hat, and carrying *The Times* under his left arm.'

*

Captain Conway caught the train, full of cigarette smoke and exhausted servicemen. They were travelling home on leave, or returning to their bases. The dreary war-time train took them slowly but faithfully through the dangerous night, travelling through air raids like a slow, patient animal labouring through passing storms.

Waiting on the platform at Euston was a man wearing a long black overcoat and a bowler. Under his left arm was a copy of *The Times*.

They shook hands, and Captain Conway studied the man carefully. He warmed to him at once. The chap had an honest and straightforward face, and a firm, clean handshake.

'Preston,' the man said. '*Charles* Preston. I'm very sorry this has happened.'

'Are you going to put me in the picture?'

'There's a British Restaurant just outside the station,' Charles Preston said. 'They do a pretty good breakfast, considering there's a War on. While you're having yours, I'll have a coffee and tell you all I know. Then I'll take you to Liverpool Street station and see you on to an early train to Great Deeping. You'll be there by mid-morning. I'll phone the RAF down there and arrange for a car to meet you at the station.'

Captain Conway breathed a sigh of relief. This was a man he could deal with.

'I've never heard of Great Deeping. Where is it?'

'The airfield is in Norfolk. Great Deeping is just across the county boundary, in the Isle of Ely.'

Captain Conway had never heard of that either. As they walked out of the station he said, 'Who do you work for?'

'MI5. I can recommend the sausage, egg and chips.'

By the time he'd eaten his breakfast Captain Conway knew all about Operation Blackout.

-52-

Consequences

In a jeep, on their way the next morning, Hilda Pritt said to Captain Rayburn, 'That local spy you told me about. Will he be able to inform . . . ?'

'Oh, yes! You can count on it. By the end of today German High Command will know all about last night's explosion.'

Good! Hilda thought. 'But how?' she said. 'Wireless?'

'Probably not. We'd be able to get a fix on radio transmissions.'

'What other ways are there?'

'Carrier pigeons, perhaps,' Rayburn said.

Hilda thought he was joking. '*Carrier pigeons!*' What an absurd idea!

But Group-Captain Rayburn wasn't laughing.

*

The questioning took place in Mrs Pickens' kitchen. The children were on trial.

It might not have been so bad if they had all felt the same.

But there was something new: suddenly everyone except Konrad distrusted Hannah. She could see it in their faces. She was Hannah the liar, the girl with secrets.

Konrad sat opposite her. They were not allowed to sit together. Mr and Mrs Pickens stood by the range, looking grim, and Ollie avoided Hannah's eye. She was set apart. Little Betty walked over to hold her hand, but her mum called her sharply back. But Hannah was most aware of Abigail, who sat at the table, very pale, and very quiet.

Then the questioning started. It was relentless and sharp. Konrad first, then Hannah. They answered every question honestly, they really did. But even so, Hannah could see that the true story – the *full* story – never quite got told. The telling of it changed what had happened. Perhaps that's always the way.

She tried to make herself feel triumphant. After all, she thought, against the odds, they had succeeded! But the truth was that she didn't feel triumphant at all. She was scared.

But Konrad, facing her across the table, felt quietly proud. Hannah knew that look on his face. He didn't care what happened next because he had done what he could to save his mother and his sister. He looked as if he *owned himself.*

Suddenly *his* confidence leapt across the table to *her*, like an electric connection. *She* was feeling *his* feelings – and none of the others knew! This used to happen before the War, a lot, both ways round. Hannah had transmitted laughter and lightness to him. This time it came from him to her – a powerful charge of *pride*.

'Now,' the senior officer said. 'We all know that the old lady did *not* detonate the explosives. So who did?'

Hannah braced herself. 'It was me,' she said.

He faced her, frowning. 'Why did you do that?'

'We had to!' she said. 'The Germans were going to execute Konrad's mother and sister.' Then she added, 'Hilda wanted to stop us.'

'Let's be absolutely clear. *You* pushed down the plunger?'

'Yes.'

'*You* committed an act of sabotage?'

'Yes.'

'But you didn't lay out the explosives. And you didn't wire up the circuit.'

'That was me,' Konrad said. Not defiantly. Just *firmly*.

'You had help?'

Mucker shuffled on his chair. 'I gave im a hand.'

The officer turned to Ollie. 'What about you?'

'Ollie wasn't there,' Hannah said quickly. 'He went to the pictures.'

'But he *was* there when we arrived,' the officer pointed out.

Ollie was at a loss. So Hannah said, 'When he got out of the cinema, he came to find us.'

'So he knew what you planned to do.'

There was no point in denying that.

'So you all knew about Operation Blackout?'

Through the window Abigail saw an RAF jeep drive on to the bridge and stop there. And she saw the two men who got out.

They all heard the sound of the vehicle, they all heard the sound of the two doors slamming shut. Only Abigail noticed the joyous look on Hannah's face.

But that's all she saw, because Hannah contained her feelings inside herself, like a wrapped parcel. Her dad would understand. She sat very still, her back straight, her head up, and her eyes shining.

The moment he walked into the room everything changed. He was in full naval uniform, and he had the manner of a man who was in charge of things. Hannah thought afterwards that's how it must have been when Lord Nelson walked into a cabin full of junior officers.

Everyone was struck by what he did. He gave the senior RAF man a quick salute, one officer to another (the Navy acknowledging the Air Force), and he kissed Hannah lightly on the top of her head. Then he went round the table and shook Konrad's hand. 'Nice to see you again, old chap,' he said. 'Sorry about your father. He was a good man.'

He pulled up a chair and sat at the table. 'Now, how can this mess be sorted out?'

That changed everything. Hannah would never forget what happened after that. It was amazing! The interrogation about *what they'd done* changed into a discussion about *what was going to happen next.*

It was a kind of bright magic. She didn't know how he managed it. People stopped being so angry, faces were no longer so red. Thoughts of treason and disgrace faded, plans were made for the future – and they were even allowed to feel that they'd done quite well.

Hannah thought how different her father was from Cyclops. Two men: one belonging to the light – open-minded, decisive, always clear; the other to the dark – ambiguous and dangerous. One saw things clearly, and was clearly seen, with no mystery about him. The other was a man of shadows, half seen, and half seeing.

She wondered if she would tell her father about Cyclops. Probably not, she thought.

Eventually, the five of them were sent outside so that the grown-ups could discuss the whole matter in private. The sky was clear and blue, and the sun was shining.

-53-
Happy Ending?

Outside in the warm afternoon sunshine Mucker demanded the full story. '*All* of it!' he said.

So Hannah told them. But although Mucker had asked the question and Ollie was listening hard, it was Abigail she was talking to.

She told them how her mum had died when she was six. And how her grandmother took her to live in London, and how she couldn't stop crying. She told them about the afternoon Konrad had turned up in her gran's front room. And how he promised he would be her best friend.

He was. And she stopped crying.

But on the night he was taken to Germany a few days before war broke out, he'd pushed a note through her letterbox.

'What did it say?' Abigail asked.

So she told them – exactly, word for word. '*We are all going to Berlin. My father has to fight for Germany. Whatever happens, we are still best friends. K.*'

Konrad stared at her. 'You remember it!' he said.

'I memorised it,' she said.

She'd never expected to see him again. So finding him in the pillbox had seemed like a weird magic – impossible, beyond belief. He was nearly thirteen, and taller than she remembered him. But she'd grown too. She was ten. He'd looked straight at her with a slight shake of his head – and she knew at once that he wanted her to keep quiet.

Perhaps Abigail understood. *She* had a best friend too, and Hannah knew they shared everything.

But Mucker was not convinced. He believed he wasn't being told the full story. 'Yew listen to me!' he said slowly. 'Yew come down ere on the train one night and git yourself settled in nice an comfy at the Pickenses' house. And then, soon after, *he* gits hisself flown in and parachuted on to the ground about a mile away!'

'Yes, that's what happened.'

'And yew expect us to believe that was just a coincidence?' he said. He pushed his face close to Hannah's as he said it.

But Konrad would not allow that. 'It was not a coincidence,' he said firmly. 'It was cause and effect.'

Mucker backed off. Hannah and Konrad together were a powerful alliance.

She tried to make them understand.

When she'd run away from London, she got on a train to Great Deeping *because those two words were written on Cyclops' bit of paper*. He'd written it there, probably because he was a spy and part of the plot to blow up the building. He too had to go to Great Deeping. It was a link in a chain. Cause and effect. It was not a coincidence at all.

But Abigail was still troubled. She was an open and generous-hearted person and she felt she'd been deceived. That was when Hannah learned that having one important friendship can mess up your others. She hadn't *wanted* to keep secrets from Abigail.

'I'm sorry I didn't tell you . . .' she began to say.

But you can never know how anyone will react. Abigail just changed the subject and gave Hannah one of her bright smiles. 'Molly's coming out today,' she said. The measles had cleared up at last, and pneumonia had not come on. 'She'll be coming to school for the last week of term. And then it will be the Easter holidays!'

*

The authorities decided to take no further action, and there were no punishments.

Konrad became the responsibility of the War Department, and it agreed to pay for him to go to a boarding school until the War was over. He didn't mind that, he said. He was used to boarding schools. But Hannah minded – and she got them to agree that he'd be a weekday boarder, and come home for weekends. *And* holidays. There were lots of boarding schools near Liverpool.

That afternoon they both left with Hannah's dad. There was never any waiting about when he was concerned. Hannah's time as an evacuee was over.

She'd been wrong about so many people – Mr Pickens wasn't as nasty as she'd thought; Mrs Pickens wasn't quite so nice; Mucker Bailey was certainly not as stupid as she'd believed. She'd even been wrong about Lavvy. People are rarely what they seem.

She said this to Abigail, who said, 'But *you* weren't what you seemed.'

Hannah was being told off. Very gently, but definitely *told off*. And Abigail was right. Hannah *was* secretive, she admitted it. She liked holding something back. Except from Konrad.

Epilogue

Cyclops – relaxing with his boss in an office somewhere in central London – reaches towards the mahogany desk and pours himself some coffee.

'That girl,' his chief says, 'tell me about her.'

'She was at the heart of it,' Cyclops says. 'Hannah – Hannah Conway. Ten years old.'

'A determined girl, I think.'

'Very! Her mother died when she was little. Her father has been in the Navy.'

'Her *risk?*'

Cyclops says slowly, 'High. *Very* high. And it was my fault. I accidentally brought her into contact with that crowd of . . .' He leaves his sentence unfinished. No word is bad enough for them.

'Don't dwell on it, old chap. We all make mistakes. Tell me about the tea-room crowd.'

'The Feelgood Tea-Rooms,' Cyclops says slowly. 'The second-in-command is a Mrs Lufton. She looks like anyone's kindly granny. But make no mistake, she's as bad as the rest.'

'Dangerous?'

'Most of them didn't have a clue! But the two women who ran it, they were a different matter. Very smart, both of them. *Ruthless* as well. They were planning to commit murder. *Child* murder. Mrs Lufton is an inspector in the War Department.'

'Not any more! They've all been rounded up, everyone on that list you got hold of.'

'I never expected to end up in Great Deeping. Once I got the list I'd planned to get out at once. But then I found out that Hannah had learned it by heart.'

'Good thing you did!'

'That Miss Feelgood,' Cyclops says. 'The local police must have known she didn't die of a heart attack. Did you instruct them to shut down the investigation?'

'Yes. It would have blown your cover.'

'When she was dead, I assumed the girl was no longer in any danger. How could I know what those children were planning to do!'

'That old lady, Mrs Pritt. How did *she* come to be involved?'

'I knew she'd grown fond of the boy. And I thought she might be able to talk them out of it. So I went to her house and woke her up. She did her best, but we got there too late to stop them.'

'A remarkable woman!'

Cyclops nods his head thoughtfully. 'You know,' he says,

'children don't take to me. My missing eye alarms them, I suppose. And I have a very poor child-side manner.'

Charles sighs and lays aside the folder as Cyclops continues.

'That girl − Hannah − she was *terrified* of me. I did everything I could . . . I tried to warn her . . . But she never gave me a chance to *explain* . . . I never got to finish what I was saying. *And* I spent several nights watching that house, in case that woman made an attempt upon the child's life. All I could do was hang about in the shadows.'

'But that's the nature of our job, isn't it?' Charles says. 'We hang about in the shadows.'

'And we deal with lies,' Cyclops says. 'All the time. Lies, lies, lies! But when I tried to tell her the *truth*, I was lost for words!' He shakes his head in bafflement. 'Charles, there's something that needs to be done.'

'What?'

'Can you get a message into Berlin?'

'Yes, if it's important. A message to whom?'

'To Frau Friedmann.'

'A-*ha*! We know about her. What's your message?' Charles holds his pen poised in his hand.

'*Your son is safe. He is at school.*'

'Is that all?'

'Yes. The poor woman must be sick with worry. I would like to set her mind at rest if it's possible.'

'That can be arranged, old chap.'

'Charles, do you think it's too late for me to get married?'

'What an extraordinary question! Of course not! Do you feel in need of a wife?'

Cyclops shakes his head thoughtfully. 'Not a wife, no,' he says. 'But I would like to have a daughter.' *Brave and stubborn*, he thinks. *About ten or eleven years old. Clever, and good at secrets.*

The End

-Author's Note-

Fact and Fiction

It is a fact that there were training schools for German spies during World War II. Anyone wanting to know more about them should read *Agent Zigzag* (Bloomsbury) by Ben Macintyre, to which I acknowledge a debt of gratitude. This absorbing book is intended for adults, but a determined young reader would find that the German authorities did, in fact, run such schools. However, it is unlikely that they would have admitted a twelve-year-old boy. That's fiction.

It is also a fact that there were high-ranking German military personnel who despised Hitler and disapproved of the way he was running the War. They were loyal to their country but not to the Führer. There were attempts to assassinate him, though the one involving Konrad's father is fictional. Similarly, Adolf Hitler definitely had relatives, but the ones in this story have been made up.

The War Department Inspectorate that Mrs Lufton belongs to in this story is entirely fictional. As far as I know, there was no such organisation. But the exceptionally severe bombing of London in the Christmas period of 1940 did take place. The new bombers that take off on the night that Konrad breaks into the empty building are Halifaxes, and they made their first operational flights in March 1941. That too is fact.

Until World War II there were many local systems for selecting children thought to be clever enough to be awarded scholarships. But ways of organising the examinations varied from one area to another. A few years after the War, a new Education Act created a regularised national system, and what became known as the Eleven-Plus was put into practice.

Great Deeping is a fictional town, loosely based on Littleport, near Ely. The Old River still existed in the 1940s and 1950s, as it is described here. It is mostly ploughed over now, but its course can still be seen when the fields are bare in winter. The narrow road alongside one of the banks is still there. This is where I learned to ride a bike when I was twelve.

VW

Join Molly, Abigail and Adam on their adventures in Great Deeping in Victor Watson's exciting WW2 series, *Paradise Barn*.

9781846470912 £6.99

Shortlisted for the Branford Boase Award

9781846471186 £6.99

9781846471469 £6.99

9781846471612 £6.99

Winner of the East Anglian Book Award - Children's Category

www.catnippublishing.co.uk